COPPER HEART

COPPER HEART

LEENA LEHTOLAINEN

Translated by Owen F. Witesman

amazon crossing

The characters and events portrayed in this book are fictitious. Any similarity to real persons, living or dead, is coincidental and not intended by the author.

Text copyright © 1994 by Leena Lehtolainen
English translation copyright © 2013 Owen F. Witesman

Published by agreement with Tammi Publishers and Elina Ahlbäck Literary Agency, Helsinki, Finland.

Printed in the United States of America.

Published by AmazonCrossing
PO Box 400818
Las Vegas, NV 89140

ISBN-13: 9781477848425
ISBN-10: 1477848428
Library of Congress Control Number: 2013909662

CAST OF CHARACTERS

LOCAL COPS

Maria Kallio...Acting Sheriff
Jussi Rantanen.. Sheriff
Järvi ....Senior Detective
"Timppa" Antikainen ....Detective
Lasarov...Senior Patrol Officer
Hopponen..Patrol Officer
Timonen ....Patrol Officer

COUNTY COPS

Arvo Järvisalo .... Detective Sergeant
Pekka Koivu................................Maria's old partner, Detective
Dr. Turunen..Medical Examiner

TOWNIES

Aniliina Flöjt .... Meritta's daughter
Meritta Flöjt, née Korhonen....................Artist, City Councilor
Pentti "Pena" Kallio.......Maria's uncle, City Council Chairman
Toivo and Eini Kallio..Maria's parents
Barbro Kivinen ....Seppo Kivinen's wife

Seppo Kivinen .... Real estate developer

Jaana Korhonen .... Jaska's sister

Jari "Jaska" Korhonen .... Guitarist, Maria's old bandmate

Meeri Korhonen .... Jaska's mother

Jarmo "Johnny" Miettinen... Personal trainer, Maria's old crush

Kaisa Miettinen .... Professional athlete

Tuija Miettinen .... Johnny's estranged wife

Mikko .... Uncle Pena's cat

Ella Virtanen .... City Arts Administrator

Matti Virtanen .... Artist, Ella's husband

SUPPORTING CAST

Mårten Flöjt .... Aniliina's father, Meritta's ex-husband

Eeva and Jarmo .... Maria's eldest sister and her husband

Saku .... Eeva's son, Maria's nephew

Helena and Petri .... Maria's sister and her husband

Antti Sarkela .... Maria's boyfriend

Einstein .... Antti's cat

1

I've always had a good memory for smells. Sometimes, even years later, I'll recall the scent of some person or place. When I think of spring, I remember the inviting smell of wet earth. Autumn I know by the heavy, plaintive perfume of wet leaves.

When the wind came from the east, spreading the acrid stench of copper and sulfuric acid from the mine's tailing ponds we called the Sump, I knew I was home. Ten years ago, before I escaped the rural town of Arpikylä, I barely noticed the smell. Back then I also never noticed the sheer majesty of the Tower, the gray rock of which dominated Arpikylä's silhouette.

As I walked down Main Street, the Tower hovered over the buildings and trees, a great gray ghost, at once ethereal and ponderous. The hill of exposed, copper-yellow bedrock below it only emphasized the Tower's menacing darkness. I had to turn my eyes away, toward the blue of the cloudless sky and the green of the birch trees below.

What was I doing here again?

I was actually getting used to being back in Arpikylä. I wasn't here to stay, after all. This was just a six-month stint, and the first two months were, mercifully, already behind me.

I was getting used to the way life tossed me from place to place without warning. A year ago I graduated from law school and started a job with a small law firm in Espoo. At first the position seemed perfect, but the firm's business practices gradually began to seem more than a little dubious. Over Christmas vacation, I decided to take a risk and resign, but before I could, the head partner died of a heart attack. As the executor of the estate got down to business, it quickly became clear that the firm was on the brink of bankruptcy. Complete liquidation was the only option, and the remaining partners sent me packing with just a few months severance in my pocket.

Finding a new job seemed impossible. I even humbled myself to the point of calling my old workplace, the Helsinki Violent Crime Unit, where I worked as a police sergeant before training as a lawyer. But they didn't have anything because the whole office was being dismantled. No one else was hiring either.

Suddenly my life lacked any fixed point of reference, especially since my boyfriend, Antti, had just left for a yearlong postdoc in Chicago. So for a while I just bummed around Antti's empty apartment, feeling sorry for myself, spending my time exercising and reading. And, yes, I found far too much time for sitting in bars. I was so desperate for a plan, I even thought about going back to graduate school.

When I couldn't come up with anything better to do, I decided to use the last of my severance to spend a month in Chicago with Antti, which meant my unemployment checks stopped coming.

Midway through my vacation in Chicago, out of the blue, I received a call from the sheriff of my hometown. Sheriff Jussi Rantanen said he had finally decided to finish his degree in forensic science and needed a deputy to stand in for a few months.

My parents and the sheriff were the driving forces behind the local chamber choir, which apparently made the Kallios' unemployed daughter a perfect candidate for his summer replacement.

I knew I had to start making payments on my student loans at the end of September, and playing sheriff at home for the summer didn't seem like the worst job imaginable. I figured I could find somewhere to live for a few months. I didn't consider moving in with my parents for even a second, and I doubted they would have liked that idea either. So I asked Jussi for two weeks to think it over. Finally I called from Chicago to accept his offer, despite Antti's skepticism.

"Do you know how many times you've told me you hate that place? Why would you want to go back there now?" Antti had asked.

"I can handle six months anywhere. And there are good people who live there too. My best friend from school, Ella, works as an arts coordinator for the city. And Koivu is in Joensuu these days, which is only half an hour away."

There was something more behind me taking the job though. Turning thirty had set off a quarter-life crisis. I wanted to find my roots. Maybe that's why I wanted to go back to Arpikylä for a while.

Arpikylä. The name of the place—*Scar Town*—was absurd. People said it came from the ragged vein of copper the color of dried blood that ran under the hill at the Old Mine. One of my high school friends, who hated the place even more than I did, said it came from no one getting out without being scarred for life. Of course it was an austere place, as all small towns based around a single industry are. During my first year at the police academy, I remember grimacing when some magazine chose Arpikylä as one of the ten most boring cities in Finland. I promised myself I would never go back.

Although being able to say you were from a place with the word "scar" in the name had a certain cachet. It sounded more interesting than Hyvinkää, Loimaa, or Kokemäki, and somehow more intense: Maria Kallio from Arpikylä, straight from Finland's Wild East. In recent years the city had been trying hard to build its image as a friendly country town. Unfortunately the campaign slogan sounded forced: "Arpikylä—the city with a heart of copper." Of course the veins of ore that once allowed the city to flourish had dried out years ago.

From the direction of the Tower, a loud beeping sound began, quickly speeding up. In concern, I stopped to watch. They weren't going to blow up the Tower, were they? I knew the explosion was supposed to be small, and it was planned to take place far from the Tower. I had signed the permit for it myself, but I couldn't help watching to make sure the old gray man would survive the jolt.

A pathetically small cloud of dust rose into the air somewhere behind and to the left of the Tower, and a reassuring, steady whistle sounded. The new owner of the Old Mine was renovating the main entrance to run tours of the shafts for visitors. The opening ceremonies were set for the coming Friday.

I waved at the Tower before turning toward the police station. The Tower just glared back as if insulted I could even entertain the idea it might fall over from a little blast like that. For a moment, the Tower looked downright frightening, commanding its environment by casting long, dark shadows over it.

Later, on my evening jog, I still had the feeling the Tower was watching me. When I came to Arpikylä, I had decided to start living a more healthy country lifestyle: lots of exercise, lots of sleep, more vegetables, and a maximum of one glass of beer on weekdays. I could already feel the results; my feet felt so light running that I was half-considering entering the Helsinki City Marathon in August. Koivu had said that the Joensuu Police Department was putting together a team and they might recruit me.

I glanced at my watch and picked up the pace. I had lit the sauna stove as I was leaving the house since I was only planning on running about six kilometers. But I had already run eight, and the trip back to the house was a good ten minutes. The fire had probably gone out by now.

My heart was beating twice as fast as the Simon & Garfunkel song playing through my headphones, but I didn't bother skipping to the next song. This part of the forest had always been a little unnerving because the pine trees grew so close together. Anything could be hiding in their dark shadows. The sound of a car approaching in the distance only heightened the sense of danger.

A muffler-challenged Nissan sprang over the hill, rattling by me and then braking suddenly. When the driver's-side door opened, I felt like turning and running in the other direction. The light of the sun setting behind the pine trees reflected off the car door directly into my eyes, preventing me from seeing the driver's face.

"Maria!"

There was something familiar in that voice. As I ran up to the car, I realized that the man behind the wheel was Johnny. I cursed my muddy tracksuit, sweaty face, and tangled hair. If I was meeting Johnny for the first time in about ten years, I wanted to look better than this.

"That's my name," I said, trying to sound casual even though the hand I extended was shaking.

"I heard from your mom that you were coming here to work. I've been meaning to come by and say hello sometime."

For a moment I said nothing and just stared. Johnny was still drop-dead gorgeous, just like he was when I was fifteen. Actually, he looked better now. He still had the muscular body of an Adonis, and his almost-too-perfect boyish face had developed sexy furrows over the years.

"Yeah, I'm acting sheriff for the summer. I'm living at my uncle Pena's farmhouse. And so what are you up to?" I asked, as if I didn't know. "Did you end up coaching?"

"More or less. I was running classes at the city rec center out in Tuusniemi for a couple of years, but then I got a job here. Me and Tuija got married about ten years ago and have two kids, but we've been separated for about six months now." Johnny smiled faintly.

"Do you have a place here?" I tried to sound nonchalant and brushed some of the red locks that had escaped my ponytail out of my eyes.

"We have a house on the west side of town, but I moved out in the spring. For the summer I've just sort of been bouncing around, but mostly I've been at my parents' place. My job has an apartment lined up for me, but it isn't available until August. It's a permanent position with the city, and they're going to pay my rent. Tuija's had a dentist office here for about five years. You know she went to dental school, right?"

I nodded. Having Johnny open up with so much so fast, as though only a couple of weeks had passed since we last saw each other, made me feel stupid. Maybe seeing me wasn't a big deal for him.

"Can I give you a lift? I'm going to pick up the kids from Tuija's parents' cabin, and your uncle's place is on the way."

"Thanks for the offer, but I think I'm going to finish my run. But next time you're in the area, stop by. You know the way. It'd be nice to catch up."

Johnny promised he would, although I wasn't sure I believed him. A few seconds after I started running, the Nissan rattled by me again. My heart pounded much harder than my pace justified as I cantered after the cloud of dust, my knees so weak I could barely run.

Over the years I had thought more times than I care to admit about what would happen if I saw Johnny again. Whatever I had imagined, it wasn't this sort of blushing teenage girl nonsense. I must have looked idiotic. Johnny had shown up in my dreams not two nights before, for hell's sake. For the past five years, I'd dreamed about him at least once a month. In the latest dream, we had run into each other in the sports department at Stockmann in Helsinki. I had been looking at soccer balls when Johnny suddenly grabbed my arms and started kissing me.

"Humiliated" was the only word for how I felt upon waking from one of those dreams. Fifteen years had passed since all of that, so why wouldn't my memories of Johnny leave me in peace?

In the final kilometer, I put the hammer down like Lasse Virén chasing the pack at the end of the ten thousand meter at the Munich Olympics. When I got home, a weak fire was still burning in the sauna stove, and when I blew on the embers, they flared up enthusiastically. A couple of logs into the firebox, and the flames were crackling again. In the yard I did some crunches, push-ups, and a few pull-ups on the rug-beating pole, then stretched and grabbed my one permitted cold beer from the cellar.

Johnny had been my first love. He played soccer and guitar, and for a while he had coached the junior soccer team I played on before my breasts grew so big I started standing out too much from the boys. At that point, I gave up soccer to play bass in an otherwise all-boy rock band. Our band, Rat Poison, practiced in the same basement as Johnny's band, the Snow Tigers. We played punk, and the Tigers played softer, folk-infused rock, but sometimes we jammed together on a Beatles song or some other classic that everybody liked. And, of course, our blowouts after practice were legendary.

I threw more water on the rocks, and the steam hissed pleasantly. It had probably been ten years since I'd last seen Johnny. His real name was Jarmo, but everyone had called him Johnny as long as I could remember. I always thought of him as Johnny, and whenever I heard someone talking about Jarmo Miettinen, it always took me a second to understand they meant Johnny.

I grabbed my beer and went outside to cool off. Mikko, my uncle Pena's beautiful gray tabby, was crouched on the roof of the sauna stalking birds. Compared to our cat, Einstein, who was enormous, Mikko looked dainty. Hopefully Einstein was getting along at Antti's parents' place in Inkoo. I tried to shake the melancholy that suddenly crept over me. I missed Antti; there was no point pretending I didn't.

Antti still had three months left in Chicago. Just before Christmas, he had defended his dissertation in mathematical category theory. My mind went back to his focused expression during his defense, and his long, graceful fingers reaching up to pull back his shoulder-length hair. Antti didn't have much in common with my stereotypical image of a talented mathematician—instead of coke-bottle glasses and thick rubber-soled shoes, he had a striking aquiline profile and almost always wore black jeans. I wondered how his style of dress was going over at an American university.

Mikko meowed at the dressing room door. He was the only cat I knew who liked being in the sauna. I let him in, and he climbed up to his usual place on the middle bench, curled his tail into a neat coil and began to purr. Did he miss Uncle Pena?

While in Chicago, I received news that half of Uncle Pena's body had been paralyzed by a brain hemorrhage and that he was lying in a hospital bed unable to speak. His heart had been acting up for years. But this time it looked as though he might never leave the hospital. That was when I came up with the solution to both our housing problems: I could look after Uncle Pena's farm and do some good old-fashioned physical labor alongside my sheriffing. And out in the country, I would have more space to contemplate the fundamental questions of my life—such as Antti's repeated marriage proposals, and why I couldn't answer with anything but "not yet."

I found it bewildering that Antti wanted to marry me. We had been dating for more than a year and a half and we had been living together for six months—I thought mostly out of necessity—and for the past four months we had had the entire Atlantic between us. But I was finding life in Arpikylä much easier than life alone in Antti's apartment in Helsinki, where everything from the dishes to the sheets constantly reminded me of him.

I threw more water on the rocks, and the hissing as it boiled off made the cat scoot down to the bottom bench. Antti took life so damn seriously. I guess that's why he wanted to get married. And have kids. I knew I loved him and I guess I wanted children someday too. I was thirty years old already; the clock was ticking. Hiding out here in the backwoods wasn't going to change any of that. But I didn't want my age or any damn clock to force me into anything I wasn't ready for.

I threw one last ladleful of water onto the rocks and continued to ruminate. Now Johnny had appeared in my life out of nowhere.

Johnny and Tuija were getting divorced. I didn't want to think about that either.

After scrubbing myself clean and dumping a bucket of well water over my head to rinse off, I went to the cellar for some of my uncle's suspiciously strong home-brewed mead and then flopped down on the couch to watch a cop show about land speculators bumping each other off in Northern California.

The following day I had lunch with Ella in the city cafeteria midway between our places of work. We ate together a couple of times a week.

Ella was gushing about the upcoming opening gala for the recently renovated Old Mine complex.

"Have you received an invitation?" she asked in concern. Good old Ella. Ella had always been there—we had lived next door to each other when we were kids and had been in the same classes all through school except for one year in junior high. However, we didn't become good friends until high school. Neither of us really fit the mold of small-town girls. One boy in our class, who didn't even like me, once said that there were only "two chicks in the class who aren't chickens too, Ella and Maria." I was still pretty flattered by that.

Ella was a different kind of tomboy than me though. She was significantly taller, with broader shoulders and smaller breasts, and she almost always dressed in brightly colored pantsuits. She kept her dark hair cut short and slicked down flat. She had traded her large glasses for contact lenses, which made her brown eyes shine softly in her round, rosy-cheeked face. Ella was practical and sensible without being motherly. She was artistically talented but not one bit bohemian. She was basically born to be the cultural affairs administrator for a small town, and had been working as such for a couple of years now after having realized she needed to get active in Social Democrat politics to secure the job. Ella's husband, Matti Virtanen, was a painter.

"Yes, I have. Kivinen's secretary invited me when she came to get the permit for the fireworks. Is Kivinen really the godsend for the city he seems to be? Where is he getting the money for the lease on the Old Mine anyway?"

"Don't you read the papers? Mostly it's money from a couple of good business deals he made with his wife's inheritance. He's from here, and I guess he feels some freakish affection for the place."

I had read a few articles about Seppo Kivinen—the main shareholder and CEO of Old Mine Ltd—and my father had told me a little about him too. When Arpikylä Travel, which was owned half by the city and half by a local entrepreneur, was headed for bankruptcy, Seppo Kivinen appeared out of nowhere with an MBA and big plans. He had a detailed analysis of how to make the Old Mine profitable again. After a complete renovation, they would have an amazing network of adventure caves, a renovated Tower, an improved and expanded mining museum, a first-class restaurant, a gold-panning sluice, an alpine slide on the hill, and who knew what else.

"Aren't adventure parks like the one he's planning kind of old news? They used to be all over the place, but it seems like most of them went under."

Ella took such a pull on her glass of buttermilk that a white mustache appeared on her upper lip.

"Kivinen has plenty of ideas—you have to hand him that. On top of all the mine-themed attractions, he plans to convert one of the big ore-processing halls into a javelin practice space for Kaisa Miettinen. And Matti and Meritta are holding a mining-themed art camp in August that's already booked solid."

"But it all takes so damn much money! Is the city backing all the loans or something?"

"There has been a lot of controversy over that. But Kivinen is employing nearly a hundred people, which means a lot in a town where the unemployment rate is almost thirty percent."

Of course I understood that, and I knew that was precisely the pretext Kivinen had used to wheedle subsidies from every source imaginable. There was the Ministry of Interior, the Ministry of Trade and Industry, and the Regional Development Fund. Apparently Kivinen had been pals with an influential government minister. Although nowadays he didn't mention the connection as often—the politician in question was doing time for insider trading.

I decided to change the subject. "By the way, guess who I ran into yesterday? Johnny Miettinen."

Ella smiled at me pityingly. Although I had gotten over my worst Johnny delirium back in high school, since then I might have forced Ella to listen to me whimper about him a few times when we were drunk.

"Does he still give you the chills?"

"Unfortunately, yes."

"He is a looker," Ella said, laughing. "Even out here in the boonies we deserve a little eye candy every now and then. Goodness knows there isn't much of it."

I shoved the last forkful of mashed potatoes into my mouth and glanced at my watch. Lunches with Ella tended to stretch longer than expected, and this one was no exception.

"I have a date with the president of a hunting club in fifteen minutes," I said, standing up. "Apparently they had some poachers last fall. Fingers crossed that I don't make a complete fool of myself. Before he shows up, I should probably speed-read the hunting act that parliament just overhauled."

Sheriff Jussi had painted a rosy picture of his work: hardly any crime—mostly little break-ins and drunks on mopeds—and some light administrative work, issuing licenses and the like. Maybe the job was easy for someone who had been living here the past ten years. But I didn't really know the marching orders around city hall or who any of the local muckety-mucks were anymore. So I had to work twice as hard. In Finland, the offices of small-town sheriffs are a sort of local government dumping ground for all sorts of legal administration from simple debt recovery and permit issuing on up to leading the police department and acting as public prosecutor.

As I was walking back to the police station along the main drag, a familiar-looking woman strode toward me. I recognized her and I almost said hi, even though we didn't know each other. After winning the silver medal in the women's javelin at the World Championships in Athletics the previous summer, Kaisa Miettinen had become a permanent celebrity. I knew she was Johnny's cousin, six years younger than me, and an outrageously talented javelin thrower. A lot of people were betting on her taking the gold medal at the European Athletics Championships later in the summer.

To my surprise, Kaisa said hi. Her smile was shy and fast. I smiled back and walked the final few yards to my workplace. The new civil service building, an addition to the old police station, had been built a few years earlier. The sheriff's office was bright and spacious. On the wall still hung a portrait of Mauno Koivisto, the previous president. I wondered whether I should change the picture. It seemed pretty stupid that the president's picture was mandated to hang on the wall of every office of every petty bureaucrat in every tiny burg in the country. Was it to serve as a reminder that Big Brother was watching? Maybe back in President Kekkonen's time during the Cold War that had been true.

I survived the hunting meeting with my self-respect intact. Fortunately the principal of my old high school had been a hunting nut who regularly played hooky on the opening days of the duck and moose seasons. The school looked the other way when students also cut class on those days, so I remembered the dates perfectly. And besides, the hunting club president didn't even have a real complaint. I got the feeling he only wanted to see what having a woman sitting behind the sheriff's desk looked like.

After our meeting, the office clerk, Hilkka, the only permanent female employee in the police station, brought in a stack of passports and drivers' licenses for me to sign. No one in the stack looked familiar; the kids getting licenses now were more than ten years younger than me and complete strangers. Now it was their turn to cruise proudly up and down Main Street, stopping in front of bars to gawk at passersby. Twelve years hadn't done anything to change how teenagers got their kicks around here.

The phone rang shrilly.

"Hey, it's me—Koivu. You remember that string of cabin break-ins last month? You had a few too, south of town out near the lake. Well, we nailed the guys. Do you remember who was handling those cases on your end?"

"No, but I could get it in two guesses," I said. The Arpikylä police department had only eight full-time cops—two detectives and six uniforms. I flipped through my binder of duty logs from the previous month. "Guy by the name of Antikainen. He should be in his office now."

"Send me over to him in a minute. One other thing first though. Um…well…Do you know what size Anita would be in those British sizes that have numbers like ten and twelve?"

"Koivu, what are you up to?"

Pekka Koivu was my old partner from my days in the Helsinki Police Department Violent Crime Unit. We had kept in touch after I left, and I was sad when he decided to move to Joensuu with his girlfriend, Anita. Koivu was clearly tired of the increasingly chaotic situation at the Helsinki PD and of his alcoholic boss, who for some reason no one could fire. Now that I was in Arpikylä though, we had reconnected; Joensuu was the county seat.

"Anita's birthday is next week and I want to buy her this nightgown…"

"Why don't you ask the salesperson?"

Koivu didn't reply. Gradually, it dawned on me what sort of nightgown he meant. "OK, hold on. Anita is pretty tall but slender…probably a size ten. Are you sure she'll like something like that?"

"Well, she's always complaining that she doesn't have any fancy lingerie like the women on TV."

"I guess you know what you're doing. But Koivu—don't buy black. White is more her style."

We agreed that Koivu would come over for a sauna the following week. I doubted Anita would be able to make it. She didn't like me any more than I liked her. Koivu insisted on introducing us, and our hostility was evident the first time we met. Antti and I had visited them at Koivu's apartment in Helsinki, and Anita had started tut-tutting when we reached just our second round of beers.

"Pekka, you shouldn't drink any more. You have work tomorrow. And isn't alcohol even more dangerous for women than for men?"

As Koivu served up meatballs, pasta salad, and coleslaw, Anita nibbled a mixture of carrots and cottage cheese; apparently she didn't eat meat. I found myself spreading unusually large amounts of butter on my bread and starting to swear. Anita's vegetarianism seemed more like fanaticism than healthy living, and she seemed to want to force Koivu to change his lifestyle too. A sharp remark about the cognac that Koivu served with the coffee—of course, Anita just had herbal tea—made me realize she was jealous. I proceeded to talk loudly about my and Antti's plans for our future and, completely out of character, snuggled up under his arm. But even that didn't help.

Now I was worried for Koivu. The poor guy was clearly head over heels and completely henpecked. Supposedly a wedding was in the offing sometime in August. Hopefully someone would be with me at the church to keep me in line so I wouldn't shout, "For God's sake, don't marry that nag!"

Detective Antikainen came by my office to announce he was leaving for Joensuu to question the cabin thieves—two Finns and one Russian. Apparently most of the stolen goods were taken across the border. The local papers would have another reason to whip up some good old ethnic hatred for our eastern neighbors. And no doubt the local petty crooks would immediately take advantage of it. Last spring, one convenience-store robber, who had already done two stretches for similar capers, seemed to think no one would suspect him if he left a few rubles on the floor at the scene of the crime. Unfortunately for him, his fingerprints happened to be on them.

As I was leaving work, I drove a little loop around the Old Mine. I hadn't been up in the Tower in ages; it had been closed for the past few years. Maybe I would get the chance at the opening party on Friday. The hill glowed copper yellow, and the bright color of the sand made the Tower look even more gloomy than usual. Its shadow loomed behind me for a long time as I drove toward my uncle's farm.

2

I had just run my evening 6K and had managed to change into a nightshirt when I heard the sound of a car in the driveway. It was already eight o'clock, so I hoped whoever was outside wasn't here on official business. A knock came at the door; before I could respond, Johnny stepped inside.

"Hi. Are you already headed for bed?" Even after fifteen years, that smile still made my legs wobbly, and I had to pinch myself mentally.

"No, I just got back from jogging. Sit down. I was just about to make some tea."

Johnny sat in Uncle Pena's rocking chair and started trying to lure Mikko onto his lap. I put the kettle on and then I slipped into my room to put on panties and a sweatshirt that hopefully would conceal my lack of a bra. As I was dressing, I noticed my hands trembling. Nervous dark-green eyes stared back at me from the mirror over the dresser.

"I thought I'd stop by since we didn't get to chat for very long yesterday," Johnny said, looking at me searchingly when I returned to the living room. "You haven't changed a bit."

"Look a little closer and you'll see all my wrinkles. And what's in my head has changed quite a bit too, thank God."

"Do you still play music?"

"Mostly by myself. Antti, my boyfriend, plays the piano, and sometimes we jam together. But I haven't played in a band since my first year of law school. And you? Are the Tigers still together?"

"No, we gave up years ago, but we still get together occasionally. Jaska plays guitar with us sometimes. But we're getting old, and my voice isn't that great after all the yelling I do leading aerobics classes at the rec center."

Johnny was four years older than me, but he didn't look the slightest bit middle-aged. His movie-star jawline was more prominent than ever, and the ten pounds he had put on seemed to be pure muscle. I wondered how Johnny had never noticed the crush I had on him fifteen years earlier, since even now I was completely useless around him.

I poured the water into the teapot, and we gossiped about our common friends and talked about books and music. Gradually, my nervousness dissipated, and I remembered why I liked being around him so much. I guess that was why I had been so infatuated with Johnny; it had never been only about how handsome he was. Yes, he was beautiful, but he had a brain too. He was just plain nice to hang out with. That was a rare combination in a town the size of Arpikylä.

"Have you and Antti been dating long?"

"A little less than two years."

"And you aren't getting tired of him yet?"

"No. I do panic every now and then though. I'm not really the mate-for-life type."

Johnny didn't say anything but kept stroking Mikko, who had finally condescended to being petted. The cat purred lazily. The scent of the summer evening wafted in through the open window. A blackbird trilled on the roof of the sauna and the wind murmured softly through the birch trees in the yard. I didn't want to say anything. All I could see of Johnny, backlit by the natural light, was his strong-jawed profile and his hands slowly caressing the cat.

The telephone interrupted the silence. I started, and Mikko jumped out of Johnny's arms onto the floor. It was my sister Eeva.

"I have a guest," I said after listening to Eeva give a five-minute report on her son Saku's first words. Eeva's stories about motherhood always made me vaguely uneasy. I didn't know anything about little kids. Was there something amazing about a child walking at eleven months and figuring out how to open a tube of toothpaste?

"Oh, a guest? You do sound a little strange. Who?"

"Do you remember Johnny Miettinen?"

"Oh, that kind of guest..." Eeva said, amusement creeping into her voice. "Do you still blush every time he talks to you?"

Flipping Eeva. Of course she had known about my crush; not noticing would have been hard for anyone. Except Johnny.

"Hi, Eeva," Johnny said loudly just before I placed the receiver back in its cradle.

In my mind's eye I could see perfectly a summer night just like this one but fifteen years earlier. I had come home clutching a single of Queen's "Bohemian Rhapsody" I had borrowed from Johnny.

Eeva had immediately noticed the name written on one corner of the record sleeve and laughed cruelly to my other sister. "Maria is stuck on Johnny, but he has a girlfriend..."

Over the following three days, I nearly wore that record out and slept with the cover under my pillow; at least I had the sense not to shove the record under there too.

"Does your other sister have kids already too?" Johnny's question snapped me out of my thoughts.

"In four months she will. It's good both my sisters are having them so my parents can get off my back about grandkids. How old are yours?"

"Tuomas is seven. He's starting school this fall. Vilma is five."

I remembered noticing Tuomas's baptismal announcement in the local paper, which my old roommate Jaana used to have mailed to our apartment in Helsinki. I had been dating Harri the Birdman at the time, but after seeing the baptismal announcement, Johnny had haunted my dreams more often for a while. Why the hell didn't I ever dream of my other old crushes or boyfriends? Not Harri or Pete the Bum, who I mooned over for two weeks after we broke up, or even Kristian, who had such a brilliant legal career ahead of him. Reminiscing about them caused only a slight nostalgia, perhaps some mild amusement. But Johnny…

As if he had read my thoughts, Johnny said, "I've wondered a lot over the years how you were doing. A couple of years ago when there was that murder and then a cop shot the killer and made her fly through a second-story window, I saw your name in the paper. It seemed like you were really living the fast life. I remember thinking that I hoped I would see you again before some drug runner capped you."

There was amusement in Johnny's voice, but his eyes were not laughing.

"I'll admit that the drunk drivers around here are clearly a safer alternative than chasing murderers in Helsinki." I drained the rest of my lukewarm tea, wanting something stronger. Go away, Johnny, before I say something stupid.

"We could get together and jam some night, you and me and Jaska at least," Johnny suggested.

"Sure, maybe. Nothing fast though. I haven't played in a while."

"Oh, we suck now. Jaska plays worse every year. He's been out of work for the last few years. He's been pretty messed up, drinking and stuff. Hopefully he can pull it together now that he has a job at the Old Mine. He never would have managed even that if Meritta hadn't lined it up for him."

"Meritta?"

"His sister, the artist. You must have read about her in the paper." Johnny's voice sounded strange. Then he changed the subject, back to his children.

It was almost midnight when Johnny left. I stood, with Mikko in my arms, staring after his rattletrap Nissan. We would see each other two days later at the Old Mine opening and talked about maybe getting together for a jam session the following week.

My mind was restless. I couldn't calm down enough to go to bed, so I just kicked a sofa cushion around the room like it was a soccer ball. Mikko watched me for a few minutes and then decided to slip out through the open window. Eventually, I tried to reach Antti, but the Spanish-sounding woman who answered his office line said that "Doctoor Saarkiila" was lecturing. So I contented myself with brewing some super-strength chamomile tea. Still, sleep didn't come until sunrise, which so close after Midsummer, meant around two thirty in the morning.

On Friday, I found myself looking forward to the grand opening gala that evening. I had definitely been living the quiet life for the past month and a half, during which time I had gone on only one pub crawl with Koivu in Joensuu, spent one night at Ella's place, and celebrated Midsummer at my parents' cabin.

In honor of the opening, I bought a new pair of lace stockings on my lunch break. As I walked past the City Kiosk, a local hot dog stand, I saw the police department's new Saab cruiser in the parking lot. Hopponen and Lasarov sat inside the car enjoying milk and hamburgers while the engine idled cheerfully.

I couldn't walk by as if I hadn't noticed anything wrong. Approaching the car, I knocked on the driver's-side window. Hopponen's ketchup-smeared face grinned out as he rolled down the window.

"Hey guys, you know there's that idling law now...It's a little difficult ticketing other people if you're breaking the law yourselves," I said, trying not to sound irritated. I had almost gotten popped in the mouth a couple of times back in Espoo for asking polluters to turn off their engines.

At first Hopponen didn't seem to realize what I was talking about.

"We have a right to our lunch hour!" he snapped so furiously that a piece of hamburger sailed onto my blouse.

"Of course, of course. I didn't mean that. You just need to turn the engine off."

"It's idling if it's running for more than two minutes," Lasarov said, enlightening his junior partner.

Hopponen's round mouth twisted as he pursed his lips. Angrily he turned the ignition key in the wrong direction, making the car give a wounded squawk. I said thanks and went on my way, wondering what names they were calling me. Nagging bitch? Tight ass? Something even juicier?

I guess I was making life difficult for myself. I knew the boys at the police station hadn't been exactly overjoyed by my temporary appointment. There was already one female deputy sheriff in the county, and five policewomen, but a lady cop still seemed like a bigger exception here in Northern Karelia than in Helsinki. The men had tried to behave politely, but their suspicion just under the surface was obvious, and every now and then it came up for air.

Almost as soon as I arrived, they took the opportunity to let me know that I didn't belong. The police department played Finnish-rules baseball in the spring and volleyball in the winter against the city employees to build community spirit. Since I wanted to get to know my colleagues better, I said I would love to participate. You would've thought I'd dropped a bomb in the break room. Finally Lasarov, the most senior officer, screwed up the courage to point out that everyone on the city team was male and in peak physical condition.

"But you should come cheer us on," he said with a forced smile. Somehow I managed to swallow my comeback about the athletic abilities of pot-bellied pigs. But after that incident, I sensed the general impression that "the Kallio chick" didn't really grasp her proper role as acting sheriff. And now I was confirming it by nitpicking. I just hated their apathy toward everything.

Not that I was a saint. Sure, every now and then I would have an attack of environmentalism and remember to take used grocery bags with me when I went to the supermarket. And whenever I obediently sorted my trash into tinder for the sauna stove, normal garbage, and biowaste for the compost heap, I felt glory shine down on me from above. And I knew the exhaust emissions of a few cars in Arpikylä, Finland, were insignificant compared to the smog hanging over Chicago, but I had to start somewhere.

That afternoon it felt like the boys were avoiding me. The break room emptied immediately when I went for my three o'clock caffeine hit. Since the evening's gala was already on my mind, I didn't pay much attention. To round off the workweek, I hung the picture of President Ahtisaari, which had come in the mail that morning, above the sofa in place of Koivisto. Should I take the old portrait to my parents as a gift? Maybe they could hang him on the wall in the outhouse at the cabin. Were there official regulations for the disposing of pictures of past presidents? Koivisto seemed to frown as I hid him temporarily in the bottom drawer of my desk.

I had biked to work that morning and planned on dropping by my parents' house to shower and change clothes after work. I assumed I would take a taxi back to the farm from the gala. After a quick trip to the liquor store across the street, I coasted down the hill to my old house on Uncle Pena's three-speed bicycle, which was in serious need of some chain oil.

The door was unlocked, but no one was inside. Strange, since my parents were planning on coming to the opening too. We did still have a couple of hours though. I stuck the bottle of gin I had bought in the freezer to chill and traipsed to the shower. The water running down my sweaty shoulders felt luxurious, but I avoided getting my hair wet. I had washed it in the sauna the previous night, even taking the time to massage in a pouch of henna to amp up its natural red.

By the time I made it out of the shower, the gin was nice and cold. I mixed it with lemon juice and had it on the rocks. The bite brought tears to my eyes, so I rummaged through my mom's cupboard for a little powdered sugar to take the edge off the bitterness. The second sip tasted much better.

I emptied my makeup bag onto the bathroom counter and set down my tumbler next to my lipstick. How many Friday nights had I looked at myself in this mirror while getting ready for a party? I tried to peer through what I saw now to the old me, the round-cheeked girl of fifteen years ago with the boyish haircut. That girl didn't have crow's-feet or three strands of gray clearly visible in the sea of red above her forehead or such broad shoulders.

Surrounded by all these memories, that silly, bubbly Friday feeling came over me again, reminding me of a time when anything could happen at a party. Everything was possible. What if tonight was the night Johnny noticed me? That was a thought from fifteen years ago, right?

I needed music. Of course my sisters and I had taken all our music with us when we moved out, so all that remained was my parents' classical and easy listening records. The radio saved me with some classic Hurriganes. "I'm a roadrunner, honey…" I took a third sip of my drink and started doing myself up. In fifteen years I'd learned a thing or two about that too.

My parents arrived while I was pouring myself a second glass of gin. I could tell by my father's face that something was wrong.

"We had to go the hospital," he explained. "Your uncle had another heart attack."

"Oh God! Is he alright?"

"He's still in pretty bad shape, but they assured us that he'd pull through. We're supposed to call later tonight." With a sigh, my father sat down on the living room couch, obviously lost in thought, and took a sip from my glass. My mother excused herself to start getting ready.

"Helena was there visiting and catching him up on the news when suddenly he just went blue," Dad said.

"Does he know about the opening gala tonight?" I asked.

Uncle Pena had been the vice chairman of the town council for the previous four terms. Despite his drinking problem, he was a trusted local politician, and ten years earlier had been within spitting distance of Parliament. Reopening the mine as a tourist attraction had been an important issue for Pena for many reasons. Before taking over the family farm, he had worked in the mine himself for nearly twelve years. As the veins of ore gradually dwindled, Pena was among the first to start looking for industries to replace the jobs the mining company would no longer be able to provide. Finding a suitable entrepreneur to restore the mine had been one of the few things keeping him almost sober before his stroke.

"I'm sure he knows, but we didn't talk about it. It would've gotten him too wound up." Dad had unconsciously emptied my glass, so I took it to the kitchen and mixed fresh drinks for both of us. For my mother I poured a glass of dry sherry.

"I imagine Pena also likes Seppo Kivinen because Seppo's father used to work in the same shaft with him," Dad said.

"Yes, Kivinen is from around here, isn't he? Did either of you ever have him as a student?" I asked my parents.

"I did in middle school." Mom had come from the shower and was standing in the middle of the kitchen in her slip. I noticed she had dropped quite a few pounds since the last time I saw her undressed. The light-blue slip hung unflatteringly from her shoulders, the skin of her arms hung loosely, and new wrinkles were visible on her face. But even so, she wore the same expression as the girl laughing in the engagement picture on the mantelpiece. Her eyes, which were just as green as mine, still twinkled.

"I remember Seppo very well. He was in the first fifth grade class I taught in the fall of sixty-two when we moved here. That was such a pleasant group of children. There wasn't anything particularly remarkable about Seppo. He was just an ordinary, quiet boy. He was a good student too, good enough that I was surprised when he decided to go to trade school instead of taking the college track."

"I understand he went to night school later to get into college and then started his MBA in his thirties," my father added. "His family didn't have the money to keep him in school. He didn't let that get in the way of his ambitions though, and I'm glad he's turned out so well."

"Let's start getting dressed so we can be on time," I said.

Going into my old room, I pulled on my purple linen dress. I had bought it for Antti's dissertation defense, and it was the most expensive piece of clothing I had ever owned. But no one had told me how easily linen wrinkles. Well, I thought, we would probably be standing for most of the gala, so I should make it through the evening relatively unrumpled.

I rolled on my new lace stockings and climbed into my four-inch heels, which I was finally learning to walk in reasonably well.

My parents were dressed in the same outfits they'd worn to Petri and Helena's wedding: my dad in a sober, gray three-piece suit; my mom in a cyan chiffon dress. They were trying hard to create a festive atmosphere, but they were clearly concerned about Uncle Pena. So was I. I was afraid I'd never again see him sitting on the steps repairing some gadget out at the farm.

"What if I call one last time…" Dad said. The family resemblance between my dad and his brother—both short with broad shoulders—was striking, and their differences were slight. Dad might have been an inch or two taller and he still had some black left in his hair, while Pena had gone gray years before. And while Dad had lost his Savo-Karelian dialect sometime during college, Pena still spoke with the elongated vowels and exaggerated consonants of their youth.

"He's better," my dad said when he returned, digging his car keys out of his pocket. "He's sleeping, and his heartbeat is regular. So I guess we can go."

"Jesus Christ, Dad, you've had two glasses of gin! All of us have been drinking. We're taking a taxi and that's final."

When Dad muttered something about how puny the servings of alcohol had been and about the waste of money, I promised I would pay for the cab. "I'm sure you can drive at least to the school in your sleep, but come on, Dad. I'm a cop. Am I supposed to write you up for drunk driving from the backseat?"

We had to wait a while for the cab to arrive, and by the time we made it up the hill to the Old Mine, the place was already crawling with people. The county governor was just starting his opening speech. A brass band was waiting in the wings to play a fanfare when the governor snipped the ribbon that stretched across the door of the Tower.

Quickly growing bored of listening to platitudes, I glanced around. In a stylish copper-brown suit, Kivinen was standing behind the governor. Apparently the woman in the green Marimekko number was his wife, Barbro. She seemed older than her husband, although she was clearly doing her all to conceal the fact. The blonde tint of her hair was nicely done—not too strong—and she had probably spent three times longer doing her makeup than I had. The governor's speech seemed even less interesting to her than it did to me: she stared off toward the mine area with an empty smile on her peach-colored lips.

Ella was busy shepherding a children's dance troupe that was scheduled to perform after the ribbon cutting and subsequent tour of the Tower. For some inexplicable reason, she was wearing the same folk costume that she had worn to our high school graudation ceremony. The blue dress with a red vest and embroidered white apron emphasized her broad shoulders and overflowing hips, and the cap, signifying that she was a married woman, appeared about to fall off. She seemed irritable, which wasn't surprising given that she was in charge of organizing at least half of the shindig.

Ella's husband, Matti, wore a caramel-colored corduroy suit designed by Vuokko Nurmesniemi; nowadays those wide, straight pant legs and Nehru jackets are practically the official uniform for artists in Finland. For once, Matti's sandy-brown hair was neatly parted, his mustache was trimmed, and his round glasses were clean of smudges. He noticed me looking at him and gave a knowing grin. I grinned back.

Behind Matti glowed someone dressed in bright orange. She was in constant motion and seemed to be eagerly explaining something to a tall man standing next to her. The man was Johnny, looking just as scrumptious as always. The woman seemed familiar, but it still took me a while to realize who she was.

Meritta Flöjt, originally Merja-Riitta Korhonen before she changed her name, was the city's most famous celebrity next to Kaisa Miettinen, the javelin thrower. Meritta specialized in figurative oil paintings. She was also a perennial topic of discussion on the pages of the women's and culture magazines. No wonder: she painted beautifully; had hyperbolic opinions about culture, the environment, and eroticism; and possessed an almost Gypsy allure. With black hair, golden eyes, and voluptuous curves, she might not have been a classic beauty, but she was definitely sexy.

When I shifted my glance a couple of yards to the right, I saw Johnny's wife, Tuija Miettinen. She gave me a crooked, slightly amused smile. We never liked each other. I was sure that Tuija had been jealous of my friendship with Johnny, even though I was the only one with any real reason to be jealous. Tuija had been the one who hooked him, after all.

Suddenly I wanted out of there, away from the party, away from Arpikylä, away from myself. But just then the horns blared and the governor cut the blue-and-white ribbon. The door to the Tower opened softly, invitingly, and the crowd pushed me along with them up the dark stairway.

3

The Tower's interior was dark and damp. Water dripped from the mortar gaps in the timeworn stone walls, and the steel-reinforced wooden staircase seemed to sag beneath the weight of the mass of people. As a child, I had been a little afraid of climbing the Tower. Was there any guarantee the stairs wouldn't break? Could the whole building collapse? Or what if I fell off the top, right over the three-foot-high railing?

The climb went slowly because people were already making their way back down. The sweet stink of perfume mixed with a sulfuric smell emanating from the walls. Johnny and Meritta passed on their way back down, and Johnny smiled, his dark-red jacket sleeve brushing my arm. Ahead I saw Matti's corduroy pants leg disappear through the hatch at the top of the stairs.

The view from the observation deck always gave me a euphoric feeling of freedom, even though there was nothing special about it—endless forest, here and there a lake reflecting the blue of the sky, the occasional patch of field with a black dot indicating the location of a house. In the summer, the view of the city was almost completely obscured behind the hill and all the tall birch trees that lined the streets. During my years in school, this view revealed a world beyond

Arpikylä, showing me the many different roads that could lead me out.

And, crazy me, here I was back again.

I went right up to the railing, playing the old "how far down do I dare to look" game. I saw Meritta Flöjt's splotch of orange down below, but Johnny had disappeared. Some people seemed to have glasses in their hands, so after a few more seconds of jostling around up top, I headed down to hunt for a drink.

As I made my descent, I tried to think of what I knew about Meritta—other than that she was my old bandmate Jaska Korhonen's sister.

Two main themes dominated Meritta's work as a painter: muscular male nudes and various phallus and vulva symbols. Meritta's male figures decorated the office walls of nearly every modern female CEO and politician in Finland who considered herself sexually liberated. Her paintings were undeniably fantastic, and the collection of pictures of ideal men that I used to keep on my dorm room wall included a few of Meritta's reproductions clipped from magazines.

Meritta said she had come back to her hometown to paint because the surroundings were so exhilarating. The Tower projecting stoutly above the city and the underground mine shafts were perfect for her paintings. Tame versions of her work hung on the walls of city hall and the library, and the most presentable were even used in city brochures.

I remembered that she was about ten years my senior and had a child who was about fifteen years old. However, the child's father, Mårten Flöjt, principal cellist for the Radio Symphony Orchestra, had dropped out of the scene several years before, when Meritta had returned to Arpikylä.

I had met Meritta a few times when her brother Jaska and I played in the same band, even though she had been studying at the Ateneum Art Academy in Helsinki at the time. Jaska had always acted sulky about his older sister, talking about how stuck-up she had gotten after getting accepted to the Ateneum. I doubted Meritta would remember me, but I thought I'd go say hi anyway. I'll admit to being curious about meeting a woman whose opinions about so many things resembled my own.

The party was in full swing in the newly opened restaurant and in the courtyard, where Ella's dance group was currently performing. I watched the performance purely out of obligation. When someone started playing a saw with a violin bow, I went inside to see if I could find anyone I knew.

One of the ore-milling buildings had been renovated to house the restaurant. A bar circled the inner wall of the fifty-foot-high hall, and later in the summer the developers intended to install a proper dance floor on the lower level. The idea was to turn the space into a kind of multipurpose gallery suitable for concerts and theater performances. The renovation and retrofitting work had to be burning ungodly amounts of money. I hoped Kivinen's projections about the increased flow of tourists would pan out.

I found Matti and Johnny in a back corner on the lower level, chatting with Meritta and a fourth person who was concealed in the shadows. From a passing tray I grabbed a handful of potato chips and a glass of punch and made my way toward them. The light flooding in obliquely from the windows along the roofline fell directly onto Meritta's dress, and for a moment she appeared to be engulfed in flames. Meritta laughed at something Johnny said, her voice ringing out over the drone of conversation and turning more than a few heads.

"Nice to see the sheriff here keeping us legal," Matti said with a grin when I approached. "Do you know everyone else?" He turned to face the rest of the group.

"Johnny is an old friend, and how could anyone not know these lovely women," I said, trying to sound playful.

"We've met before, haven't we? You played in my brother's punk band." Meritta extended her hand. "Meritta Flöjt. I've been meaning to come pay a visit to our new lady sheriff. It's a shame your post is only temporary."

"Meritta wants more feminists around here to keep us men in line," Matti said mockingly.

"Oh, the men around here aren't all bad. Your uncle is a perfectly reasonable person." It took me a few moments before I realized Meritta was talking about Pena. They were both on the city council. Meritta had been the first person from the Green Party ever to win a seat.

The fourth person in the entourage still hadn't said a word, trying to hide between her cousin Johnny and the wall. The attempt at concealment was a little pathetic since Kaisa Miettinen was only an inch shorter than her six-foot-two cousin and stunningly handsome in her own right. For a javelin thrower, she was quite slim, which I guess was why the sports journalists had christened her the Javelin Fairy. Blonde curls extending to her shoulders and a shy smile emphasized her elfin, somehow sexless look. At least one person at *Sports Update* and another in the *Helsingin Sanomat* newsroom must have been infatuated with her, because news coverage about her was much more detailed than usual for female athletes. After winning silver at the previous summer's World Championships, she had been named one of Finland's best medal hopefuls for the European Athletics Championships in Helsinki and the Atlanta

Olympics. I thought Kaisa would have been at her training camp by now.

Kaisa's eyes were the same as Johnny's: bluebell colored with flecks of gold surrounding the irises. At the same height and with similar slim, muscular builds, they could have been twins. But Kaisa was a good ten years younger than Johnny. Her eyes lacked the tired circles, and the laugh lines at the corners of her mouth disappeared with the smile that created them. Johnny, on the other hand, was looking more worn-out than usual.

"Couldn't we finish the painting next week?" Johnny asked Meritta, apparently continuing the conversation my arrival had interrupted. "I promised to help my dad reroof his house this weekend. And Kaisa shouldn't be letting her muscles stiffen up posing since she's got the Grand Prix coming up."

"Kaisa doesn't have to pose, just you. I want to capture Kaisa in motion. For your portrait I want to show almost every follicle of hair on that beautiful body..." Meritta turned to me again. "I'm doing a series of panels I'm calling Apollo and Artemis, and Kaisa and Johnny are my models. Pretty perfect specimens, don't you think?"

Both Johnny and Kaisa seemed self-conscious, so Matti and I turned the conversation to the renovation work on the Old Mine.

"I think the best thing is that we'll get to go in the tunnels again," Matti said. "The feeling down there is like nothing else I've ever experienced. You've painted down there, haven't you, Meritta? Are those ones done yet? And what lighting did you use?"

"I used old mining lights called jack lamps. All of the paintings are in Helsinki on sale in my gallery. Strange I forgot to invite you to come see them before I shipped them off. I painted them almost right on the edge of the cave-in area, which gave everything an extra eerie ambiance. And I liked going down there just for the adventure," Meritta said with a grin.

"Well you won't catch me going down there," Johnny said almost angrily. "You know the city had to close half a street and empty all the houses because the ground there is still slipping toward the shaft, right?"

"Of course I do. But that's just one part. The rest of the tunnels are fine."

"At least that's what the geologists say," Matti added. "Have the rest of you been down there?"

"In school," Johnny, Kaisa, and I said nearly in unison. In ninth grade I went on a field trip to the mine with our guidance counselor. We had been told to bring rubber boots to school, and before we entered the elevator, the engineer leading the tour distributed yellow helmets to everyone. I was a little disappointed that the helmets didn't have the headlamps I had seen in pictures.

Just the elevator ride a few hundred feet down the shaft turned the weaker-kneed students a sickly shade of green. Down below, the tunnel walls loomed in on us. The worst thing was the darkness. Even with the lights on you could still sense it. And then there was the silence, broken only by drips of water falling from the ceiling. Everyone automatically started whispering. And then from somewhere nearby came an explosive drilling sound, answered by another one farther off, making the walls seem to shake and the ceiling appear on the verge of crashing down...

I remembered resurfacing aboveground. The wind had felt deliciously dry, the sound of sparrows miraculous, the sun seemed brighter than it ever had been. The boys gaped at each other with looks of "I'm never working down there." That night I called Uncle Pena and asked him how many years he had spent in the mine. When he answered more than ten, I hung up astonished.

Sounds of tinkling glasses came from the swarm of people near the bar. A moment earlier Seppo Kivinen had walked past us and climbed the stairs, and now he stood stiff as a statue in his copper-colored suit.

His unamplified voice echoed in the cavernous room. "Ladies and gentlemen! Friends! I thought I wouldn't have to say anything tonight, that this amazing space would do the talking for me, but c'est la vie...I would just like to say how truly happy I am to see the Old Mine full of people and life again. The ore under these hills has brought wealth to Arpikylä for more than eighty years now, and despite a recent small hiccup, I believe it will again. I grew up here, at the base of the Tower in fact, in the subsidence area on Lavakatu. My father worked in the mine for thirty-seven years. I hope the reopening of the mine tunnels and the museum can serve as a tribute to him and everyone like him, whose work and sweat built this town. A toast to those brave men!"

Kivinen seemed genuinely moved. Meritta was biting her lip, but I wasn't quite sure whether she was touched or amused.

"I'm empty..." Matti said, staring at his glass glumly. "Shall I bring everyone another round?"

"No, I have something I need to take care of," Meritta said and vanished right after Matti left for a refill. Suddenly I was glad Kaisa was there with Johnny and me. Talking about sports was easy, and Kaisa didn't seem so shy anymore.

"I prefer training here at home," she said. Her perfectly preserved country dialect was in cheerful contrast to the rest of her polished image. "There ain't no traffic here, and the field and weight room are always free. And especially now, with the games here in Finland, it wouldn't make no sense going to Portugal or somewhere and getting my muscles too used to being warm."

"I've been helping out as a sort of assistant coach lately, since Kaisa's real coach lives down south in Vantaa and can't be here all the time," Johnny said. "Or at least I operate the video camera so Kaisa can watch footage of her throws later."

"I could probably only throw it twenty meters," I said. "How far can you send it, Johnny?"

"Have you seen my mom?" a young, angry voice suddenly asked from behind Kaisa. When the speaker came into view, I saw a frighteningly skinny girl; a shaved head and baggy sportswear emphasized the concentration camp prisoner look.

"I left my fucking keys at home. Johnny, don't you have keys to our place?"

"Why would I?" Johnny seemed genuinely bewildered.

"Mom always gives one to the guys she screws. There's gotta be dozens of keys to our house strewn across the world. Aren't you up to bat right now?"

"What the hell are you talking about, Aniliina! I just model for your mom."

"Oh come on. I'm not blind. Never mind, I see the bitch now."

With that, Aniliina strode off toward the exit, where Meritta was caught up in the crowd. We couldn't hear their exact exchange over the buzz of conversation, but it was clearly angry.

"Johnny, are you in a relationship with Meritta?" Kaisa asked suddenly, intensely, as if her life depended on his answer.

"Come off it, Kaisa. Of course not. I just—"

A high-pitched scream from Aniliina cut off Johnny's sentence. "Eat shit, bitch!"

When we turned to look, we saw her with two fists full of Meritta's hair, pulling as hard as she could. Aniliina's shirt was stained with punch, as if Meritta had emptied her glass on her daughter. The chatter in the restaurant had ceased, and people stared in bewilderment at the Flöjt domestic dispute, which to a law enforcement officer looked out of hand. Forcefully pushing my way through the crowd, I shook Aniliina free of her mother. The girl was alarmingly light—she couldn't have weighed more than ninety pounds.

"Get the fuck off me. I'm gonna kill that bitch," she snarled at me.

"I'm not giving you the keys unless you bring them back," Meritta hissed.

"Borrow one from one of your man-whores! And you let me go, goddamn it. Who do you think you are?"

"She's a cop," Kaisa said surprisingly loudly from just behind me. "Why won't you bring the keys back, Aniliina?"

"I want to go for a walk in the woods."

"I've got my bike. I'll take you and I can bring the keys back to Meritta. OK?" Kaisa asked.

"If this pig will let go of me."

With that I released Aniliina, who was still dripping punch. She put out her hand to receive the keys from her mother, then loped down the stairs with Kaisa trailing after. With a snort, Meritta shrugged, making the heart-shaped copper earring hanging from her left ear bounce, and continued her conversation with the mayor as if nothing had happened.

Suddenly feeling like I didn't belong, I walked out onto the terrace. The tailing field at the base of the hill glowed an intense copper color in the light of the setting sun, and the small pond in the center sparkled like sweet red wine. The colors were right out of a surrealist painting. Comparatively, the natural colors of the birch trees on the slopes of the hill where the mine buildings stood looked as if they had escaped from another piece of art entirely.

I wondered whether there was anything to what Aniliina said, whether there really was something between Meritta and Johnny. And what if there was? I wasn't going to be jealous of a crush I had fifteen years ago, was I?

I wondered how much Meritta would charge for the paintings of Johnny. And what Antti would say if I hung one on my wall. Then I started thinking about which wall would be best. Suddenly my old bandmate Jaska appeared at my side.

"Can I offer the sheriff a drink?" he asked, pulling a bottle of cheap vodka out of his antediluvian leather jacket.

"Why not." Tipping the bottle back, I took a good swig, wondering how many bottles of vodka just like this we had emptied together. "Table vodka"—the absolute cheapest, strongest liquor the state store sold—had always been his drink of choice.

"So, Uncle Jaska, can you tell me why Meritta and Aniliina aren't getting along?"

Jaska took a gulp from the bottle and wiped his mouth before answering.

"Hard to say which one of them is crazier. Aniliina has that eating disorder, anorexia, I guess. And Meritta has always been horrible. If only she would have stayed in Helsinki."

Jaska hadn't bothered putting his party clothes on. His perennial punk rocker uniform—tight, worn-out jeans, leather jacket, and dirty sneakers—had to do for every occasion. With his dark hair now significantly receded and his beer belly hanging over his waistband, Jaska's skinny legs made him look insect-like. When we had first seen each other again, his face was the thing that frightened me most. It was so badly swollen that his previously cute brown eyes appeared to sink deep under folds of skin. My old classmate looked at least forty.

"What are you annoyed with her for? Didn't your sister get you a job here?"

"Why does she always have to stick her nose in my business! Yeah, she got me a job working for nothing, wearing a tie, sitting in a little box tearing people's tickets. I'm stuck there for at least six months since I lost my unemployment. And I haven't been able to book any gigs lately."

"Oh, what band are you with now?"

"I play with Johnny and those guys sometimes. And this band in Liperi wants me to join them. They play some kind of heavy metal…"

As long as I could remember, Jaska had always been in some band or another, each better than the last, and once he had almost landed a recording deal. But nothing ever came of it. Jaska's greatest achievement seemed to be a blurry picture in the bottom-left corner of a free calendar of summer concerts that came with a subscription to *Sound* magazine.

"Johnny said you guys were talking about getting together for a jam session." Jaska pushed the bottle at me again, but I shook my head. I was pretty sure the town's unwritten code of conduct did not include female sheriffs appearing drunk in public. Jaska, on the other hand, drained about a quarter of the bottle, which went down without so much as a burp.

"And I sure as shit don't want to be working for my sister's lover even if the rest of town thinks he's some sort of miracle man. This mine business is bullshit—I can feel it in my bones."

"You mean that Meritta and this Kivinen guy…" For some reason this revelation delighted me.

"Have you seen his old lady? It ain't no wonder he's screwing around. And you know Meritta…"

"What about me?" Meritta's orange dress appeared next to me, and I turned to see Seppo Kivinen standing behind her in his copper-hued suit. Without a word, Jaska suddenly took off running. Meritta's derisive laughter seemed to propel him even faster down the hill.

"How drunk is he?" Meritta asked.

"How often is he sober nowadays?" I asked in return. I didn't like Meritta laughing at him.

"Never, as far as I know. By the way, have you two met yet? Seppo Kivinen—Maria Kallio, our summer sheriff."

Kivinen's handshake was cold and firm. His eyes locked into mine in an attempt to appear interested. He clearly chose his topic of conversation according to his company, which in my case was the security arrangements at the mine. Before long the governor and mayor came over and I was able to escape.

I would have liked to climb back up the Tower, but the door was locked. The iron surface of the heavy door handle felt cold to the touch. A lighthearted, old-fashioned fox-trot was playing inside the restaurant, which seemed to clash with the threatening rock wall of the Tower and the unreal yellow of the hill's gravel. I wondered about Jaska, Aniliina's bizarre behavior, and Johnny's tired face. I didn't feel in a very festive mood anymore. But I marched back inside, finding Ella and Matti near the door. They seemed to be arguing over which of them should go relieve Ella's mother from babysitting at home.

"They're leaving tomorrow morning to drive to Tampere, and you promised I could stay for the party," Ella said, clearly furious.

"Couldn't she sleep at our place just as easily? I don't want to leave yet either—"

"Well, you can call and ask!" she said before turning her attention toward me. "Maria, think carefully before you get yourself a man and have kids. Everything has to be so damn complicated!" Ella angrily fingered the brooch on her folk costume. "Men are always trying to wriggle out of promises…"

"I'll call her and I'll go home if she can't stay over." Matti's brown velvet suit disappeared into the swarm of humanity.

"All he ever does is run around the country doing workshops and going to Artists' Association meetings. And if he can't come up with anything better, he's sitting with Meritta in the Copper Cup planning their arts camp. And then the one time I'm supposed to get to have a good time, he's like this!" Ella's face was glowing red, and I got the impression that the root of her irritation was something other than a dispute over whose turn it was to watch their kids. "And then I had to put on this stupid getup because Viivi poured milk on the front of my only party dress."

"Let's get some punch. Based on the smell, there must be some sort of food here too. And then let's do something crazy. Go ask the mayor to dance or something." I was trying to cheer up both of us.

A few minutes later we were standing on the restaurant terrace, looking down at the crowd below and trying to decide whose head to pour punch on, when I noticed Johnny's light-brown curls directly below us.

"Think I could hit him…"

I was already tipping my glass when Ella squealed, "Look out, Johnny!"

Johnny looked up and shouted something that didn't carry over the blare of the music, now a waltz. He looked for the nearest stairs and started to climb up toward us.

"You two look like you're up to no good." Although Johnny tried to grin, his face still looked tired.

"Not me. It was Maria. She was going to dump punch on your head."

"What the hell for?"

"Boring party. We have to spice things up somehow."

"Let's go dance." Without waiting for me to reply, Johnny grabbed my wrist.

"Do I have to pour punch on someone's head too?" Ella yelled after us.

By the time we made it downstairs, the music had switched to Procol Harum's "A Whiter Shade of Pale." Johnny smelled familiar, and I remembered how at one time just dancing with him had been enough to satisfy me for weeks. As Johnny's body against mine invited me to press closer, suddenly the party ceased to be so boring. The feelings that had surged in me fifteen years ago rose to the surface, and I had no desire to resist. I had already made myself a laughingstock once because of Johnny, so why not again?

Another slow song came on. Johnny's hand on my waist was warm and heavy, his expression relaxed. In the crush of people, we collided with Ella and Matti, who appeared to have made peace, and somewhere in the crowd I saw my mother looking at me with a puzzled expression. How was it any of her business who I danced with?

I was annoyed when another quick fox-trot came on. When we left in search of more punch, Johnny kept his arm around my waist. We snuck out of the restaurant the back way to the base of the Tower. A narrow sliver of summer moon hung next to the Tower, the sky the same bluebell color as Johnny's eyes.

"You look a little tired," I said probingly.

"I spent all last night with Tuija thrashing out practical stuff about the kids. In theory we have joint custody, but she's been griping about them staying with me. Tuomas woke up to us screaming at each other and it took an hour to get him calmed down again. I thought Tuija would be here, but I haven't seen her."

"She was earlier. So what got between you guys?"

Johnny looked down the hill, his dark-red suit outlined clearly against the sky. Apollo indeed.

"We were too young. We were seventeen when we started dating, and I was a totally different guy then. I want more out of life now than...teaching other people's brats how to do somersaults. I've been doing the same thing for ten years, and I have another thirty ahead of me. I'm going nowhere."

"Well what do you want to do?"

"I don't know. Something else." Johnny stripped some leaves from a young birch tree, crushing them with his hand and scattering the green chaff across the copper-colored sand. "I don't have it in me to be a musician anymore, but I think I could try coaching soccer again or sports reporting or...Now you're going to laugh for sure...I'd like to study photography. Travel the world taking pictures. The dreams of a thirty-four-year-old man!" Johnny hurled the rest of the birch leaf bits down the hill.

"I'm not laughing. I get it."

"I don't think you've ever laughed at me." The look in Johnny's eyes was hard to bear as his face came closer to mine, our lips almost touching, but then the sound of footsteps behind us made him pull away.

"Am I interrupting?" Kaisa looked just as confused as I was.

"Did you get Aniliina calmed down?" Johnny had turned to stare down the hill again.

"She didn't calm down; she just went for one of her crazy long runs. She's been getting worse again since she's out of school and her therapist is on vacation. I almost think they should send her back to the hospital…"

"So her anorexia is really that bad?"

"Isn't it obvious!" Johnny snorted. "She's nothing but skin and bones."

"Where does that strange name—Aniliina—come from?"

"Aniliina Violetta, in fact. Apparently she was completely purple when she was born," Kaisa said.

A dark silhouette appeared from behind the Tower.

Suddenly Tuija reappeared out of nowhere and motioned for Johnny to come with her. "Here you are, Johnny. I have something I need to talk to you about." Without a word, Johnny left. Kaisa turned to watch Johnny go, and I couldn't quite interpret her expression. Was that anger I was seeing?

My arms had goose bumps. "I think I'll go inside. It's getting a bit cold out here," I said, and Kaisa followed me in. Inside I bumped into Ella and Matti again and a host of other acquaintances. As I exchanged news with approximately half the town, I succeeded in limiting myself to only one more glass of punch. The program included a relatively tame fireworks display around midnight, after which the party really began to die down, and no after-party seemed in the offing. As Ella and Matti were leaving to finally let her mom go home to bed, I walked with them down the hill. The moon had risen above the Tower, casting a frosty glow onto the dark-gray stone as if tiny lights were shining all along its walls.

"Phosphorus," Matti explained. "The rock was quarried from the top of the hill. The glow of the phosphorus was what made people believe trolls lived under the hill."

I snorted. "I still believe that," I said, thinking of the odd feeling I had been experiencing most of the night.

I left Matti and Ella in front of the church and continued walking down the street toward the taxi station. Downtown was quiet and dark, the sole light shining from the police station. A muffled thumping came from the dance floor at the hotel restaurant. When I reached the bookstore, I heard a bicycle bell behind me. Johnny was coasting down the street on an old yellow Jopo. With its high handlebars and diminutive wheels, the one-speed bicycle looked ridiculous under him.

"Hi, Maria. Where did you disappear to?" Johnny jumped off his bike to walk beside me.

"Did I disappear? And, by the way, you need a bike light on that piece of junk."

"Oh yeah, you're the sheriff. I promise to walk it the rest of the way. It's my dad's. I haven't picked up mine from Tuija's place yet."

"Are you going to your parents' house tonight?"

"Yeah, we're starting the roofing project in the morning. Are you going to your mom and dad's place too?"

"I thought I'd take a cab out to the farm, but it doesn't look like there are any at the station." The city's three taxis must have been out on other runs. That wasn't any surprise, of course, with it being Friday, the night of the Old Mine gala, and closing time at the bars. No buses ran after six p.m.

"I can wait with you." The shadows under Johnny's eyes had deepened even further, and I could tell what the look on his face meant. He wanted someone to talk to—not about his problems, just about something insignificant to help him calm down.

So we talked music again. And photography, which I didn't know the first thing about. When no taxi showed up after fifteen minutes, I decided to try Plan B.

"I think I'll walk to my parents' house and grab my bike. It's only six kilometers out to the farm."

"I'll come with you. It's almost on the way."

That was a familiar line. Back before Johnny had a driver's license, we had spent many hours after soccer practice leaning on our bikes on the corner down the street from my house. Of course only when Johnny wasn't going to Tuija's house. After he got his license, sometimes he dropped me off at home in his dad's car. But I still anticipated the nights when he didn't have the car and had to bike.

Johnny tried to talk me into riding on his luggage rack, teasing me for being overzealous, which only got worse after I told him about the idling incident that morning.

He wasn't in the habit of laughing at me either. That had probably prolonged my infatuation. If he had ever treated me like an irritating little kid instead of a friend, my feelings would have faded much faster. Especially during junior high when I had a fairly hard time making friends. I guess I was a freak. Girls in Arpikylä weren't supposed to play soccer or play in rock bands. Eventually I did get pushed out of soccer when some of the parents started hinting not so subtly to Johnny that keeping a girl on the team was ridiculous. As the boys grew, they argued that I wasn't going to be able to take the hits they would be dishing out. And supposedly the other teams would make fun of us for not having enough boys who could play.

What was Johnny—an eighteen-year-old kid—supposed to say? That I could handle anything as well as anyone else on the team? Of course they tackled me harder—fifteen-year-old boys weren't about to let any opportunity to grope a girl pass by. Penalties were the furthest thing from their minds when they were trying to get the ball from me. I chalked it up to the male superiority instilled in small-town boys. I guess Johnny realized I was turning into a problem for the team. So when I told him I had decided to give up soccer, he didn't stand in my way. I said I was having difficulty balancing schoolwork with sports, which was about the most see-through excuse I could have used. Even though I never did homework, my GPA was still well over nine out of ten. He did wheedle the real reason out of me eventually though.

"My parents," I explained at last. They didn't like me playing soccer either. When I complained to them about people trying to get me kicked off the team, my mother simply said, "It does seem like you're just trying to get attention. You'd have an easier time making friends if you tried to be more like the other girls. You could play volleyball. We have a perfectly good girls' team."

"But I'm better at soccer, Mom!" I yelled, which was followed by the slamming of doors and the sure knowledge that no one in the entire world understood me. Of course, I had hoped Johnny would try to convince me to stay. But all he did was comfort me clumsily, saying that at least *he* wanted me on the team and that at least we would still see each other at band practice.

And no one was going to get me to quit Rat Poison, even though the message was clear enough that piano and voice lessons were more appropriate than rock bands for girls. If I had been a sexy lead singer or something, people would've been more able to understand. But all I did was stand in the back corner strumming my bass guitar. I never even shook my hips, and I sang backup vocals only in emergencies. So I didn't fit the mold of a music chick either. But Johnny liked me, and that got me pretty far. Although "liking" never turned into anything more.

"Why did you come back?" Johnny asked as we turned onto my old street.

"The job. Money. I don't know…I just had this feeling that I needed to come here for a while. Maybe it's a turning-thirty crisis." One reason undoubtedly was that I wanted to get to know my parents again, which hadn't occurred to me until just then.

"Turning thirty…What am I having then? A turning-thirty-four crisis?"

"I think it's good you want to do something different with your life. I, for one, am happy I haven't gotten stuck in one permanent job yet."

"And what about this Antti of yours? How permanent is that?"

For a moment I felt like playing Peter and denying all the promises I had made to wait for Antti and all the talk about getting married. But I had learned a little in fifteen years.

"I guess we're pretty permanent. We'll make a final decision about whether to get married or not in August when Antti gets back to Finland."

We walked in silence to the intersection. The Tower behind us still glowed silver in the light of the moon, now high in the sky. A pale Big Dipper struggled to stay visible above it.

"But he isn't here now," Johnny said, pulling me to him.

Our first kiss tasted like potato chips. And I guess I really had learned something in fifteen years, because I didn't faint like I always thought I would. But, after retrieving my bike from my parents' place, I did sing Beatles songs at the top of my lungs all the way back to the farm.

4

The ringing phone seemed awfully far away. It had to be Antti, who was probably drinking in Chicago on a Friday night and calling me without realizing that, in Finland, it was seven o'clock Saturday morning. My mouth felt gummy as I dragged myself toward Uncle Pena's old black rotary-dial phone, preparing to rip Antti a new one.

"Morning, Kallio. Antikainen here."

"Morning. What's up?" Oh, hell, work. Automatically my free hand started fumbling with the coffeemaker.

"It's up at the Old Mine. Someone found"—Antikainen paused dramatically—"a body."

"What? Where are you?" Suddenly my hand was shaking. Half the coffee grounds spilled onto the floor as I tried to scoop them into the filter.

"In a patrol car outside the mine restaurant. Lasarov is over with the...body. What should we do?"

"I'll be there as soon as I can. You need to get a doctor. Call the county and they'll line someone up." The coffeemaker began its reassuring burbling. "Can you tell who it is? The person who died?"

"The dog walker who found the body already identified her. Orange dress and lots of jewelry. It's that artist, Meritta—"

"Call the county. I'll be right there." After quickly counting how many hours had passed since my last drink, I decided I was good to drive. When I stepped outside, Mikko slipped out after me and took off running toward the edge of the field. I pumped a couple of bucketfuls of deliciously cold water from the well and dumped them over me. So, my hair would get a little wet; now was no time for primping. I acted without thinking, robotically putting on a no-nonsense, comfortable pantsuit, pouring the coffee into Uncle Pena's hunting thermos, and packing a couple of sandwiches for the road. This was going to be a long Saturday.

Alternately slurping coffee and wolfing down the sandwiches, I began driving slowly along the deserted forest road. With half a quart of coffee in my belly, the world started looking less fuzzy. Still, I didn't let myself think about the fact that someone I knew had died. Whatever shock was churning my insides, I couldn't let it take over, not yet. The time for that would be once I was back home, alone.

On the way to the scene of the crime, the only living things I saw were six cows watching the world with relief after their morning milking. The parking lot at the Old Mine was empty. The gates to the museum complex were locked, but I quickly climbed over them and rushed up the stairs toward the main building. At around the thirtieth step, I started feeling the effects of having stayed up too late the previous night, but I kept up my pace all the way to the top, imagining that if I ran fast enough, I could still bring Meritta back to life.

The base of the Tower was quiet. The white-and-bluish-black police van appeared abandoned. I realized I could have driven up the back way too. Then I noticed Antikainen and Lasarov nearer the Tower with something orange at their feet. Her body strangely twisted, Meritta looked as though she had fallen from the sky.

I looked up the face of the Tower. Nearly a one-hundred-foot drop. The fact that Meritta's body was so intact, that her face was still recognizable, was a little surprising. Her orange hippy dress was spread around her like a Krishna robe, and I noticed the copper heart that had hung from her left ear was missing.

"Who called it in?"

Antikainen shuffled through his papers.

"Ritva Matikainen. She lives just down the hill. She was out with her German shepherd and the dog found...um...Ms. Flöjt."

"And where is Ms. Matikainen now?"

"She wanted to go home." Antikainen looked worried that he might have made a mistake. I nodded to show I understood. I would have wanted to go home after finding a body too.

Just then the sun topped the trees and began streaming into our eyes, igniting a strip of blazing orange on Meritta's dress. The gravel surrounding the dress looked pale in comparison. I tried to concentrate on how the routine was supposed to unfold, thinking about how the county forensics team would need to go up the Tower to check for any evidence of what might have caused Meritta's fall. Should we call in some detectives from the county as well? With any luck Koivu would be on duty. I wouldn't have any turf issues with him. But did we need outsiders involved? Most likely it was just an accident. As I recalled, Meritta had still been at the party when I left.

"What was someone doing walking their dog around here? Aren't all the gates locked?"

"The north side just has a boom across the road. People walk up here all the time. Kivinen says he's going to eventually build a fence."

I sighed. So anyone could have been here. But not many of them would have had keys to the Tower. How did Meritta get up after the tour was over and the doors locked?

As I remembered, the Old Mine was scheduled to open at ten today. With the official opening the day before, plenty of tourists would be showing up before too long. But we had to close part of the area, at least around the Tower. I had to call Kivinen directly. He could decide what would be best for the rest of the attraction. We couldn't let flocks of curious tourists come gawk at the site of the accident.

"I think we're going to need reinforcements. Call the rest of the boys in. And someone needs to tell the family what happened. Her daughter and brother...and I think her mother's still alive too."

"Actually, Meeri Korhonen, her mom, is my neighbor," Lasarov said slowly.

"Maybe it would be best to notify her first and then let her tell Aniliina...Doesn't Jaska—doesn't Jari Korhonen still live with his mother? Lasarov, could you handle it once someone comes to relieve you? Since they are your neighbors."

Lasarov nodded and then walked a short distance away from us, back to Meritta's corpse. His lips moved as if he was practicing what he would say to her mother. I wouldn't have wanted to trade places with him. Antikainen's phone beeped and then he began giving driving directions to the county forensics team and medical examiner. I found myself thinking of them as rescuers. They would arrive and tell us that Meritta fell by accident and we had no reason to launch a criminal investigation.

Forensics...They would need keys to the Tower, since the door was locked. Information gave me Seppo Kivinen's number. As I waited for someone to answer the phone, Detective Järvi and Officer Hopponen drove up with Officer Timonen in the backseat. Trading places with Timonen, Lasarov jumped into the cruiser and they set off to break the bad news to Mrs. Korhonen.

Antikainen started rummaging around in the back of his police van and emerged with a roll of yellow police tape with the words "Police line do not cross." After about ten rings, Kivinen answered. I wondered whether he had stayed until the end of the party, as a good host should.

"You can't be serious!" He groaned after I stated the reason for the call. "A body...Meritta Flöjt! How did she die?"

"She's lying at the base of the Tower. We can't say anything definite before the medical examination, but based on her position, we assume she fell from the top."

Kivinen sounded appropriately upset, but when I explained to him that the police would be forced to close at least part of the mine area, he grew angry.

"Unacceptable! The whole day is already booked solid with museum tours, and we have busloads of retirees coming in from Kuopio. We can't close down now. Just think of the cost..."

"The sooner we find out what happened, the faster everything will return to normal. At the very least we'll need the keys to the Tower and the guest list from last night. It would be best if you could come down here right away."

After ending the call with Kivinen, I saw the county forensics van turn the corner at the bottom of the hill and head toward us. It was eight thirty and in town I could already see morning traffic. Stores would be opening. People would soon be getting into motion. As would rumors, which spread quickly in towns this size. Two hours from now, everyone would know that a body had turned up at the Old Mine.

The county medical examiner, Doctor Turunen, was about fifty years old, thin, and taciturn. As I watched him get down to work, I found myself expecting some sort of miracle, as if he could simply glance at Meritta and declare that she had fallen accidentally. The county police photographer snapped pictures of Meritta, and Antikainen began combing the area around the Tower with the rest of the forensics team. Suddenly Kivinen's dark-blue Volvo was also in front of the restaurant. I hoped he would say Meritta had been drunk. Maybe he would know why Meritta had been in the Tower in the first place.

But Kivinen still wasn't interested in Meritta, only the tour buses full of senior citizens that would be arriving at eleven o'clock. As I listened to him grumble for five minutes about how we were getting in the way of his business, I silently counted to ten over and over to soothe my irritation. It didn't help.

"Mr. Kivinen, has it occurred to you that we're trying to do our jobs here too?" Yelling at a man whose guest I had been the night before was a bit of a drag. "I understand you knew the victim. Aren't you the slightest bit interested in how she died? Now cough up those keys and get me that guest list!"

"The Tower is safe. To fall you'd have to climb over the railing. You can't blame us for this!" Kivinen dropped the pathetically small-looking key to the sturdy Tower door into Detective Järvi's waiting hand. "And what are you going to do with the guest list? Do you intend to interview all two hundred people who attended the party? Including the mayor and the governor?"

"We just want to find out who last saw Meritta Flöjt alive. And how she got into the Tower. I tried the door at around nine o'clock, and it was locked."

"She had her own key," Kivinen said as if it were self-evident.
"What?"

"I gave it to her months ago. She—she enjoyed being in the Tower, especially at sunrise and sunset. She was talking about painting the landscape someday. She had my permission to move about the property freely, and she came and went as she pleased. Her paintings are great publicity." Now Kivinen was starting to sound apologetic. His eyes even began to wander, flitting between the hillside and the medical examiner, who was still busy inspecting Meritta's body. No longer cold, Kivinen's toffee-colored eyes looked more frightened now. A few minutes later, I thought I detected sorrow in them. I had seen the same phenomenon before: when faced with tragic news, people try to keep busy with something inconsequential as if that could make the reason for their shock disappear. Then the pain would suddenly hit them. Kivinen seemed to be experiencing that now. Walking a little way toward Meritta, he suddenly turned back and sat on the hood of his car, digging in his pockets as if searching for a cigarette but coming up with only a packet of gum, which he stared at in bewilderment for a moment before popping a piece in his mouth. I realized he was trying not to look at Meritta but couldn't help himself. It was as if the corpse was drawing him to it. I remembered Jaska's insinuations about a relationship between them.

"Can I see her?" Kivinen asked finally.

"As soon as the doctor's done. Do you have that guest list?"

Detective Järvi and the forensics team were in the Tower, and it sounded as though they were arguing about something. I glanced up. One of the county investigators was sitting on the edge of the Tower with Järvi holding on to his arm.

"Let's go into the restaurant," Kivinen said, looking as though he might be sick. I turned to follow him, but the medical examiner's voice stopped me.

"Come over here for a second, Kallio!"

"You go inside. I'll be in in a minute," I told Kivinen and started walking back toward the Tower and Meritta.

"I can tell you something already," Doctor Turunen explained slowly, almost whispering in his Savo dialect. "As far as I can tell, the cause of death was a broken neck. That's generally what happens in a collision like a traffic accident or a long fall. The spine is also probably broken. The hips are bent very strangely. You don't end up in a position like that from only a blow to the head. And I don't see any other contusions on the head that could have resulted in death. Based on the amount of rigor mortis, she's been dead only a few hours. If I had to make a guess, I'd say she died between three and four a.m."

"So you do think she fell?"

Turunen's brow wrinkled. I hadn't ever met him before, so I didn't know how quick he was to draw conclusions.

"Fell...or was pushed," he whispered. "The body does show bruises likely inflicted prior to death. A couple of the fingernails are broken. You should have the guys up top look for them. The knuckles on her right hand are swollen...She may have hit someone before she died. So yes, she may have fallen of her own accord, but it's just as likely that someone pushed her over after a struggle. I'll take her to the lab in Joensuu and have a closer look. If I were you, I'd assume she was pushed...although I can't say that with certainty."

I didn't feel like running up the Tower, so I just called the guys up on top and told them what to look for. Signs of a struggle. Pieces of fingernails. He was trying to hide it, but I could hear astonishment in Detective Järvi's voice.

Inside the restaurant, Kivinen was speaking heatedly into his cell phone. He seemed to have pulled himself together again. Judging by the smell, that effort had required a shot or two of whiskey. "You can go see Meritta now," I said when he hung up.

"I don't think I want to anymore. You wouldn't happen to have a cigarette on you?"

"I don't smoke."

"I don't either anymore…theoretically." Kivinen dug more nicotine gum out of his pocket. "There's the guest list. I left sometime around one, and there weren't many people left at that point. I can try to remember who if you want. I am pretty sure Meritta was still at the party. The place was empty by the time my secretary left at two thirty. She didn't go in the Tower, though, so Meritta could have been up there."

"And the night watchmen? Aren't they supposed to drive by once an hour?"

"I've tried to call the company, but no one is answering."

Kivinen had told me that security at the Old Mine was handled by a company run by a couple of young local men who had promised to patrol the area several times a night.

"How well did you know Meritta Flöjt, Mr. Kivinen?" My voice echoed in the empty, stone-walled restaurant.

"Isn't it a city ordinance that we're all supposed to be on a first-name basis? Call me Seppo." Kivinen extended his hand, which I shook, though I was a little taken aback as I muttered my first name. Under the circumstances, Kivinen's familiarity seemed out of place, even though I could tell he wasn't joking about the city ordinance. Small towns had a habit of passing peculiar laws, and this one was instituted while I was in high school. My art teacher had been one of the main opponents of the measure, arguing that we didn't have to copy every idiotic idea the Swedes dreamed up.

"Yes, I knew her…She was a member of the committee that helped develop the concept for the Old Mine renovation, the same committee that your uncle Pena was on. And…well…There's no point trying to hide it, since someone will tell you eventually anyway. Last winter Meritta and I spent a few nights together. It wasn't anything serious. I'm married and I intend to stay that way." Kivinen didn't seem the slightest bit uncomfortable talking about his relationship with Meritta. That didn't mean anything though. People cheated on their spouses without any qualms all the time. So why was I so messed up over one friendly kiss with Johnny?

"Your relationship was over, then?"

"Yes. I think she was with someone else this spring. And there wasn't any love between us, so we weren't bitter. You saw yourself yesterday how well we got along."

"Yes, I did." I didn't want to think about Meritta's other male companion.

Next we quickly ran through the guest list and then began discussing which areas on the property to cordon off. Without too much resistance, Kivinen agreed to close the Tower and delay opening the restaurant until the evening. In order to cause as little inconvenience as possible, the lower area where the museum and other attractions were located would continue operating as planned.

When I came out of the restaurant, Meritta's body had disappeared, and Lasarov and Hopponen had returned from reporting her death to her next of kin. The local cops were powwowing intensely with the county police. The photographer was still snapping away up above.

"There were all sorts of neat things up there," Detective Antikainen said. "The pieces of fingernail you were expecting, a little blood…" Cheerfully Antikainen waved a transparent evidence bag with something orange inside, which one of the county forensic technicians grabbed out of his hand and added to his collection of samples. "That piece of cloth is probably from our vic's skirt. And this Kalevala brooch must be hers…"

Horrified, I stared at the heavy medieval-reproduction brooch in the other bag Antikainen was holding up. The palmette ornamentation was unmistakable; I knew I had seen someone wearing it yesterday, but not Meritta. Ella had been wearing it as part of her folk costume.

"Well, what did the ME say? Do we have a murder on our hands?" Antikainen asked blithely. Lasarov coughed, and Järvi also seemed irritated with him. To date, the high point of Antikainen's police career had been a knife fight between two rival Gypsy gangs that resulted in two fatalities.

I felt sick to my stomach. "Let's have Forensics and our detectives meet down at the station. Lasarov, you come too to represent Patrol. Timonen and Hopponen, will you be OK here? We'll keep the Tower closed until further notice, and we'll send someone up at noon to relieve you so you can go eat."

Descending the stairs back to my car felt unreal. The lightning rod on top of the Tower, shining innocently in the morning sun, reflected beams of light directly into my face. It was almost as if the Tower were winking at me. And the blood up there—was it Meritta's or someone else's? Meritta's murderer? Then there were the pieces of fingernail. And Ella's brooch? What the hell was happening? Had I come back to my boring old hometown just to get caught up in another murder of an acquaintance?

Everyone else was already waiting in the break room by the time I arrived. Detective Järvi was looking downcast at the empty coffeemaker. "There isn't even any coffee," he said to me in an accusatory tone.

"So go ahead and make some. You must know how." Goddamn it. I was Järvi's boss. Did he really expect me to handle the coffee just because I was a woman?

Järvi glanced at me with a slight frown and then slipped out to get some water for the coffeemaker. I did feel a bit ashamed of myself. Bossing around a guy who had been a cop almost as long as

I had been alive felt gauche. And besides, growing up, everyone had always known him as the nice cop in town. He came to our elementary school and taught us to look both ways before we crossed the street. He came to our junior high to warn us about shoplifting and souping up our mopeds. He came to our high school to lecture us about drinking and driving. Always just as thin and gray, he had looked more or less the same for as long as I had known him. Fortunately, the cop who had once written me a ticket for riding my bike at night without a light had retired a few years earlier.

"Otherwise we had a pretty quiet Friday night," Järvi observed as he poured the coffee grounds into the filter. "There isn't anybody in the tank. Antikainen and I don't really have a backlog either, so we can start the investigation immediately. I don't think we need the county at all. If we need reinforcements, we can call guys in from other nearby towns."

"I don't see how that's an *if*," I said, "when the first thing we have to do is interview nearly two hundred people."

"But most of them are just going to say they left before you did. And when you left, Flöjt was still there," Antikainen pointed out. "And the boys can help."

By "the boys" presumably he meant the local patrol officers.

"They have Karttunen and Säkkinen out on vacation already. And the rest of you are supposed to be taking your summer breaks soon. And there's the comp time you've been building up. I don't see what the problem is with working with the county. Do you have some issue with them?"

"What's your problem?" Antikainen suddenly yelled. "You go spend a few years in Helsinki and now you think us local cops are a bunch of yokels who don't know how to do anything?"

"Maybe she doesn't want to have to lead the investigation," Järvi suggested.

I couldn't help nodding, since Järvi had hit the nail on the head. If the brooch we had found in the Tower was Ella's, and if the rumors about Meritta and Johnny's relationship were true...I couldn't handle a third summer in a row of rummaging around in my friends' dirty laundry. Approaching Meritta's possible murder professionally would be impossible. Based on my two previous experiences, I knew how investigating a murder felt when my own emotions were in play. Even though I had handled both incidences well enough and good things had come of them—the first case had reintroduced me to Antti and in the second case, a relative of Antti's sister would have ended up in jail if it weren't for me—recovering had still taken time.

"I was at the party myself, as were my parents and a few of my friends. I may not be a suspect, but someone will still have to question me. And are any of you really looking forward to running around grilling your friends and neighbors?"

"That's all we ever do. I even had to lock up my brother-in-law once when we caught him drunk and waving a knife around," Lasarov said.

Still, I decided to stick to my guns. "The county is a resource, not a liability. They aren't going to take over the case. I'll call them in a few minutes. In the meantime, let's figure out what we need to do first."

The county forensics team took the evidence back to their laboratory in Joensuu. Antikainen and Järvi stayed behind to gather addresses for everyone on the guest list, and Lasarov went to spell the guards at the Tower while they took their lunch break. I retreated to my office to call the county crime division. Their lead detective, a Sergeant Järvisalo, promised to come and bring another detective provided that the medical examiner's final report indicated a crime had in fact occurred. So I stayed in my office to drink coffee and wait. I imagined Mikko would have found himself something to eat by now. I only hoped the front porch wouldn't be covered with bird carcasses when I got home.

I may have nodded off at my desk, because Antikainen's shrill voice outside my door snapped me out of a strange, dazed state. "You can't go in there!"

"Just try to stop me." When I lifted my eyes, Johnny was standing at my door, looking like he hadn't slept in a year.

"Maria. I had to come. Is it true what they're saying in town about Meritta?"

"What are they saying?" I motioned for Johnny to sit. How had he managed to grow three days of stubble in one night? When I looked into his eyes and saw their empty depth, I knew the truth about his relationship with Meritta.

"That Meritta is dead. That she fell off the Tower."

"It's true," I said. I didn't move around the desk to hug him, even though I should have. We hadn't hugged the previous night, so why should we now?

"Goddamn it. I knew this would happen someday if she kept sitting on that railing when she was drunk!" Johnny hid his head in his hands, and I moved toward him, but the police officer in me overcame the person.

"What did you say? You saw Meritta sitting on the edge of the Tower?"

"She always sat up there. She'd swing her legs and laugh and make fun of anyone who was afraid of heights. She said it was like sitting on top of the world..." Johnny's shoulders were heaving. Now I remembered a newspaper story from a couple of years before with a picture of Meritta sitting on the railing of the Tower with her black hair shining against a backdrop of white clouds and blue sky.

"Did you see her go up in the Tower last night?"

"No. I did talk to her a little before I left. She said she wanted to be alone."

Well, well. Just like in high school. Johnny couldn't get Meritta to leave with him, so he had nothing better to do than walk me home. I didn't know which annoyed me more, that he was still using me as his fallback or that I still cared.

"Was that a change of plans? Had you arranged to leave together?" My voice must have been sharper than normal because Johnny glanced at me with a puzzled look.

"We hadn't arranged anything. So you know that…"

"That you two were involved. At least that's what everyone says." My voice was still too cold, almost angry. "Do I understand correctly that you think Meritta was drunk, climbed up the Tower, and fell by accident?"

"Yeah, I guess so…I'd been up there before with her to watch the sunrise."

"But you weren't with her this time?" I asked, watching Johnny closely. Under his beard shone a fresh-looking bruise, and the knuckles of his right hand were split. I closed my eyes, but when I opened them, the injuries were still there.

"How did you get banged up?" The tremor in my voice made me sound angry, although really it was from fear.

"I fell off that stupid Jopo on our lane. I didn't realize its little tires wouldn't go over the rocks like a mountain bike. Why do you ask?"

"So you didn't get that bruise…last night at the Tower, for example? Do you have any injuries other than on your jaw and hand?"

"What the hell are you implying?" Johnny's tone was even angrier than mine, and all the color had drained from his face.

I was ashamed of myself. "Sorry, forget I said that. I'm tired too. I saw you leave for home. I just feel so crappy about Meritta, even though she was almost a stranger, and I feel bad for you too. Go home and rest. We'll call you if we have any more questions."

Johnny left without saying good-bye. I poured my seventh cup of coffee from the thermos, and had almost finished it when the medical examiner called. Some of the contusions on Meritta's body had come from before her death, probably in a "wrestling match," as Doctor Turunen put it. The scratches on her back indicated that she had been pushed over the edge of the Tower. The blood type of the samples taken from the Tower matched Meritta's, and they were conducting further analysis as we spoke.

"We ain't had no murders in a while now," Turunen concluded in his broad Savo dialect. Before I could relay the results to Detectives Järvi and Antikainen, the phone rang again.

"Hey, it's Koivu. I'm with Sergeant Järvisalo headed your way. Oh, Turunen called you too? Can we meet up at the Tower in half an hour?"

At least there was one bright light in all this misery. I was going to get to work with my old partner Pekka Koivu again. My desires to the contrary notwithstanding, I knew that the case was going to pull me in even if the county detectives did take primary responsibility for the investigation. Koivu would want my help because I knew the town. And I knew myself. No matter how difficult it was, I wasn't going to be able to stand on the sidelines. Even if it meant arresting Ella or Johnny in the end.

5

The phone rang just as I was leaving to go back to the Tower.

"Is it true that Meritta Flöjt has been murdered?" a female voice dripping with curiosity asked before I could even say my name.

"Hi, Mom. She's dead, but...That's all I can say so far."

"Even to me?" My mother sounded incredulous. I had heard those words before, like when I used to cry over Johnny but refused to tell anyone what was bothering me. God, why did I ever come back to this stupid town?

"So you're going to have to investigate?"

"Yeah, a little, but other people will be handling most of it." My decision to go into the police academy had always horrified my parents. The law was a much more appropriate profession in their eyes, even though I would be dealing with the same dirty business. Although lawyers never needed to handle dead bodies.

"Do you have time to come out to the cabin tonight? Eeva and Saku are coming."

"I'll try. It would be nice to see Saku. He's growing so fast. Oh, by the way...What time did you and Dad leave the party last night?"

"Who, us? Right after the fireworks. Don't you remember? Why do you ask?"

"No reason." Someone else could handle interviewing my parents. "I have to go now, but I'll see you tonight."

Flocks of curious onlookers had gathered at the base of the Tower, some willing to pay the entrance fee to the mine area just to get closer to the crime scene. Apparently having a murder on opening day wasn't such bad publicity for Kivinen's business after all. A few of the rubberneckers, apparently reporters, were armed with professional cameras. Who had tipped them off? Kivinen? Had he realized the news value of a mysterious death after all? One of the people who looked like a journalist started accosting Antikainen, who was in uniform, but he sent the journalist my way. After the reporter identified himself as a representative of the county paper, I said something evasive, wishing I were somewhere else.

When Koivu finally stepped out of the shiny county Saab cruiser, I felt like throwing my arms around his neck. At least with him I didn't need to put on an act. The detective sergeant, a heavyweight wrestler type in his forties who spoke in a southwestern Tampere drawl, immediately went up the Tower with Antikainen and Järvi while Koivu and I hung back on the second-to-last landing and chatted.

Koivu's blond hair was mussed and he looked more tired than usual, like a bear cub woken up in the middle of his winter sleep.

"I only got an hour and a half of sleep before Järvisalo called. You probably haven't heard yet that we had a real knock-down, drag-out last night in Joensuu—Somalis on skinheads. Luckily no one died, but three from each side are in the hospital. I was questioning them all night. I know the Somalis aren't little lambs and I have no doubt some of them are just sponging off the government, but I still don't get skinheads. One of them said to me last night with a totally straight face that Hitler was an 'awesome dude.' And I thought I was getting away from all the crazies by coming out here to the country."

"And I thought I was getting away from all the murders, at least ones where I know people involved. And now…" I didn't really know what to say. "The victim, Meritta Flöjt, was dating a man who…well, was my biggest crush during high school. And her brother used to play with me in a band."

I still didn't want to mention Ella to anyone until I verified that the brooch really was hers. Koivu grinned wearily and then swung his right arm around my shoulders.

"Don't worry. We'll get through this."

"What are you two dawdling for?" Antikainen put his head down through the hatch, and Koivu recoiled from me as if he had been doing something wrong. Antikainen looked at us strangely but fortunately didn't say anything.

The top of the Tower was windy, and clouds were gathering. Especially to the north, the landscape had begun to darken. The pond to the southwest was like a gaping wound. At the north end of the pond, where the other mine tower used to stand, was now just a hole. A few years before, the mining company had tried to unload the mine for next to nothing, but of course no one was interested at any price because the deal also would have included millions in liability for rehabilitating the sinkhole area. The mining company hadn't wanted to invest their money in any kind of restoration work, so they leveled the mine buildings with explosives. But without the other tower, the landscape looked strangely barren, like a face missing an eye. Rising farther off in the distance, the tower of the third local mine awaited the same fate. Fortunately, Kivinen had come to rescue the main mining complex.

"I've heard our victim used to sit up on that railing," I said to Detective Sergeant Järvisalo. "Maybe she did just fall."

"The ME thinks otherwise, based on her bruises."

"Maybe we'll find some other explanation for them after we interview the party guests."

Silently I wondered what Järvi and Antikainen were still doing up in the Tower instead of starting the questioning, which would have been a better use of their time.

"She could have been sitting on the railing, and the killer started to push her off, and there was a fight," Koivu suggested. "In that case, the killer could be of any size and strength. On the other hand…If both of them were standing here, and the vic was resisting, getting her up and over the railing would definitely have required some muscle. Should we try it, Maria? Wasn't Flöjt about your size?"

"A little taller, but more slender. Probably about the same weight."

Koivu and I staged a demonstration fight, which ended with him dangling me headfirst over the railing. The yellow sand below was awfully far away, yet simultaneously seemed to call me back into the arms of Mother Earth. I wondered whether Meritta hung like this, trying to keep a grip on her attacker, or whether she clung desperately to the railing as someone struggled to break her hold…I felt like screaming. Had Meritta screamed? Did she imagine she was flying for a moment as she fell?

"Koivu, that's enough!"

I felt sick. For a few minutes I had to sit on the bench in the middle of the observation deck and breathe deeply, waiting for the shaking in my legs to stop. It wasn't until everyone else started talking about going to lunch that I realized I was hungry too. Detective Järvi suggested that we have pizza delivered to the station. After that, he, Antikainen, and Koivu would head out to start questioning party guests. Sergeant Järvisalo was in a hurry to get back to Joensuu and promised to call on Monday unless something important came to light before then.

Well then. County Detective Sergeant Arvo Järvisalo was supposed to head up the investigation. But he wasn't going to be here. So in reality, Maria Kallio, summer sheriff, was in charge. That was exactly what I had been afraid of. Detectives Antikainen and Järvi, on the other hand, seemed pleased.

As we went back to the cars, I noticed someone wearing a familiar leather jacket standing near the restaurant.

"Save me a couple of slices. I'll be there in a minute," I said to Koivu and then went over to chat with my old bandmate.

Jaska's face was swollen, and I could smell the stench of liquor on his breath from three feet away. A plastic bag with clinking bottles inside hung from his wrist.

"Hi. Are you working?" I asked when I couldn't think of any other way to start the conversation.

"No. Kivinen gave me the day off."

"I'm sorry about your sister."

"I know. Where did they take her?"

"To Joensuu for an autopsy."

Pulling a beer out of his bag, Jaska tried to open it with his teeth.

"Don't start drinking here. Come on. I'll give you a ride. Do you want me to take you home?"

"Is this you expressing your condolences or is it a police interrogation?"

"Both."

"Not home then. Let's just drive around."

Back behind the Old Mine, I turned toward the Sump and then drove through the cemetery. Jaska stared at his bag of beer but still hadn't successfully opened a bottle.

"Forget about the condolences," he said as we turned onto the highway and headed out of town. "It was good Meritta died."

"Why?" I didn't recognize Jaska's voice. I had never heard him so bitter.

"I hated Meritta! At least sometimes," Jaska said. "She just had to come back here and show off what a big success she was. If she would have just stayed in Helsinki. Or kept her damn trap shut about her musically gifted little brother who never got his big break. Shit!" As he talked, Jaska tried to open a bottle with his teeth again, but it slipped and the cap left a nasty-looking cut on his lip.

"Be careful. Here's an opener." I threw my house keys to Jaska, who was suddenly as white as a sheet. Blood was running down his coat, so I pulled a handkerchief out of my pocket too.

"Goddamn Meritta! Just talking about her makes things go wrong. She always said she cared about my future. But instead of helping, she just bitched about my 'failed rock 'n' roll dream.'"

He must have swallowed some blood along with the beer, because he gagged after the first swig. The second went down easier. "Is there anyone else who could have been fed up with her enough to push her off the Tower, or do you think she jumped? Maybe she finally realized that the best thing she could do for everyone was die. At least for me and Aniliina…"

"We don't know yet. By the way, what were you doing at the Old Mine yesterday?"

"Gate-crashing, of course! They don't invite ordinary working stiffs to parties like that." Jaska was already opening his second bottle of beer. I wondered how many he had already gone through.

"Where did you go from there?"

"To the Copper Cup to get wasted. I was there until closing at two. Then I guess I went home. I don't really remember. Ask my mom what time I got home. She usually knows."

Blood was still flowing from Jaska's lip, with drops falling onto his dingy gray T-shirt. Stopping at an intersection with a side road, I turned the car back toward town. When Jaska was in a mood like this, talking to him was pointless. I remembered the Jaska from our school days, the boy who everyone supposedly kept down. School went badly for him because he said the teachers played favorites. Band practice had to end early because his fingers were sore or his head hurt. His mom didn't give him enough money, and the boss at his summer job was a dick. His girlfriend, when he happened to have one, never understood.

Jaska had repeated the tenth grade but then somehow managed to wriggle his way through the matriculation examination. After the army, he tried technical school, but it wasn't interesting enough. The only thing that did hold his attention was playing guitar. He had to have known he wasn't very talented, but he still kept his dreams of rock stardom alive. Year after year those dreams became more tattered. Jaska was still grasping at the shreds though, trying to make himself believe he was something other than an alcoholic amateur musician in his thirties with no salable skills whatsoever.

Although he was never the type to make friends with women, we had nevertheless been good pals during school. I knew his tantrums, and I knew he easily could have shoved his sister over the railing if she was laughing at him—especially if he was drunk. Maybe he didn't even remember doing it. Or didn't want to remember.

Here I was again, full speed ahead, suspecting my friends and acquaintances of murder. Jaska, Ella, Johnny...Who else? As we passed a little hill, the Tower came into sight again. It would watch over us for the entire ride back into town. Meritta wouldn't have wanted to die anywhere less public. Was it possible no one had seen what happened?

"How are your mother and Aniliina coping?" I asked as I pulled onto the main drag.

"At first Mom was hysterical and then she started planning the funeral. I guess my other sisters and my brother's wife are coming tomorrow to help. I don't know about Aniliina. She won't come over to our house. Just wants to be at home. Maybe her dad will come if anyone can get a hold of him."

"Is Aniliina all alone now then?"

"No, Kaisa Miettinen is there. She's the only person Aniliina can stand these days."

"How long has Aniliina been anorexic?"

"Just last summer she was still a little butterball. She wasn't a total fatso; her tits and ass were just a little too big for her age. Then she just started shrinking. This spring she was even in the hospital for a while because she wasn't eating anything at all. Maybe now she'll get better because her crazy bitch mother is gone. I saw a program on TV once that said anorexia comes from a bad relationship with your mother." Jaska said this last part cheerfully.

I snorted. "I'm surprised they haven't decided hemorrhoids are caused by a bad relationship with your mother," I said. When we drove by the Copper Cup Bar & Grill, Jaska asked me to drop him off.

At the police station, only Lasarov remained. Everyone else had left to start doing interviews. After eating the remaining pepperoni pizza, which had long since grown cold, I left Koivu a message and headed home. I needed to feed Mikko since I had decided that I might stay over at my parents' cabin. At least the idea of a sauna, a few cold beers, and my mother's cooking was tempting. And seeing Saku, my eleven-month-old nephew, would be fun.

Mikko purred and rubbed up against my legs as if I had been away for days. I plunked down a full can of cat food and a cup of milk and left the bathroom window open a crack so he could get out in case of an emergency. He could survive one summer night under the stars if he did get shut out. I wondered how many mice Einstein had caught in Inkoo at Antti's parents' home. And how Antti's work was going in Chicago. Two months left now. He had promised to bum around here with me for the last few weeks of my summer job when he came home.

I looked at my naked left ring finger. Was it missing something? Antti thought that if we wanted to continue our relationship and live together, we should just go ahead and get married immediately. The thought of me with a veil on my head was so ridiculous that I laughed out loud. Mikko glanced at me, looking hurt.

"Silly kitty, I'm not laughing at you. And I wouldn't wear a veil anyway. Antti doesn't even belong to the church. Maybe the courthouse and regular clothes will do…"

I drove the back roads to my parents' lakeside cabin, avoiding the center of town. I was deliberately avoiding driving past the police station, knowing the temptation to stop in hopes of getting new information was too great. Driving down the dirt roads, I pretended I was Mika Häkkinen going for a Formula One victory in Monaco. The cows applauded as I drifted the rear end of the Russian Lada station wagon, spraying gravel into the fields.

As I was making the final turn, I suddenly realized we hadn't found Meritta's handbag. That was a bit odd. Wouldn't you expect a woman who had so carefully painted her eyelids copper to bring something to touch up her makeup during the course of the evening? And she had to have kept her key to the Tower somewhere. Where had her purse ended up?

My parents' cabin had no phone, so I would have to leave the mystery of the purse for the next day. I parked Uncle Pena's Lada behind my parents' red Opel and was barely out of the car before Saku was careening toward me.

The poor child appeared to have inherited the Kallio family snub nose, which looked especially funny on an eleven-month-old. Tousled blond hair had also started sprouting on his head. Scooping Saku up and throwing him over my shoulder, I carried him back to the sand pile where he had been playing with my father. Mom and Eeva were sitting on the garden swing.

"Where's Jarmo?" I asked, since I didn't see Eeva's husband.

"He stayed in Joensuu. He had some sauna night to go to. Something about foreign guests at work. It's nice to see you on time for once." Eeva was knitting a tiny pale-blue cotton sweater, and my mother was crocheting lace. A hammer had always felt better in my hand than a crochet hook, although I did know how to darn socks.

"What time does Saku go to sleep?"

"Sometime around nine."

"I should have time for a little jog, then. Should I start the sauna stove first?"

"It's already burning. Is there any new information about Meritta's death? Timo Antikainen already stopped by our house asking if we saw anything."

"Yeah, since this is an unexplained death, it's routine to question everyone who was at the party. We want to know why and when Meritta went up in the Tower."

"Was it an accident or murder?" Eeva asked curiously.

"We still don't know," I said evasively.

"My sister the police hero is solving another murder," Eeva said, her voice dripping with sarcasm. "Why doesn't anyone call me a hero for changing Saku's diaper before I've had my morning coffee?"

I laughed. "I certainly would. I'm going running now, and then hopefully I can have a sauna with Saku before bedtime."

Besides the birds, the forest road was quiet. A lone frog hopped out of my way into a ditch. After running just a mile, I again was reminded that I'd slept only four hours the night before. My legs burned, and my breathing was labored. Slowing my pace, I eventually turned back a little earlier than I had planned. Still, running was relaxing. The past twenty-four hours had contained altogether too many emotional ups and downs, and I was drained.

I dipped myself in the lake before going into the sauna. For Saku, sauna meant sitting on the floor in the largest washbasin at the cabin, splashing water all around. The hissing of the rocks when I threw water on them made him laugh. The only thing that upset him was when I wouldn't give him a taste of my beer.

"He's a pretty dangerous little guy," I said to Eeva as we were drying Saku in the dressing room. He peered at us beneath the hood of his towel, his eyes already a little sleepy.

"Are you starting to want one? You should just do it. Or does Antti have something against kids?"

"It's more about me. It changes your life so much."

"You're right, but once they come, you get used to the change. Actually, Saku, you might as well have your bedtime milk right now." With that, Eeva took her son to her breast, and Saku smiled in satisfaction before latching on and becoming one with his mother. Slightly bewildered, I watched their symbiosis. The thought of another person getting food directly from my body was beyond strange.

"I hear you and Johnny were pretty hot and heavy on the dance floor last night," Eeva said teasingly. "Mom says his wife didn't like it one bit."

"They're getting a divorce. And don't be stupid. Anyone can dance with whoever they want!" Startled by the irritation in my tone, Saku disengaged. My family seemed to think I was ready to give Antti the old heave-ho for some guy from a million years ago who might have murdered his mistress…Damn it, Johnny. Get out of my head!

After the sauna, I took a walk out to the boat dock, watched for a few seconds as the tiny fish rose in the lake, and then dunked myself again. The water was cool but not cold. A hopeful tern dove at the fish now and then. After a few attempts, it rose, satisfied, into the sky, carrying its prey in its beak.

After my parents came out of the sauna and Saku had fallen asleep, the conversation quickly drifted back to Meritta's death.

"I'm worried about Aniliina," my mother said as she dished freshly smoked whitefish onto our plates. "That girl has had enough hard things in her life already. She's as smart as can be, just like Meritta was, but in many respects completely different from her mother."

My parents, who had taught for more than thirty years at the only middle school in town and then at the junior high and high schools after the grades in the schools were combined, were walking encyclopedias on the lives of local residents. Almost every person under the age of forty-five had been in one of their classrooms, and they were well into their second generation of pupils. I wondered whether my own tendency to stick my nose in other people's business was a result of all those conversations around the dinner table about the day's dramatic events, including all their students' backstories. Sometimes our parents' occupation was a pain for us girls, since we could never cut class without our parents finding out, and sometimes other kids accused us of getting good grades simply because our parents were teachers. All of us had also shamelessly exploited the situation, secretly reading our crushes' English essays, as I had done with Johnny's papers—ambitious attempts at stringing dictionary words together. Mom probably would have killed us if she had ever found out.

"Aniliina is going to high school with the best GPA in the school, despite her hospital stay," said my father. "Her report card is almost straight tens."

"And last year she won a national art competition. She does take after her mother in some ways. And her father too, I imagine. She is an extremely good violinist," my mother added.

"Sounds bad," I said with a grin. "Isn't it the smart girls who usually get anorexia?"

"When Aniliina got sick, I talked with Meritta about it, since her daughter was in my class," said my father. "There have been a concerning number of these cases in our school in the last few years. And yes, the ones afflicted with it are usually good students. Meritta seemed to think her daughter's sickness was caused by pressure to conform to outdated beauty ideals from when women filled more traditional roles."

"That's one theory. We have anorexic students in our school too," Eeva interjected. "Is Aniliina's father interested in his daughter's welfare at all?"

"He's coming, but I hear that Kaisa Miettinen is with Aniliina right now. I imagine Kaisa and Meritta were good friends, which is odd, since they seemed so different on the outside," I said.

"They were both serious about what they did though," said my father. "Hopefully this won't get in the way of Kaisa's training for the European Championships."

"Doesn't Kaisa have pretty strong nerves?" I asked. "Last summer at the World Championships she was in second. Then in the final round, that German threw a couple of centimeters past her. So for her final throw, Kaisa threw ten centimeters even farther out and took home the silver. I've always thought she was so calm, except during interviews."

Kaisa's calm, reticent nature seemed to intrigue reporters. She never talked about her private life, and answered questions about whether she had a boyfriend with a cool smile. Apparently at the Presidential Ball on Independence Day she had basically run away from all the cadets eager to dance with her. But sometimes in competition you could catch a glimpse of a different Kaisa, of a woman who sent her javelin flying through the air with the focused expression of a hunter. That was the woman who let loose the widest grin you've ever seen after winning that silver medal. I also remembered the intensity in Kaisa's voice when she had demanded to know whether Johnny and Meritta were in a relationship. Why had Johnny lied?

Was Kaisa in love with her cousin? The thought just popped into my head all of a sudden, and just as fast it seemed like the most obvious thing in the world. Was that why Kaisa was training out here in the middle of nowhere instead of near a beach somewhere warm? To be near Johnny?

"Kaisa studied sports psychology. Maybe that helps with Aniliina," my mother suggested before ordering us all to bed.

Saku would be waking us up early, she reminded us. Sneaking into the spare bedroom, Eeva and I found Saku snoring quietly with a teddy bear under his arm and his blanket balled up under his belly. My parents' low voices and the rattling of dishes from the main room sounded strangely familiar—memories coming back to life.

I still didn't know how to start getting to know my parents as an adult. I didn't even know whether I really wanted to know them other than as the people who had controlled my life for those first nineteen years. What good would it do anyone to unload my childhood traumas onto them since no one could change the past? I guess I had thought that if I knew my parents better, I could learn to understand Maria Kallio's wants and needs better too. But I wasn't sure whether I dared anymore to take the plunge into myself.

6

In the morning, I awoke to something small and smelling of milk crawling on me and yelling "Antee-tee-tee!" and "Upuh-upuh!" Then it grabbed my hair and started pulling. Opening my eyes, I saw Saku's grinning, slobbery face hovering above my head.

I swam for fifteen minutes and ate about three times more breakfast than usual before departing for town. I had decided to stop by Ella's house before going to work. I had to be the one to ask Ella directly about the brooch. Hopefully Koivu was coming from Joensuu again to help with the interviews, because I wanted someone to bounce ideas off of.

Ella's family lived in a slightly run-down wooden house right on the edge of the sinkhole zone. The house was originally one of the homes the mining company built for its workers, and was intended for two families. Ella's husband, Matti, had turned half of it into an art studio by pulling down some of the interior walls. The yard with its unmowed grass was a permanent art exhibit for a group of steel sculptures created during a period when Matti was obsessed with "giving material form." This was a departure from the standard themes of his paintings—triangles and cubes. Typically, he painted these shapes in distinctive three-dimensional arrangements that made recognizing his work fairly easy. I had received one of his paintings as a present on my thirtieth birthday.

After knocking, I walked in without waiting for a reply. The children, Ville and Viivi, were sitting in the living room watching *The Moomins* cartoons. Ella was busy with something in the kitchen, and Matti was nowhere in sight.

"Morning! Tea?" Judging by her bedhead and the wrinkles in her nightgown, Ella had just woken up.

"Sure. Is Matti still asleep?"

"No, he's been in the studio since eight. I don't know whether he slept at all given this whole Meritta thing..." Ella crossed the kitchen to close the door. "He's barely done anything but cry since he heard."

"Were they that close?"

"They've known each other for at least fifteen years. They studied together at the Ateneum." Ella poured me a cup. Her tea was usually much stronger than I preferred, so I mixed in a good amount of milk.

I always forgot that Matti was ten years older than Ella and me. He was so childlike somehow. Ella and Matti met at the Workers' Academy, where Ella had been studying to become an arts administrator and Matti was teaching painting. Ella, who had never been the type to fall head-over-heels for anyone, would have accepted a marriage proposal from Matti the very next week.

Matti was a nice guy. He could be a bit frivolous, but I got the impression that was just an artistic role he was playing. He was a talker, and sometimes even I had a hard time getting a word in edgewise. Usually he was brimming with enthusiasm for some scheme or another. Although he was a respected artist, he was still eager to teach and help out at the Finnish Artists' Association. The young students at the local art school and the community center painting circle were lucky to have such a qualified teacher. And Matti enjoyed teaching and organizing art camps, which were a good counterbalance to the solitude of painting.

Ella drank her tea silently while I sipped mine and wondered desperately how to start the conversation about the brooch. I was sure Ella had been wearing it when I was joking about pouring punch on Johnny's head. And at that point, the Tower had been locked.

"Hey, Ella, the night before last you were wearing a Kalevala brooch on your folk costume. My sister's birthday is in a few weeks, and I was thinking she might like something similar. Could you show it to me?"

Ella looked at me as if she didn't have any idea what I was talking about, but then she stood up and went to go look for the piece of jewelry. From the living room I could hear Little My laughing hysterically on the television and Ville and Viivi joining in. I hated the sugary-pastel Japanese animation of *The Moomins*, which were so ubiquitous nowadays I was surprised they weren't being printed on toilet paper. Identifying the wistful optimism of Tove Jansson's original characters in these bubble-gum versions was difficult.

Ella came back empty-handed. "I can't find it. Last night I washed the blouse that goes with the outfit, so the brooch might be in the washing machine." Ella nodded toward the bathroom, where I could hear the rumbling of the machine. "I've been so upset myself that I dumped the kids' leftover cereal in the laundry basket instead of the trash this morning." Ella's voice was pleading, as if begging me not to ask about the brooch.

"Won't it get ruined in the wash?"

"It won't hurt silver. I use a natural soap," she said before shoving a big piece of bread in her mouth. Stirring my tea, I hoped Ella's brooch really was in the washing machine and not at the Joensuu police station. You couldn't buy Kalevala jewelry in town—you had to go somewhere bigger like Joensuu, to a real jewelry shop. Eventually during an interview someone would remember Ella wearing it. I would have to keep an eye on the family's travel and watch for the brooch to reappear in Ella's wardrobe.

"Your friend Pekka Koivu stopped by yesterday. He's nice. He asked when we left the party."

"He probably didn't press you very hard after you said you left with me."

"No, he didn't. Having friends in the police is good." Ella laughed, but the pleading was still there in her voice.

"Thanks for the tea. I should get to work. Tell Matti to take care."

I walked through the living room, past the TV where the Snork Maiden was sniffling and Little My was still laughing. Out in the yard, violets and daisies were blooming in pleasant disarray, a chipped porcelain plate lay on the ground with a few drops of milk left in it, perhaps put out for the hedgehogs. I felt like going back in and asking Ella to open the washing machine. If she was lying, why?

Because the direct route was closed due to the unstable ground around the cave-in, I had to drive around the Tower to get to the police station. The parking lot at the Old Mine was full, including several charter buses. Maybe news of the murder in the county paper that morning had attracted extra tourists. Had Sergeant Järvisalo given permission to reopen the Tower already? I slowed down enough to be able to glance up, but all I could see was the sunlight reflecting off the Tower windows.

Hopponen was lounging in the break room at the station and reading the sports pages. This was his idea of playing duty officer.

"That guy from the county is in your office. Everybody else is out doing interviews," he said. Over his shoulder, I glanced at the soccer results and the quarter-page ad under them with Kaisa Miettinen launching a javelin into the distance. That spring Kaisa had landed a hefty sponsorship contract—for a female athlete—with one of the long-distance phone companies. I wondered why a phone company would choose Kaisa, since she didn't seem like the type to spend time chatting on the phone.

"Ave Maria," Koivu said, looking concerned as I stepped into the office. "It's good you came. Um...Did you go home with a man named Jarmo Miettinen Friday night?"

"I did." I hoped Koivu didn't notice me blushing.

"And this Miettinen is an old flame of yours?" When I nodded, now even redder, Koivu continued. "When I went to question him yesterday, he said he went to his parents' house for the night and that you were together most of the way. He even mentioned being relieved to have such a reliable witness. Then just a few minutes ago, I happened to talk to one of the last people to leave the party, at two thirty, who said that he saw Miettinen on his way back toward the Old Mine around that time. Three people were leaving right around then, and they all report seeing Miettinen."

"Bloody hell!"

"And that's not all. I started looking through the notes your boys have been compiling, and I saw that Järvi interviewed Miettinen's estranged wife. She says she saw Miettinen at their house at about three fifteen, apparently picking up his mountain bike. Mrs. Miettinen heard noise outside and got up to check on things, at which point she saw her husband and went back to sleep."

My head roaring, I sat down on my green sofa under President Ahtisaari's portrait. I felt like an idiot. I hadn't even been a substitute for Meritta, just an alibi.

"Johnny...I mean, Miettinen, paid me a visit here yesterday. He had some bruises and claimed he fell off the little Jopo he had ridden earlier in the night. Let's bring him in. Arrest him. Put him in handcuffs and lock him up."

"Maria..."

"I can't stand being taken advantage of like that! OK, fine, let's go talk to him. I want to hear why he lied. Can you drive?"

Only once my hands had stopped shaking and Koivu and I were sitting in one of the station's two Saab blue-and-whites, did I notice how tired Koivu looked.

"Were you up late last night with all these interviews?"

"No. I was home by eight, but then Anita and I had a huge fight." Koivu sighed, trying not to look miserable. "It was actually over something pretty big. At first, she was angry because I have to work over the weekend again, but then she started talking about those skinheads we arrested Friday night. The one who got hurt the worst, the real monster Nazi of the bunch, is Anita's patient. I'm still having a hard time believing this"—Koivu paused to look me in the eyes before turning his head toward the windy back road that leads to the lake—"but Anita defended him. Apparently he's a 'nice guy,' a health nut just like she is, who doesn't drink or smoke and only eats food grown in Finland. He doesn't want to pollute his body with anything foreign. Anita thinks the skinheads are right and that we don't need any refugees here. She thinks the Finnish police should be on the Finns' side." Koivu's voice was shaking.

"Anita's always been proud of you being a police officer, hasn't she?"

"Yeah, she's always had a thing for cops. We protect people from the bad guys. But now I'm the wrong kind of cop. Can you understand how that feels?"

I nodded. "My first real boyfriend dumped me because I was a cop and therefore represented the organized society he was trying to rebel against. Slightly different reasoning, but basically the same thing."

"So things are going pretty well for us," Koivu said as we parked in the Miettinens' yard. "For both of us," he added, smiling dejectedly. I smiled back, glad that I had Koivu—and not anyone else—sitting next to me at that moment.

"You're the lead interrogator. I'm just here as a witness," I reminded him as we climbed out of the car.

The day was already hot, especially in my jeans, and the sun was blinding. At first, I couldn't see clearly what was making all the clattering up on the roof.

Three men were on the roof. Johnny's dad was pulling up shingles next to the chimney, and another man I didn't recognize was dropping them into some sort of chute that carried them down to the yard. Johnny was nailing down new sheathing on the west side of the roof, and his body sharply silhouetted against the cloudless blue sky. An ugly yellow baseball cap with Arpikylä Athletics on it balanced backward on his head, and light brown curls were damp at his neck. His face had smears of black and his lightly tanned skin glowed in the sun, the muscles of his shoulders and upper back oscillating in time with his hammering. A trail of sweat running down his back disappeared into the waist-band of his cutoff shorts. When he noticed us, Johnny stood up, and the yellow down that covered his calves and thighs glittered in the sun, adding definition to his perfect leg muscles.

For a second all I could do was stare, and I'm sure my mouth was open too. I felt a floating sensation, as if I might glide right up onto the roof and into Johnny's arms, taste his warm, sweaty skin, inspect every muscle as I removed his shorts and tennis shoes, moving that terrible ball cap to my own head...

"Jarmo Miettinen, your account of your movements on Friday night could use some clarification." Koivu's cool voice was like a bucket of well water dumped on my head. And it had the same effect on Johnny too. The hammer slid from his hand onto and off of the roof, landing almost on Koivu's toes. Johnny himself didn't seem to notice. He just stared at his hands for a moment before sitting, then swung down to hang from his arms before dropping from the roof. The arrogance in the way he carried himself was the thing that finally brought me to my senses. I stared angrily into those gold-flecked blue eyes.

"What's this all about?" Johnny's voice was gravelly, and with the back of his hand he smeared the tar on his cheek as he tried to wipe the sweat from his forehead.

"You made a statement to the police yesterday that you arrived at your parents' home at approximately one thirty a.m. But four witnesses claim to have seen you in the center of town after two thirty," Koivu said.

Johnny's eyes broke contact with mine and moved to the tips of his shoes.

"Can anyone confirm the time you arrived at your parents' house Friday night?" Koivu's voice was calm and firm.

"We aren't in the habit of spying on grown men's comings and goings," Johnny's father yelled from the roof. "The missus and I were both sleeping."

"Is your wife at home, Mr. Miettinen?" Koivu asked. Johnny's father pointed inside to the kitchen, and Koivu disappeared.

Johnny was standing so close to me that I could feel the tension radiating from his body. His sweaty skin smelled of brazen masculinity and the heat of the sun. Up close, I could see bruises on Johnny's left side, and his left knee was also scraped. The men on the roof had stopped working, and I could feel their gazes on me, at once accusatory and fearful. A moment later, Koivu reappeared. Standing in the doorway, he said, "Miettinen, put some clothes on. We're going down to the station to sort this out."

Johnny first looked at me, then Koivu, then me again. I tried to look as if none of this was having any effect on me.

"Are you arresting me, Maria?"

"This isn't an arrest," Koivu said, his voice still cool, and I could almost believe he was enjoying the situation. "You're just coming in to clarify your statement."

Johnny went inside compliantly, asking Koivu for permission to shower as he went. I waited in the yard.

"Um…Is the boy mixed up in that artist's death somehow?" Johnny's father sounded confused. I didn't know if he remembered that I used to be Johnny's friend. As recently as Friday night.

"We just want to check a few things." How normal my voice sounded surprised me. It was funny, because fifteen years earlier I had hated Johnny's father, the man who thought his son should concentrate on his schoolwork instead of wasting his time playing in a band. He had approved of soccer at least. Their fights had been epic, at least the way Johnny told it, painting his dad as a regular domestic tyrant. I wondered what their relationship was like now, since his father clearly had no interest in providing Johnny with an alibi.

Johnny came out with his hair wet and slicked back. A blue shirt hung unbuttoned on his shoulders, but thankfully, his faded blue jeans were buttoned and buckled tight. I slipped behind the wheel, hoping that driving would give me a good excuse not to talk. Koivu sat in the back next to Johnny just to keep him uncomfortable.

I wondered whether Johnny's distress the day before had been an act. I thought I knew him, and he had always been open with me almost to the point of transparency. But of course a thirty-four-year-old is different from a nineteen-year-old. All of our minds now had growth rings, making them harder to penetrate with each passing year.

We sat in silence all the way to the police station. Once there, we marched Johnny into my office. I ensconced myself behind my desk, and Koivu sat in the armchair next to it and asked Johnny to take a seat across from us on the sofa.

I took notes as Koivu began repeating Johnny's first statement and noting conflicts with the testimony given by the other witnesses. When Koivu said that Tuija had testified that she had seen her husband in their yard, Johnny snorted.

"My soon-to-be-ex wife isn't exactly an impartial witness! We almost got into a fistfight at the party on Friday."

"So you deny visiting your wife's home the night of the death?"

"No…I was there. I was feeling kind of antsy after the party." Johnny glanced at me, but when I stared back impassively, he bit his lip and continued. "And then I fell off my bike just after I dropped Maria off at her parents' house. I bent the front wheel and had a helluva hard time riding it after that. I thought it would be easier to get a better bike at our house."

"What are you talking about? It's almost the same distance to your parents' house as to your wife's house. Of course, we can check on that bent bike wheel. But the people who saw you didn't mention anything about a broken bicycle. You're going to have to come up with a better story than that, Johnny." I couldn't keep my mouth shut any longer. It was so obvious that Johnny was lying.

Koivu continued ladling out the questions. "You had a relationship with Meritta Flöjt. Is that correct?"

"Yes."

"Was that the reason for your marital troubles?"

I would have wanted to ask Johnny the same questions myself, but I never would have had the nerve.

"No."

Koivu jumped to a new question before Johnny could reply with more than a single syllable. "Did you intend to marry Meritta Flöjt once your divorce was finalized?"

"We never talked about it. Do you think this is fun?" Johnny was addressing me again. When I didn't answer, he jumped off the couch and walked right up to my desk.

"I did not kill Meritta. I didn't see her at all after I left the Old Mine. What are you driving at here?"

"Why do you keep lying?" I said, throwing the words in his face and then pointedly staring at the damaged knuckles of his right hand squeezing the edge of my desk. If the bruises on his jaw and torso were on the left side, then why were the knuckles of his right hand split open? You would think he would have smashed his left hand if he really did fall off his bike.

"What I just told you is the truth." Johnny backed away from me toward the sofa. "I could still ride the Jopo, just not very well. Maybe the people who saw me didn't notice the bike was broken since I passed them going uphill, which is difficult even when not on a broken bike. But that Jopo is ready for the junk heap. Go and look. Be my guests! It's probably still in Tuija's yard."

Johnny's eyes flickered nervously between Koivu and me. I remembered Johnny hemming and hawing as he thanked me for my contribution to our soccer team, trying to hide his relief that he didn't have to ask me to leave. Every word he had said just dug the hole deeper. And now it was happening again.

We didn't have any reason to arrest Johnny. The fact that he had lied didn't make him a murderer. But was he lying to protect himself or someone else?

Fifteen years ago, I often dreamed of helping Johnny get off the hook for something. The daydreams always went something like this: Johnny was the passive victim in distress, and I was the savior. I braved all sorts of dangers from lightning storms to assassins, and my reward, of course, was the handsome prince. My favorite fairy tales were always the ones where the girl saved the boy, like in *The Snow Queen* and *Beauty and the Beast*. I couldn't imagine myself sitting on some glass mountain waiting for someone to save me or sleeping for a hundred years until a prince woke me with a kiss.

But if Johnny was a murderer, I wouldn't be able to save him. And I wouldn't want to.

"I guess that's all for now, Miettinen. Of course, we'll check on the bike. Someone will contact you to sign an affidavit based on your statement. It's best you don't leave the city without notifying us though. Do you need a ride home?"

"You mean I don't get to see the inside of a cell?" Johnny said, pretending to be disappointed. He glanced at me as if he was going to say something, but then changed his mind and just left.

"I'm surprised his nose didn't start growing, he was lying so much," I said to Koivu before the door had even swung all the way shut. After I explained my doubts about Johnny's pattern of bruising, we went over the events of Friday night again. When I told him my suspicions about Ella's brooch, Koivu suggested that we check with the county lab to see whether they had found any fingerprints on it.

After hanging up the phone with the county lab, Koivu said, "At least three sets, one of them our vic's. Flöjt's fingerprint pattern indicates she only held it momentarily, possibly tearing it off. The other prints are more from fiddling with it, and one set probably belongs to a male."

"Those could be Matti's...We should figure out some excuse for getting his and Ella's prints. Do you still have a lot to do? Do we have time to eat?"

"At the mine restaurant?" Koivu asked, grinning.

"Yeah, right. No, let's go to the Copper Cup."

At the restaurant, we were the only customers sitting on the grill side, which was no wonder, since the Wiener schnitzel they served was totally dry. The windows of the pub opened onto the main drag, which was devoid of traffic. As we were finishing our Sunday lunch, I saw Matti Virtanen enter the Copper Cup through the bar-side door.

I found him at the bar nursing a vodka tonic, his face red and swollen. Matti's eyes were barely visible between his sausage-like eyelids. He looked as though he had been drinking for several days straight. Or crying. Or both. Replying listlessly to my greeting and obviously ashamed to be seen in such a state, he proceeded to explain that he didn't usually drink in the middle of the day. "But I—I can't even paint. Or sleep. Meritta...," he said, his voice shaking and his hand trembling as he moved the glass to his lips, splashing some of the drink onto the table.

"Wouldn't it be better to see a doctor? You're a mess. They could give you something to calm you down."

"I'm going to try this booze first. Have you found anything out?" Matti asked, noticing Koivu behind me, who had hung back to pay the bill.

"Nothing conclusive yet." In his condition, nothing was going to come of asking him about the brooch. I dug a single midazolam out of my bag.

"This is really mild. Finish your drink, go home, and take this. Try to sleep. The drug should relax you." I also handed him my compact mirror. "Look at yourself. You need sleep, not alcohol."

For a moment, Matti stared at his image in my smeared mirror, then shook his head and promised to try. I grabbed the mirror and, instead of shoving it back in my bag, I fished out the plastic baggie that I usually used to store my eye shadow palette with the broken cover.

"Fingerprints," I said as we walked back toward the station.

"And I thought you were just trying to be friendly."

"Among other things."

Detectives Antikainen and Järvi had come back from their break, which gave us a chance to review the interviews, which were increasingly peculiar. No one had seen Meritta after two a.m. No one had seen her leave the mine area, and no one had spoken to her after Kaisa left the party at around one thirty.

About thirty names remained on the list to be interviewed, and I promised to handle some of them myself. The afternoon didn't yield much new information though. None of us found out anything more significant than that the handlebars of Johnny's bike were indeed bent, but it was still rideable.

When I returned to the police station, Koivu was there, having just arranged a meeting with his boss and our detectives for nine thirty the following morning, at which point we would decide how to proceed with the investigation.

"I tried calling Anita too, but she slammed the phone in my ear," Koivu said. "So I don't really feel like going home."

"Well, if you have to be back here in the morning anyway, why don't you come to my place for the night? We can heat the sauna, and I still have half a bottle of Jack Daniels left. I don't really feel like being alone either."

"You talked me into it."

Koivu lit the fire in the sauna stove while I fed Mikko, who seemed irritated with me. Before heading into the sauna, we decided to run off the pressure of the day, so Koivu borrowed a ludicrously small tracksuit from my uncle's closet. Jogging with someone felt strange since I had always preferred running alone. Antti wasn't much of a runner. He preferred to keep himself in shape by biking, chopping wood, and skiing during the winters when that was possible down south. I had always liked running precisely because the solitude and silence allowed me to think. That was why I usually didn't even listen to music. Running with another person easily turned into a competition. You always had to run a little faster than normal and listen for when they started breathing more heavily.

With Koivu it wasn't so bad though. We were pretty well matched in endurance events, and we both liked to start out slow and end sprinting. And Koivu knew how to keep his mouth shut. I figured he was thinking about Anita as we ran past the thickest stand of pine trees on my route, the Tower still peeking through in the background. Today it was dark and mysterious, as if mocking us for our inability to discover what had happened beneath its watchful eyes the night of Meritta's death. My own head was full of Johnny, Matti, and Ella. And Kaisa Miettinen, who was the last person to see Meritta alive. I found myself wanting to interrogate her myself.

When we got back, the sauna was ready. After stretching, I started stripping off my sweaty clothes, but Koivu stood staring at the sky. Then, obviously a little embarrassed, he asked, "Um... Are we going in together?"

I hadn't even considered another option since it would be idiotic to make one person sit outside all sticky with sweat while the other one squatted alone in the sauna. I guess I forgot we were the opposite sex.

"That's what I was thinking. Should I get you a beer too?"

When I returned, Koivu had his clothes off and was hiding himself in the darkest corner of the sauna. We had been in a sauna together before, but always with other people. Out of courtesy, I made sure to look only at his face the whole time we were in the sauna, although I have to admit the situation amused me a little. I didn't remember that I was four years older than Koivu very often, but it did cross my mind then. Mikko the cat perched on the lower bench, occasionally rubbing his head against Koivu's hairy ankle.

I had just poured our first shots of Black Jack after coming out of the sauna when the phone rang. Antti's voice seemed as though he were just a few feet away.

"Hi Maria, are you OK? My mom called and said there was a murder in Arpikylä."

"I'm fine. We're not even sure it was a murder. How are you?"

Antti's colorful description of a recent trip to New York made me jealous.

"You remember Hans, the one I was supposed to go to California with at the end my fellowship? Well, he broke his leg. He's flying back to Germany in July. I don't think I'll bother going alone, so I'm going to come home a couple of weeks early if I can get my plane ticket changed. Do you have anything against that?"

"Of course not, stupid!" Suddenly I felt bubbly inside. "By the way, Koivu is here. Should I say hi for you?"

"Oh, so you've taken up with Pekka, have you?" Antti's feigned distrust didn't sound very believable. He knew Koivu and me too well. "By the way, was the person who died someone you knew?"

"Kind of. But don't worry about that. Have you run into Warshawski?"

Searching for V.I. Warshawski and the bar she frequented in Sara Paretsky's novels had been one of our favorite diversions while I was visiting Chicago.

"I haven't had time. I'd rather see you anyway."

When I heard that, I hurried to end the call before how much I missed him really had a chance to hit me.

After two whiskeys, Koivu decided to call Anita again. At least this time she answered and didn't hang up on him until he told her where he was.

"What's her problem?" I asked, not daring to suggest that the obvious answer was a case of chronic bitchiness.

"Our relationship has been on the rocks for a while now," Koivu said, cramming his mouth full of Uncle Pena's homemade sauerkraut, which we were eating for dinner along with the whiskey and a few bratwurst from the freezer. "We almost set a wedding date for the end of August, but then Anita decided it would be nice to get married in the winter, sometime just before Christmas when there would be snow…Now she's not even talking about that."

"Do you still want to marry her?"

"Yeah, I guess. I don't know. Sometimes she's so fanatical. You know I don't like sissy girls, but Anita is so absolute about everything. And I had no idea she was some sort of racist sympathizer."

"Can you have a sensible conversation with her?"

"She isn't a very good listener. She just preaches and I agree." Koivu looked miserable. Once again, I was feeling as though I should tell him to run and never look back, but I had the good sense to keep quiet. Koivu needed a listening ear more than advice.

We talked until almost two before I headed to bed, me in my room and Koivu on the living room couch. Apparently his cares didn't weigh on his ability to sleep because within just a few minutes I could hear his contented, snuffly whiskey snores coming from the other room. As I watched the pale stars winking through the gap in the curtains, I wondered whether anyone had found Meritta's purse.

7

Detective Sergeant Järvisalo took a long pause before stating, "In light of the forensic investigation so far, it appears highly probable that this was a homicide." He looked around the room, pleased with the impact of this statement. Detective Antikainen was flushed with excitement, and Detective Järvi stared, stunned, at the Sergeant. I was sure my own expression was just as odd. Only Koivu appeared calm.

"But, of course, what we don't know yet is whether we're looking at murder or manslaughter," Järvisalo clarified. Apparently he was practicing for his interview with the local radio station. "In any case, this was a violent death and not by the victim's own hand."

Even Järvisalo's theatric delivery couldn't dispel the cold feeling I had inside. "Here we go again," I said to Koivu, who was sitting next to me. He squeezed my hand under the table, and my internal temperature rose a few degrees.

"I have a search warrant, so we can investigate the deceased's residence. Maria, could you come along? The victim's daughter is likely to be present…"

Child welfare was one of the few things that wasn't part of my job, but I agreed to go anyway. I was curious to see Meritta's house, especially her studio. And Aniliina.

The Flöjts also lived on the border of the subsidence zone. From their yard you could see the Old Mine hill glowing yellow. The shadow of the Tower seemed nearly to reach their house.

When Aniliina came to the door, Sergeant Järvisalo was speechless. She looked more dead than alive. Wearing a tight black sweater and thick black tights, her ribs and pelvic bones protruded alarmingly. Her face was white, her hands so transparent, so thin, that you could almost see the doorknob through her left palm. Only her eyes were alive, dark, and angry.

"Hi, Aniliina, I'm Maria Kallio. This is Arvo Järvisalo and Pekka Koivu from the police," I said. "We need to search your house. Is Kaisa here?"

"She left for practice. Do you have a search warrant?"

Still disoriented, Järvisalo dug the form out of his pocket, and Aniliina inspected it closely before nodding. I guess she was trying to act the way she had seen people do in cop shows. Maybe acting out a role that could fit on a little screen made the pain easier to bear.

"What exactly are you looking for?" she asked as she handed the warrant back to Järvisalo.

"Anything that could help us solve your mother's death. She painted here, right?"

"That side over there is the studio. And make sure you clean up after yourselves!" Aniliina beckoned us inside, trying to look tough, like an adult. From the street, the house looked like just one of the thousands of one-and-a-half-story houses built after the war, and the kitchen was like any other. But in place of the living room was an open space that stretched all the way to the roof, penetrated with light from an enormous skylight. In the studio was also some sort of sleeping loft, apparently for Meritta.

"My room is over there, but you probably don't need to see it, right?"

Järvisalo shook his head, as if bewitched by this emaciated apparition. He seemed to breathe a sigh of relief when she went into her room, slamming the door behind her.

Koivu and I went into the kitchen. It was excruciatingly clean and sterile, and looked recently renovated. The pantry was crammed full of flour, bran, sunflower seeds, and assorted tins of tea. The refrigerator was full of cheese and vegetables, as well as various products for the health conscious: diet soda, nonfat yogurt, light margarine, low-fat cheese.

"Looks just like our fridge," Koivu said with a grimace.

The kitchen appeared to be a place where people spent a lot of time. Spacious enough to accommodate a pull-out sofa and an armchair, the centerpiece of the room was a large oak dining table. A small television had been stuffed into a cupboard and was visible from the couch. Perhaps the kitchen also functioned as the Flöjts' living room. Meritta's dishes were colorful ceramics, and I remembered seeing a picture in a women's magazine of an Easter table setting she had done for a contest. Stored on the counter above the cupboard that held the pots and pans were a couple of full bottles of cognac, imports judging from the labels. Otherwise we didn't find anything worth mentioning in the kitchen.

Järvisalo was investigating the bookshelf in the sleeping loft with surprising care. When I climbed up beside him, he suddenly put down a book on Japanese erotica.

"Could you take a look at the sauna and bathroom?" he asked. "You understand women's stuff better than any of us."

"I know the difference between a drill and a chainsaw too," I groused before heading downstairs to the bathroom, which, along with the sauna, looked to have been built within the last few years. The tub was round and jetted, and an orange telephone was mounted on the wall above it. The toiletries and cosmetics were not luxury brands by any means. Meritta had clearly been a loyal Body Shop customer, but all her products had one thing in common, all claimed to be free of animal testing. The laundry detergent was an eco brand, and instead of tampons or pads, I found a strange contraption that appeared to be a reusable sanitary alternative.

But something was missing. Nowhere did I see mascara or a powder box, even though Meritta clearly had used both products. But, of course, most women kept those things in their purses.

"Has anyone found Flöjt's purse?" I asked after climbing the stairs back up to the studio.

"Purse? No. We didn't find a wallet or keys either. Did she usually carry a purse?" Detective Järvisalo raised himself off the floor of the sleeping loft where it appeared he had been peeking under Meritta's double bed.

I had tried feverishly to recall whether Meritta had been carrying a handbag with her at the party, but I just couldn't remember. Best to ask Aniliina.

The reply to my knock on her door was an angry "What?" I entered and found Aniliina squatting on a low stool next to the radiator and reading some sort of chart, which she quickly hid. The room was stiflingly hot, but I still got the impression Aniliina was freezing.

"Yes, she had a purse. Orange suede. Maybe the size of a normal book. She used it to carry her makeup, keys, wallet, and a little notebook. She never went anywhere without it. Didn't she have it with her when she…" Aniliina couldn't complete her sentence; instead she wrapped her bony arms around her waist as if to protect herself.

"We haven't found it."

"Where is it then?" There was fear in Aniliina's voice.

"Good question." I didn't like the situation. If Meritta's house keys were missing, whoever had them could get at Aniliina any time of the night or day. I wondered how I could suggest changing the locks without alarming her.

Then Koivu yelled for me from the studio. "I thought you'd want to see this," he said, displaying an oil painting nearly six feet tall.

It was Johnny, in the nude. Meritta had painted him obliquely from the rear with his waist twisted as he turned to look toward the viewer. His eyes looked directly into mine over his shoulder as if in challenge. Meritta had succeeded brilliantly in capturing the rotating movement of the body, the light gleaming on the muscles, the arcing shadows of the limbs. Although Johnny was clearly identifiable, Meritta had obviously approached him as a model and not as a subject for realistic portraiture. The painting conveyed something akin to an ancient Greek or Roman statue, an arousing masculine radiance that reminded me once again of Johnny's smell and the feel of those glowing muscles under my hands.

"There are more of the same over there," Koivu said, motioning toward a corner of the room under the loft that seemed to function as a storage area. Just then Detective Järvisalo's cell phone rang. He said a few curt words into the phone and then turned to Koivu, looking serious.

"We have to get back to Joensuu. It's those Somalis and neo-Nazis from Friday night again…Knife fight in the hospital."

"Any dead?" Koivu's face had gone white.

"One of the skinheads. A nurse got a knife in the side, but she's not in any danger."

I could see from his face that Koivu was thinking of Anita. He was already halfway to the door before Järvisalo realized he should follow. Grabbing the cell phone, Koivu yelled a few words at the duty officer in Joensuu. The answer he was looking for came as he opened the car door, and I could tell by the way his body relaxed that the wounded nurse was not Anita.

"I can wrap this up," I yelled after them.

Now I had time to look around the studio properly. At more than four hundred square feet, the room had a ceiling at least fifteen feet high at its tallest, with windows opening in two directions in addition to the skylight. The smallest window had a view of the Tower. Meritta had looked at it every day as she painted, not knowing her life would end at its base.

The studio also had an armchair and sofa, between them a small smoking table. Other furniture included only a couple of supply cabinets and easels of various sizes, two of which supported blank primed canvases. Meritta had clearly been actively working. Climbing up to the sleeping loft, all I found was an armoire, a bookshelf, and a bed about six feet wide covered with an orange duvet. In addition to women's poetry, the bookshelf held a large collection of books on erotic art. Picking one at random, I flipped through it. On one page two men with skin the color of chocolate kissed each other, and on the next two women with skin one shade darker did the same. The book, which was printed in black and white, was meant to illustrate contrasting skin tones with sexy and amusing photographs. I decided to buy it if I could find a copy at the Academic Bookstore in Helsinki.

I returned to Meritta's paintings down in the studio. In the first stack, I found a few familiar images, some powerful landscapes of the Old Mine, and a series of pencil sketches of Kaisa throwing the javelin. On the bottom of the first stack, I found a grotesque picture of Meritta's brother. I doubted Jaska had agreed to sit for Meritta, so she had probably painted it from memory. Jaska was in his rocker uniform of worn-out jeans, a leather jacket, and a black T-shirt. A guitar hung around his neck. He was posing on stage with his legs spread in classic axman stance. His alcohol-swollen face wore a smug expression.

It was a spiteful painting, perfectly merging how Jaska viewed himself with how the rest of us saw him. I hoped Jaska would never see it. Actually, I wished I had never seen it.

The second stack was mostly Meritta's series of Kaisa and Johnny. In some of the paintings they were together, and Meritta used light and shadow to play with the similarities and differences of the male and female form. Some of the paintings depicted Kaisa with her javelin. Depending on the mood of the piece, the spear sometimes seemed like a phallic plaything and at other times like a weapon. In one of the pictures, Johnny, barely recognizable because he was covered in so much mud, stretched to reach a soccer ball.

I don't understand much about art, but I liked Meritta's work instinctively. Something told me it was high-quality work. The way she could transform familiar people into images that portrayed so much more than the models themselves was fascinating.

Did the paintings belong to Aniliina now? I wondered what price they would fetch.

On the bottom of the second stack were two more paintings. At first glance they were almost black, but upon closer inspection the minimal light in them revealed holes, tunnels, and endless caverns. They were at once disturbing and familiar.

Meritta had told Matti that all of her mine-themed paintings were in her gallery in Helsinki. But what else could these be, and why had Meritta lied? Did she want to conceal them from Matti for some reason?

I stared at the paintings for so long that their blackness made my eyes throb.

"So all the men left?"

I jumped. Aniliina had crept up behind me. She ran her thin hands through her tangled hair, and her mouth appeared almost blue in her wan face. Everything about her conveyed one simple message: I am miserable. And the misery had begun long before Meritta's death.

"Yeah, and I'm about done too. But before I go, would you mind answering a few questions? You must have known your mother best."

"I didn't know her at all. And she didn't know me."

Nevertheless, Aniliina led me into the kitchen, where we sat down, I on the couch and she curled up in the armchair in the sun. Compared to Aniliina, talking to Ella and Johnny had been easy.

I thanked my lucky stars I wasn't fifteen or even nineteen anymore. Especially at fifteen, life had been pure misery. I was desperately in love with Johnny, wanted to leave home, didn't know what I wanted to be when I grew up, and didn't recognize my own body. While choosing a career was still difficult, and loving Antti was tricky, all in all life felt much better now than it had fifteen years earlier. Maybe that was growing up.

"I feel like coffee. Can I make some?" I asked Aniliina, nodding toward the coffeemaker. "Do you want some too? Coffee or something else?"

"I don't want anything."

"You really should try to eat."

"No I shouldn't!" Aniliina's voice was furious, as if I had attacked her. I considered what I actually knew about anorexia. Why wasn't Aniliina in the hospital anymore? She looked appallingly thin.

"I don't want to end up a fat-ass like my mom or my grandma. They're so ugly. How can you even stand having breasts?" Aniliina looked curiously at my body, which I considered only moderately curvy although clearly feminine.

When the coffee was ready, I poured Aniliina a cup anyway.

Aniliina got up and went into the kitchen. "There's some *pulla* and cake here if you want it with your coffee." She pulled the pastries out of the cupboard and practically pushed them at me. "Grandma's chocolate cake is to die for. Have a taste."

I took a piece of the delicious-looking cake as Aniliina stared at me triumphantly. I wondered what my acceptance signified to her. Sure, I knew lots of women who watched what they and others ate, like my sister Helena or Koivu's girlfriend, Anita, but I had never experienced anything this intense.

"Had Meritta been acting strange lately? Was she happier or more depressed than usual?"

"She was fucking thrilled just like she always is when she's painting something new. And of course her new man, that Johnny guy, was keeping her all cheery. Mom was really into him."

"So everything was good?"

"Except me." Aniliina rubbed her coffee cup between her palms like a hiker might on a cold winter day, sipping gingerly. "Me, she just screamed at. First she wanted me out of that prison—the hospital, I mean—and then she was constantly threatening to send me back. And I'm not going back there, not ever!" Aniliina's dark eyes burned in their sockets.

"Are you here all alone now or is Kaisa coming to stay the night again?"

"Kaisa's flying to Helsinki tonight. The Grand Prix starts tomorrow. Dad said he might come if they finish their recording session today. But I can manage just fine on my own," Aniliina said a little more graciously. "At least better than with Grandma and my drunk-ass uncle. Grandma just cries and goes on about how she always knew something bad would happen to her poor little baby girl. I'd have to agree with her on that."

"Why?" I asked more sharply than I had intended.

"She means all the men and the paintings Mom did. I mean how she irritated almost everyone. I've always wondered why someone never killed her before. She was such a fucking bitch."

With this, tears began flowing down her cheeks, which she tried to pretend weren't there. Gradually, she started rocking back and forth, curling up like a snowman melting in the rain. Her empty coffee cup fell to the floor. I pulled a handkerchief out of my bag and ended up wiping away her tears. To my surprise, she didn't resist and even let me stroke her hair.

"She was still my mom though," Aniliina finally stammered. Then, as if ashamed of her outburst, she straightened up. "Did you have anything else? I need to go for a jog."

"Do you know where I can find Kaisa before she leaves for Helsinki?"

"Yes, she's supposed to be at the field practicing until three."

Leaving Aniliina alone felt awful. Hopefully her father was on his way.

"If you remember anything that seems important, call me anytime. Even if you just want to talk…" I didn't want to force myself on Aniliina, but I wanted her to know I was at her disposal. Leaving her both my home and work numbers, I decided to talk to her father, Mårten, about changing the locks as soon as he arrived.

From their house, the sports field was only a quarter of a mile away. Seeing it filled me with memories of shouting and sweat, the sudden pain of a tackle, and the tingling excitement of my team scoring a goal. But seeing the field so quiet, with only a couple of old men rounding the track, felt strange. Then I saw a solitary tall figure on the javelin runway. Choosing a javelin from the rack, Kaisa hefted it in her hand, looked down at her check marks, and then walked slowly to the other end of the runway to start her takeoff. First a couple of slow, almost exploratory steps, then an explosive spurt that brought her throwing hand back. The spurt came to a halt just before the white scratch line, from which she hurled the javelin into the air. The arc of the projectile was smooth and powerful, and it seemed like ages before it touched the ground several meters past the thickest white line drawn across the field. Was that the fifty-meter line? Or sixty? If that was the case, that was a phenomenal practice throw.

When I saw the coach rush to Kaisa from his observation post, I was sure it must be the sixty-meter line. Both seemed satisfied. Kaisa jogged a quick lap around the grass, stretching her shoulders and waiting until the runners had passed before taking off again. Her second throw also sailed past the thick white line, but not as far as the first.

The sports announcers on TV always commented on the purity of Kaisa's technique. I wasn't really familiar with the finer points of the javelin throw, but I could see that her takeoff was precise, her throwing hand stayed in a good position, and she put her whole body into the throw, not just her shoulder and arm.

The third throw landed just short of the line, making Kaisa shake her head. I walked closer. From fifty feet away it would have been difficult to tell the thrower's sex if I hadn't already known. That slender, broad-shouldered, narrow-hipped body could have belonged to any young athlete. Only closer up could I make out the rise of her pert breasts under her training shirt, the smooth skin of her face, and the graceful line of her jaw. Kaisa wasn't one of those female athletes who bothered with makeup or sexy sports outfits. But even with mussed hair and normal sweat pants, she exuded an unself-conscious charm. Back when she won her first Finnish Championship, she still walked hunched over, a teenage girl obviously ashamed of her height, who seemed to stand up straight only while on the throwing runway. Now she walked with her head held high and her back straight, but still she hated all the media attention.

I didn't know whether interrupting Kaisa in the middle of practice would be considered lèse-majesté. Detective Antikainen had already interviewed her on Saturday. She had been one of the last people to talk to Meritta before she died. Even though Kaisa's statement didn't contain anything out of the ordinary, something was still bothering me—her intense look Friday night when she asked Johnny if he and Meritta were in a relationship, and the fact that Johnny had lied to her about it.

I also wanted to talk to her about Aniliina. Apparently she had been good friends with both the mother and the daughter.

Kaisa and her coach seemed to be taking a break. He ambled toward the maintenance shack, and she collapsed onto the high-jump pit and started slurping a sports drink out of a green plastic bottle.

"Hi. You got a second?"

"I'm on my break." Kaisa sounded irritated, but not unwelcoming.

"Nice throws. How far out is that thick white line?"

"Sixty-two. The cutoff distance for the first round in Helsinki."

"But then you must have thrown at least seventy that one time…"

"Tomorrow at the Grand Prix I need to throw the top distance for the summer," Kaisa said as someone else might say they needed to go grocery shopping the next day.

"Hopefully they'll show it on TV. I'm just coming from the Flöjts' house. Aniliina said I would find you here. While I was over there, I noticed Meritta had painted some pretty impressive pictures of you. How long have you been modeling for her?"

"We started sometime in the winter. I didn't really pose though. She mostly just came here to the field and painted, even in the sleet."

Kaisa didn't seem to consider it anything special that *she* had practiced in the sleet.

"Were you friends?"

"Yes." Tears welled in Kaisa's eyes, and she wiped them with the back of her hand. "I ain't never met anyone who understood me so well. She *got* why I throw and everything else too…Why did she have to go and fall? I hate that Tower! They should tear it down and stomp on the pieces!" Kaisa slammed the ground with her hand. "But I guess I just have to go on like everybody else. That's what Meritta would have wanted me to do."

"Did Meritta seem like herself Friday night?"

"No, she didn't. She was angry about something. When I left, she said that hopefully she'd be in a better mood the next day. She was supposed to paint me the next day, on Saturday."

Kaisa claimed she didn't know the cause of Meritta's anger. We had just moved on to talking about Aniliina when the coach returned and glared at me with a look that said I should make myself scarce. I obliged, heading toward the cafeteria at city hall in hopes they might still have something decent to eat.

Paperwork took up the rest of the day. Luckily when I arrived home, a letter from Antti was waiting in the mailbox. He was an excellent letter writer. Occasionally I wondered whether I had fallen in love with him just because of a letter I read while solving my first murder. In his letters, Antti was both more direct and gentler than he was in person. And he wrote lovely long missives, often a page in the morning, another during the day, a couple in the evening, and then another batch of pages the following day.

Reading the letter, I giggled at Antti's description of an Episcopal Church bazaar that some university colleague had dragged him to. Then I came to a passage that abruptly smothered my merriment:

> I usually don't even notice jewelry. But at the bazaar
> I saw this ring made by a local jewelry designer.
> Suddenly I found myself thinking that an emerald
> like that would look perfect on your finger. I mean
> what I'm writing. Let's get married as soon as I get
> out of here. Being away from you has made every-
> thing so clear. I know that you are the one I want.

Even before he left, Antti had wanted to get engaged, but I dragged my feet. I thought that being apart would help me see what I really wanted. But so far all I had learned was that I could live without Antti and still be happy. Loneliness didn't bother me. And to me that felt like a good prerequisite for sharing a life with someone: I loved Antti, but I wasn't dependent on him. Five days out of seven I would have said yes if he proposed. But on the other two days, even the thought of getting married made me shudder.

I spent that whole night trying to get my thoughts down on paper, but I wasn't really sure what I wanted to say. Finally I fell asleep frustrated, even though Mikko had tried to cheer me up by dragging an enormous mouse inside the house.

At around one a.m. I woke to the sound of the phone ringing. After answering, I started pulling on my jeans with my free hand.

"Hi. It's Aniliina. There's someone here. Upstairs...He had a key."

"Stay where you are. Lock the doors to the downstairs if you can. Don't even try to go see who is there." I dialed our patrol car's number on the rotary phone, but no one answered. After ten rings, the call transferred to county dispatch. As I pulled on a shirt without a bra—there wasn't time—I explained the situation. The on-call officer at the county promised to keep trying to reach the patrol car.

I grabbed the crowbar I had been using as a dumbbell, threw it in the back of the Lada and put the pedal to the metal. The summer night was at its darkest, the birds momentarily silent. I reached the center of town in six minutes, taking another minute to navigate to Aniliina's street. Only a lone wino staggering down the sidewalk witnessed my reckless dash. The whole drive I berated myself for not changing the locks at the house even though we knew Meritta's keys were missing. If something happened to Aniliina, it would be my fault.

When I arrived, I didn't see the patrol car or any other vehicles. The house was dark and eerily quiet. I left the iron bar in the car but inside my pocket I squeezed the small knife that I always carried. Slowly I crept toward the front door, which was open. With my ears straining like a cat's listening for a mouse, I stepped into the entryway.

From the studio came quiet sounds of movement and a strange, muffled metal rattling as if someone were trying to open a lock. In the darkness I could just make out a vaguely human shape crouched in front of the cabinet where Meritta stored her paint. I crept from the door toward the stacks of paintings.

Then we both froze when we heard the siren of an approaching police cruiser. Suddenly I was blinded by a flashlight and left momentarily helpless as the figure rushed past and out the door. Although he had only a two-second head start, by the time my eyes readjusted to the dark, he had already disappeared into the small grove of trees behind the house that lead to the Sump.

The sound of the siren grew louder, and then the patrol car careened into the yard with lights flashing. Just as it stopped, I heard the sound of another car engine starting in the Sump.

I screamed at Järvi and Timonen as they vaulted out of the car. "Are your dipshit brains really so small that you don't know not to run your sirens at full blast when you're chasing a burglar! And the lights? Really?"

"But the county said the Flöjt girl might be in danger...We just thought we'd let the burglar know the police were on their way and he'd better clear out," Timonen said in their defense.

Aniliina! For a moment I had completely forgotten about her. Running back inside, I threw myself down the stairs and found the door to the sauna suite locked.

"Aniliina! It's me, Maria. Are you OK?"

When the girl opened the door, she was visibly shaking.

"It's alright. He's gone. And I'm staying with you the rest of the night. Now what happened?" I asked.

Aniliina said she hadn't been able to sleep, so she decided to take a bath. She had just finished drawing the water when she heard something upstairs. She explained she had turned off all the lights in the house except for in the bathroom, which was windowless. The intruder might have thought she was sleeping or away from home.

Even though I promised to stay with her and assured her that the police would come by regularly to check on the house, Aniliina didn't want to stay. And she wouldn't listen to a word about going to her grandmother's house.

Finally I said, "I have a free sofa at my place. You can stay with me if you're not allergic to cats."

She agreed and went to get her stuff. While I waited, Detective Järvi appeared in the studio carrying an orange suede bag.

"He brought this back," he said excitedly. "It was the murderer, wasn't it?"

"Yep. If you would've just kept your goddamn siren off!"

I tried to sketch the dark, hunched figure in my mind, but all I could recall was a vague shape doing its best to conceal its features. He—or she, since there wasn't really any way to know—had been wearing a ski mask that concealed his face and hair. He had been a little taller than me—I was sure of that judging from the sound of his panting as he rushed past me. And his smell... Was there something familiar about it?

"Will you grab some gloves from the car?" I asked Detective Järvi. "Let's take a look in that purse. Then you can give it to county forensics when they come tomorrow to dust for prints."

Carefully I picked up Meritta's purse by the handles. A faint hint of perfume still clung to the suede, mixed with the stronger, stuffy aroma of tobacco smoke. Strange. Meritta didn't smoke. On the side of the handbag was a dark stain, and I remembered the punch Aniliina had spilled at the party.

Aniliina couldn't take her eyes off the purse, as if the orange gemstone fastened to its lock were the mesmerizing eye of a cobra. Was she thinking of her final encounter with her mother, that terrible fight? When Detective Järvi returned, I moved over to the smoking table and put on disposable gloves before opening the bag.

Nothing out of the ordinary inside, just birth control pills, a wallet, and makeup. Powder, mascara, an orange-and-gold-toned eye shadow palette, an eyeliner pencil, and vermilion lipstick. The wallet contained a Visa debit card, a library card, a few member cards, a picture of a round-cheeked Aniliina at about age six, and a little cash. But no keys.

"Is anything missing but the keys?" I asked Aniliina, who was still staring.

"Her sketchbook," she finally said. "Mom always had it with her, even though she didn't use it much for sketching. She wrote grocery lists and phone numbers in it mostly. But I think that's all…"

"What keys did your mom carry?"

"Besides our house key, she had ones for the art school and the Old Mine. I guess she probably had some little keys too, for her suitcase, the padlock on the woodshed, and stuff like that."

Aniliina looked so exhausted that I decided to finish asking questions in the morning. Before leaving for my uncle's house, I forced her to take a sleeping pill. Since she barely weighed ninety pounds, it made her pass out on the couch almost as soon as we arrived. Mikko curled up protectively beside her. As for myself, I took a big shot of whiskey to help settle my rage, but it didn't work.

What had the intruder been looking for in Meritta's house? Why had he brought back the purse? And his smell…Why did it seem so familiar?

8

The next morning I awoke to the sweet smell of coffee and the sound of someone clattering around in the main room. A second passed before I remembered what had happened the previous night.

Looking a little shy, Aniliina smiled when I stepped into the room.

"Fresh coffee first thing in the morning? I'm in heaven," I said and then proceeded to make myself a sandwich and spoon yogurt into a bowl. To my astonishment, Aniliina also ate an orange and a cup of yogurt, even though it wasn't nonfat.

"That cat is really nice. He slept by my feet the whole night. I want a cat too, but Mom's allergic." When Aniliina realized what she had said, her eyes welled up. "Well, now I can get a cat," she muttered. "Mom did like cats though. She felt bad that we couldn't...Maybe I won't because of..."

Aniliina didn't resist as I pulled her into my arms. I could feel her spine and collarbone through the violet fabric of her winter pajamas. The muscles around her vertebrae felt like little more than dry tendons, her close-cropped hair like hemp fiber bristles, as if I were holding a desiccated plant in my arms. Aniliina cried a little and then, after calming down, announced that she wanted to go home.

"I won't be afraid during the day, and those policemen will stop and check on me sometimes. And I'm sure Dad will be here tonight. He said he would be."

When I dropped her off, I came in to have another look at Meritta's paintings and asked Aniliina if I could take a few with me to the police station, feeling like they might be important.

After digging the mine paintings out of the stack, I stared at Johnny's portrait again. Apparently noticing my expression, Aniliina said bitterly, "Mom always drooled over him the same way you are. I guess he was better than the ass-grabber from last summer though."

"One of your mom's boyfriends did that to you?"

"Yeah. I think his last name was Hiltunen. He said I had almost as good an ass as my mom. She saw it and threw him out on his own ass."

I could imagine. Meritta had definitely liked erotica, but she had also lobbied against sexual harassment and brothels. I had a hard time imagining her socializing with the kind of men who went around pinching underage girls.

"The guys at school do the same thing. They call me princess of porn and think that means they can touch me any way they want. Mom didn't have a clue about all the stuff that got thrown at me because of the crap she said in the news."

"Maybe they were just jealous because your mom was famous."

"Bullshit! Maybe they would have been if Mom had been like Kaisa. A sports star or something. Maybe it would have been better if she only did impressionism. If they couldn't tell what she was painting, they would have just thought she was strange, not perverted."

I wondered whether that was what made Aniliina sick, the fear of being different and the need to be accepted. Since she couldn't control anything else about her life, maybe she tried to compensate by controlling her weight. If the pressure to fit in was as strong as when I was a kid, I thought I could understand Aniliina a little better. Because she didn't have a natural rebellious streak like I did, she turned all her anger and anxiety against her own body.

Back at the station, it was quiet, so I ground away at my paperwork for a while. Jussi had left me with quite the backlog of cases from over the winter. A surprising number of criminal indictments were still in their initial stages, and there was plenty of catch-up to do issuing liens for unpaid fines. Maybe he had needed a rest more than he needed a study sabbatical. And here I thought temping for a small-town sheriff was going to be boring.

Koivu called around noon.

"I have news. You probably aren't going to be happy to hear that one of the sets of prints from that brooch are Matti Virtanen's."

"Shit! I never should have handed him that mirror!"

"You don't really mean that. You'd want to know the truth anyway. I'm going to interview the Virtanens as soon as I can, but things are a little exciting around here at the moment. You heard that those skinheads and Somalis were fighting in the hospital. Some visitors, who weren't checked properly at the door, brought in weapons. And, of course, both sides are telling completely different stories."

"What about Anita?"

"I haven't really seen her. She was on graveyard. Tomorrow is her birthday though. I guess I should try to come up with something."

"Good luck. Did you already hear what happened at the Flöjts' last night?"

Koivu hadn't, so I brought him up to speed, and then we chewed the fat until the duty officer notified him that he had another call.

I called Ella to see if she was free for lunch, but found myself almost relieved when the city switchboard said she had gone to Kuopio for the day for a seminar. So, lacking anything better to do, I stopped by the corner store for some potato salad and a bag of Pirate Doubloons *salmiakki*, and then continued through my pile of paperwork. I've always been convinced the ammonium chloride in salty licorice improves your ability to think.

As I was gnawing on one particularly tough piece, a knock came at my door and Mr. Kivinen walked in. Today he was wearing a dull-silver suit with a tie bright as the clear blue sky above the Tower. Quickly I tried to swallow the candy, but it stuck nastily in my throat.

"Could I bother you for a moment?" he asked.

When I nodded, he sat down under President Ahtisaari. "I just wanted to come and thank you for how well you've handled this investigation so far. It hasn't interfered with our operations at all. Quite the opposite. You know how curious people are."

I nodded.

"And I'm also glad that you've kept our discussion at the restaurant that morning just between the two of us. I forgot to mention that my wife doesn't know about what happened between Meritta and me. The detective who interviewed her—I think his name was Koivu—was very discreet."

"It's nice to hear that, even though I'm not actually leading the investigation. Detective Sergeant Järvisalo from the county police unit is."

"Oh, I know how much the local authorities influence these things. I wanted to try to thank you somehow...Would you ever be interested in touring the mine tunnels? We weren't able to show them during the opening. And then perhaps I could offer you lunch in our restaurant."

"Actually, I'd love to visit the edge of the cave-in. Meritta said the excavations there are amazing." I was thinking of Meritta's mine paintings. Was the killer's motive hiding in them somewhere? Could going to the place where she painted them tell me what it was?

"Unfortunately the cave-in area would be too dangerous, so we can't go there. But we'll see. Would tomorrow work, perhaps around eleven thirty? Then I could show you around myself."

For the sake of appearances, I glanced at my calendar, even though I knew I was free then. After Kivinen left, I gagged the candy the rest of the way down my throat. What did he want from me? Why had he come to tell me that his wife didn't know about his relationship with Meritta? Was he trying to protect his wife? I remembered a bored-looking woman in a Marimekko dress and then made a mental note to dig out Koivu's interview notes as soon as I finished the stack of forms I was working on.

Then I dove into the Saastamoinen Construction Company bankruptcy filing. The time it had taken to file this fraud indictment was completely unacceptable. Why had Jussi let this sit on his desk for six months? In order to focus, I kept munching on my skull-and-crossbones *salmiakki* coins, which seemed to have dried out pretty thoroughly. Suddenly I felt a dull ache in my left molar. Damn, a filling was caught!

I was in luck though, managing to land an appointment at Tuija Miettinen's dental clinic that afternoon due to an unexpected cancellation. Located just a few doors down from the police station, Tuija's office was in the same place I remembered going to the dentist when I was in school. The only difference was that the sign on the door said Miettinen now instead of Sorsa.

I had never been one of those people who was afraid of going to the dentist, but I didn't love it either. However, now I was nervous. Being Tuija's patient somehow felt strange. I had barely had a chance to flip through the previous week's *Donald Duck* comic book in the waiting room before they called me in.

The dentist's coat suited Tuija. Against the bright white, her pallid cheeks seemed to have color, and the sheen of her short, dark hair was stronger than usual. The dental hygienist, a woman in her forties, seemed a nervous sort.

"Hi, Maria. Let's take a look at that filling," Tuija said, motioning me to the chair. "How did it come loose?"

"Chewing dried-out Pirate Doubloons." I was mortified, caught eating silly candy like a little kid!

As she poked and prodded, Tuija narrated to her assistant. "Mesial-occlusal portion of amalgam on #18 chipped, no signs of decay and no other cracks noted on surrounding tooth structure. OK, Maria, now I'll just check for anything on your other teeth while we're here."

"There shouldn't be anything," I muttered with my mouth full of mirrors and instruments of torture. Tuija continued listing off tooth codes, but didn't find any tartar buildup.

Then she turned to her hygienist. "OK, Maija, you can go. There's just this one filling, and I can handle that myself."

Tuija explained that her assistant had already set another appointment after their previous client cancelled.

I nodded, even though no one was asking my permission.

"Let's get some anesthetic in those gums. You aren't allergic to anything, are you?" Her mask hid the lower half of her face and the glare on her glasses concealed her eyes, making her expression unreadable. Tuija tilted the chair farther back. From the reception area came a quick "Bye" and the thud of a door closing. As the syringe approached my mouth, I turned my eyes away. What was the syringe really filled with? I felt a wave of fear. I was completely at Tuija's mercy, but then in the blink of an eye the injection was done.

"Now we just wait. Is there news on Meritta's case?"

"Not really."

"Is Johnny a suspect?" she asked, taking off her face mask. Her face looked pale again. "You can bet he was sugarcoating what he was really doing Friday night."

"You knew about their relationship?"

"Of course. It's been a long time since Johnny bothered hiding his women from me."

"Were you jealous?"

"Of Meritta?" Tuija laughed in a way that was more like a series of snorting sounds. "I've spent so many years watching Johnny with other women that I don't bother being jealous anymore. I don't care. But Meritta did. She wanted Johnny for herself."

Tuija's face was just as serious as it had been fifteen years ago. She was such a dull grind that we all had wondered what Johnny saw in her. I still didn't really understand.

"Can you still feel anything?" Tuija asked, inserting something in my mouth.

"What? Oh, in my tooth? No."

With that, Tuija got to work. I was so tense that the only place that hurt was my neck. Once the drill stopped whining and Tuija finished cramming filling material into my tooth, she started talking again.

"So you can stop suspecting me of anything. Of course I'm sure Johnny has told you his sob story too, about his horrible wife who just doesn't understand. And he's right; I don't. You'd think four years would be long enough to get over turning thirty. That man has such a hard time living with himself that no one else can stand to be with him either. I guess he's disappointed with his life. But I'm not disappointed with mine. I like my job and my kids, and I'm satisfied being a normal person living a normal life. Johnny says he wants adventure, but he doesn't actually dare do anything with his life except for womanizing endlessly."

I grunted something, but my mouth was so full of stuff that saying anything intelligible was impossible. I imagine Tuija enjoyed that. I couldn't remember her ever saying this much to me at once. Tuija squirted my mouth full of water, and a little went down the wrong pipe, coming straight back up onto Tuija's face mask. But she didn't seem to even notice as she continued suctioning the water out of my mouth. Maybe the squirting and sucking were usually the dental hygienist's job.

"I don't want a man who's only ever half-present, who only does work around the house when he's asked. I'm sick of explaining to our kids why he's always gone. And honestly, I feel less lonely since he moved out." Tuija began raising my chair, which hid her face from view again.

"It might be a little sore tonight when the anesthetic wears off. Take painkillers as needed. And don't eat anything for a couple of hours."

As I stood up, Tuija had her back to me as she washed her hands. My cheek felt three times larger than normal, and talking was difficult.

"If you're trying to convince me that you didn't kill Meritta, you're talking to the wrong person. I'm not in charge of the investigation. The county detectives are."

"I didn't mean that. I just want to say that you can have Johnny. Isn't that what you've wanted the last fifteen years?"

Turning toward me, Tuija's face was one of amused spite. "It's pathetic how obvious it is."

I fled the room, not sticking around to hear any more. The tears came as soon as I got outside. I felt like a stupid teenager again.

"Did it hurt that bad?" asked Officer Lasarov, who was sitting behind the Plexiglas at the duty desk when I returned to the police station to gather my things.

"She hit a nerve."

Lasarov nodded sympathetically. Even for a police officer, visiting the dentist was an acceptable reason to complain about pain. Knowing that the best remedy for pain was more pain, I headed to the weight room in the basement of the local swimming club.

It was literally just a weight room, a small, sweaty cellar with mostly barbells and benches. A few machines had been added recently, apparently at Kaisa's request. That one of the best javelin throwers in the world worked out in this sorry excuse for a gym was incredible. Didn't she bring the city loads of positive publicity? Or was she the wrong sex for that to matter?

But there was nothing wrong with the leg extension or curl machines. As I slaved away for a good hour on my usual routine, I watched in amusement as the guys grunted with their weights. Twenty more pounds on the bar than normal and a nice, long pose after racking it. Clearly they were laying it on because a new girl was in the gym, even if she was a familiar face.

After soaking in the shower for ten minutes, I was ready to meet Jaska. I had a feeling that Jaska had to know more than he was sharing about Meritta's death. I wouldn't have been the least bit surprised if he had been the intruder from the night before. The only thing was that he could have gone into his sister's house anytime he wanted.

Jaska and his mother lived in what everyone called the "high-rises" near my old school. They were only three stories tall, but at the time of construction, they were the first multi-story apartment buildings in town. Hence the name. When I rang the bell, Jaska's younger sister, Jaana, opened the door and reported that her brother was at band practice.

"They're still practicing in the same basement you guys used. I don't know who he's playing with, but you can go and see." Jaana also told me that Aniliina's father had arrived in town a few hours earlier.

I wondered whether I should bother interrupting band practice. Johnny might be there too. I was nervous, but I decided not to be completely spineless. Seeing the cave where I spent the best times of my high school years was going to be weird. In reality, the room we used was the high school's bomb shelter. No sound passed through the thick door that led down to the practice room.

When I opened it and started down the stairs, I could hear that at least some of the dials were turned up to eleven. The hallway had that familiar smell of cigarettes, beer, and French fries, and the pale-yellow paint had peeled away to almost nothing. Descending those concrete steps felt like walking back through time to puberty.

Five musicians were playing: Jaska on guitar; Johnny on vocals and guitar; Pasi, another former Tiger, on drums; a fifteen-year-old on bass; and another vaguely familiar-looking guy on keyboards. All men. Typical. They all stared at me in astonishment—all except Johnny, who turned his eyes to the ceiling.

"Hi. Jaska, I need to talk to you."

"Are you in a hurry? Tumppi has to leave in an hour," Jaska said, motioning to the bassist. "If not, sit down and have a listen."

I didn't really know what I was supposed to do. Pasi lit a cigarette, which instantly filled the low-ceilinged room with smoke. Empty beer bottles served as ashtrays, as they had fifteen years earlier. Johnny sat on a table, tuning the top string of his guitar. Then suddenly his E-string broke with a twang and he swore.

"I have a spare," Jaska said.

Had anything changed? Jaska always carried a couple of extra sets of strings, sometimes even a set for the bass, along with a bunch of picks, a pitch pipe, tape for fixing drumheads, and just about everything else a band could need to keep on playing. Before I used to think his attention to detail was funny, but now it just felt sad. His own body was in complete crap shape, but you could bet he would have a spare guitar string.

"We have a gig coming up in July. Popeda is playing at Ilosaarirock and we're the second warm-up act," Jaska said proudly.

"Yeah, half an hour at seven o'clock in exchange for free oxygen," Pasi added sardonically.

I'd heard this conversation before. A major music festival, a chance at a big break, and everyone but Jaska knowing that nothing would come of it.

Johnny had his guitar fixed.

"Should we try these songs you and Jaska have been working on?" Johnny asked Pasi. All of a sudden, Jaska seemed to stand a little taller.

The first piece began with a flamboyant organ solo on the keyboard, followed by Jaska singing lyrics in elementary-school

English delivered in a you're-squeezing-my-testicles parody of Meatloaf.

The songs were horrible. I didn't know which of them was responsible for the words and which the melody, but no one knew what they were doing. Jaska still didn't know how to play, and his attempted imitation of classic heavy metal vocals was appalling. The bass player was quite good, and I couldn't tell about the keyboardist because the part they had written for him was such an irritating mishmash. Johnny played lazily. I wished I had gone home after all.

"Well, what did you think?" Jaska asked after the three-song set. His swollen eyes were aglow with anticipation.

"It was different than I expected. A little like Meatloaf with some Ramones mixed in. The organ part was pretty interesting…" I met Johnny's mocking gaze that seemed to say, *So, you don't dare tell him the truth either.*

Next the guys played a mixed bag of covers, including ZZ Top and Led Zeppelin. An almost healthy cast had appeared on Jaska's face, and his eyes were full of life. The scar behind his left cheek, which he had gotten from falling on a beer bottle while drunk, burned a dark red. Occasionally his enthusiastic hands would slip on the neck of the guitar. The others had better technique, but no one could match Jaska's passion. Playing with them would have been more fun than listening. Then at least I could have concentrated on making my own part as good as possible and enjoyed melting into the larger sound. Gradually, I felt myself getting into the music, and my hand started drumming on the edge of the table. When I noticed a tambourine on the couch, I picked it up and started shaking it, not giving a damn that it didn't fit with the song they were attacking, the Hurriganeses' "Get On" with its "Johnny B. Goode" intro riff. Even though

I hadn't sung much during my Rat Poison days, I found myself adding background vocals for Johnny and Jaska.

Over the years, the band cave had gained some new furniture—a table and a couple of chairs. The couch was still the same one that Johnny had once passed out on, the same one where I had sat while Jaska copied my language arts and math homework between class periods. Even then it had been ready for the landfill. I doubted anyone had cleaned it in all these years.

"I gotta go now," Tumppi said after we wrapped up "Get On."

"He has to get back to the base, and the last bus leaves soon," Jaska explained, lifting a bag of beer out from behind the drum kit.

"He's in the army? I thought he looked about fifteen."

"Fifteen or nineteen, what do we care?" Johnny laughed. "Hey, Jaska, don't start drinking yet. Let's play some more. Maria can do bass."

"I haven't played in a hundred years! Don't expect me to be good anymore." Still, I picked up the bass guitar off the couch, plugged the cord into the amplifier, and adjusted the shoulder strap. I liked feeling the hard surface of the instrument against my thighs again. The strings were warm under my fingers, a little stiffer than what I was used to. Experimentally I plucked a few scales and then threw out a boogie-woogie lick. After just a few scraps of melody, I could feel my fingertips on my left hand begin to sting. But I didn't care. Finally, I was home.

"I don't even remember any songs," I said for the sake of appearances.

"We have sheet music. Here." Johnny tossed a book of Beatles music we had stolen from the town library eons ago onto the table.

I grimaced. Coming back here and playing with Johnny, Jaska, and Pasi the same songs we had jammed to half a lifetime ago was both fun and grotesque. Of course Jaska had always turned his nose up at anything like the Beatles, Simon & Garfunkel, or Hector. He had thought they were too tame and, judging from his expression, he still did. But I thought they were perfect for three thirtysomethings walking down memory lane together.

"How about this?" Johnny had turned to "Can't Buy Me Love."

Getting into the right rhythmic flow took me a while. Johnny's voice wasn't as clear as it had been back in the late seventies when he was the dulcet lead singer for the Snow Tigers. Our singer for Rat Poison, on the other hand, was the guy with the roughest voice we could find. But when we all jammed together, the singer was whoever got there first, sometimes even me.

We played a few more familiar Beatles tunes. Even though my fingers were stiff and I was nervous, it was still fun. Playing in a rock band was different from anything else I had ever done. The adrenaline rush was just like running. But in a band, I was one with the other musicians, a part of the music itself, my heart beating in time with the drums. After "I Saw Her Standing There," I realized that I really missed this.

Then we changed to Hector, some classic Finnish folk rock. First we played his translation of Buffy Sainte-Marie's "Universal Soldier" and then "The Snow Made an Angel"—two of our old standbys. I had always liked the latter's scale-like bass lines that launched into each succeeding phrase. I sang with Johnny and the keyboardist right up until the chorus of the second verse:

> And Daddy went to Sweden,
> Mommy flew to heaven.

And the priest got to drink his coffee again.
And brother was drunk,
I saw him crying in pain.

A strange pling came from Jaska's guitar, and I wondered whether he was thinking about Aniliina too. Or was he thinking of the twisted orange angel lying on the gravel at the base of the Tower? Only the keyboardist and drummer carried the song through to the end.

Johnny had turned toward the music shelf. I didn't know whether he was really looking for something or if he just wanted to hide his face. When he turned back toward us, his expression was suddenly mischievous.

"Do you remember this, Maria?"

It was a handwritten Finnish adaptation of CCR's "Who'll Stop the Rain." The boys in the Snow Tigers had played it one year for the battle of the bands during the town festival and had taken the top prize. But one of the big men from the mining company had been in attendance and got all wound up over the verse: "My daddy done died, fallen down in the mine. I guess the boss and his men couldn't get him up in time. That was the day, made up my mind, I ain't goin' down that hole." The local director of the mining company called Johnny directly and forbade him from playing the piece at the county music competition. I couldn't remember exactly what the threat was, but he succeeded in getting Johnny to promise not to play the song.

At the county festival, I remembered sitting with sweaty palms in the audience, nervous for the Tigers and nervous about whether Johnny would play the banned song. When the familiar opening riffs blasted over the speakers and Johnny started to sing, I almost cried. Johnny was a hero. No one could tell him what he could and couldn't play! Afterward, we had been pretty disappointed when no one made a big deal about it.

I would have known this bass line even if you woke me up in the middle of the night. C, E, F, A. Da-da-da. Da-da-da. I smiled at Johnny. When he smiled back, my knees went weak and my mouth dried up. We all screamed the refrain, "I ain't goin' down that hole!" Even though we ended up laughing, there was something melancholy about it. When we were kids, we thought we really had a choice. We just had to shape our lives to be exactly what we wanted. Life would hand us everything on a silver platter if we just got out of this little town.

"Now some noise," Jaska demanded when we finished a John Fogerty song. So we ran through a few early Eppu Normaali and Pelle Miljoona pieces, which left the ankle biter on the keyboard completely out in the cold. Then Johnny sat down on the edge of the table, clamped a capo on the neck of his guitar and started plucking, repeating an E-minor arpeggio sequence. I listened for a few seconds and then began strumming the bass tonic and then the melody.

"Are you going to Scarborough Fair…" The boyish brightness was back in Johnny's voice. "Scarborough Fair" was one of the few songs we had always sung together. This was exactly the song that made me feel connected to Johnny; whenever I heard it, I thought of him, my Johnny Guitar. I couldn't help looking at him as we sang, his focused yet contemplative expression and his hand stroking the guitar strings. They were the same, although the years had made the joints and the veins in his arms more prominent. I wished he were stroking me instead of the guitar. Then I saw the Band-Aids on the knuckles of his right hand, and the enchantment melted away.

Now it was Pasi's turn to leave.

"Did you have something you wanted to talk about? Let's go down to the Copper Cup for a beer and we can watch Kaisa's meet," Jaska suggested.

"No, I'm fine." I didn't want to step back into my police role and ruin such a fun night by harping on my suspicions. I wanted to go home and pretend for a while that everything was still the way it used to be. I wanted to forget that I no longer believed singing could change the world.

If only I had known how much I would regret that decision two days later.

"Oh, you have your car? Could you drop me off at home so I don't miss the beginning of the javelin throw?" Johnny asked when he saw my uncle's rattletrap in the parking lot. I didn't know what to say, so I just nodded toward the car.

We sat in silence for the first mile and then Johnny opened his mouth. "Maria, do you think I was lying to you about Friday night? I didn't see Meritta after the party. I went back out for a bike ride because I was messed up. Because of you."

I tried to upshift, but my feet fumbled with the gas and clutch, making the affronted gearbox snarl.

"I just rode around thinking about what life would have been like if fifteen years ago we would have…My relationship with Meritta was drying up. I was just material for her art. She only wanted me until she got bored and found something new to paint. She didn't need me, not really. But, Maria, couldn't we still give it a try?"

I had imagined Johnny saying those words so often in my daydreams. Now I realized how completely absurd they sounded. I had never loved the real Johnny. I loved the image I had built up around him. He was just good material for my adolescent dreams, the same way he had been good material for Meritta's paintings.

"It wouldn't work. And I wouldn't have been able to make your life any better."

"Don't you believe me?" Johnny's voice was raspy now.

"Maybe I don't." I turned the car into the Miettinens' yard and forced myself to look into Johnny's yellow-flecked blue eyes. "Let's have this discussion again after Sergeant Järvisalo has caught Meritta's murderer."

Johnny got out, slamming the car door shut behind him.

I swung the Lada so hard into the turn onto the highway that the tires screamed and I dented the line of mailboxes. Really? I had just been offered the thing I once wanted more than anything else in the world, and now I was ready to just toss it away with some vicious words thrown in for good measure?

For a fleeting moment, I decided to turn back and tell Johnny that I had changed my mind. I imagined what it would feel like to make love with him, how he would taste, how he would smell next to me every morning.

But instead I drove home, lured Mikko into my arms, and sat on the steps listening to the evening trilling of the skylarks. This was definitely one of the two days of the week when I would have turned down a proposal from Antti. Mikko purred contentedly as I told him that I probably wouldn't say yes to Johnny on even one day out of seven.

9

The evening ended nicely with Kaisa winning the Helsinki World Grand Prix with the best throw of the summer, 71.74 meters. The next morning the papers were all atwitter with "delicate, charming Kaisa's" rock-solid conditioning. *The Karelian* declared her the absolute favorite for European Championships gold. In the picture, Kaisa was just releasing a javelin, but compared to Meritta's paintings, the photograph felt strangely lifeless.

My first customer of the day was the manager of the Copper Cup Bar & Grill, the mother of a former classmate who always made sure minors didn't have any business trying to get into her pub. Although Marsa still didn't have a single hair out of place, her face, despite her makeup, was now wrinkled and gray. The worst thing about returning to Arpikylä was that everyone I knew had aged eleven years, and looked as if they were wearing masks.

"So I have an entertainment permit application to submit," she began hesitantly after we were done with small talk. "Our owner is worried that Kivinen's restaurant at the mine is going to eat up all our customers. Apparently we have to come up with new ways to draw the crowds. So…well…There's this stripper who's going to start coming in on Saturday nights." Marsa handed me a brochure. Posing on the front was a woman with large breasts and freckled skin, who went by the stage name Miss Miranda. All she was wearing were thigh-high pink vinyl boots and a matching sequined G-string.

"If this brings the customers back, the owner intends to try topless waitresses," Marsa continued, her voice filled with despair.

"What does the staff think about it?" The brochure promised a high-class erotic show and "unforgettable experiences."

"Well, no one who works there now is going to take off her shirt! And who would want to look at old ladies like us anyway? Kivinen already hired away all the best-looking girls in town."

So not all of the townsfolk were completely on board with Kivinen's massive project. I understood full well that a burg the size of Arpikylä didn't have space for three restaurants. The Old Mine and the Copper Cup were competing for the same clientele, since the Matador was a greasy spoon best visited only after you were drunk.

"Do you happen to have the Cup's business license with you?" I asked.

Marsa dug it out of her bag. Looking it over, I couldn't find anything in it that would give me grounds for refusing to grant a permit for the stripper, since it seemed as though that was what Marsa was hoping. The Copper Cup Bar & Grill was authorized for dancing and dinner shows, which also gave them more flexibility in pricing than if they had simply sold alcohol.

"Unfortunately I don't have any legal basis for rejecting this application. But I'll be there on Saturday, and if things don't go exactly as the law prescribes, then we'll see. But I think you should start gathering signatures for a petition against this. Tell female customers to boycott the restaurant." I knew that sounded a little desperate since women around here didn't spend much time sitting in bars anyway, at least not without their husbands.

"The staff can't start a campaign against our own employer. He'll just throw us out...And that's probably what he wants anyway so he can get these topless girls to replace us. I have talked to a few of the women city council members though. Meritta Flöjt had promised to do something, and then there was that Christian member of Parliament..."

"Contact her again."

Meritta was the one we needed here, since she wasn't sex-shy like that Christian old maid. Arpikylä's first parliamentarian's most notable accomplishment so far had been proclaiming that every Member of Parliament who supported gay rights was going to hell. And no doubt she had been involved in arranging Kivinen's development subsidies for the Old Mine.

Grimacing, I signed the permit. When was I going to find a job where I didn't have to constantly violate my own principles? Marsa looked disappointed, as if she were thinking that having a woman sheriff wasn't much use after all. But the same laws were in effect regardless.

And now on Saturday nights, Jaska and his ilk in town would be sitting in the Copper Cup drooling over Miss Miranda's shapely butt...which brought to mind the sexy nightgown Koivu had bought for Anita's birthday. Today was the day. How had Anita reacted to her gift?

Before I could pick up the phone, it rang. My mother. They were leaving for Joensuu to see Uncle Pena—a call had come from the hospital reporting that he had experienced some sort of attack again.

At first I thought I would have to cancel my meeting with Kivinen, but my mother assured me that Pena wasn't going to die in the next few hours. Each attack seemed to be carrying him closer to the end though.

"I'll come at four," I promised. "We can drop in on Eeva and Saku too while we're there."

On my office couch, Meritta's mine paintings radiated blackness. I thought of Uncle Pena, who had spent ten years of his life in that pit. I imagine you got used to it, that it was only dramatic seeing it for the first time. After my grandfather died, Pena took over the family farm. He had never married or fathered any children. His cat, liquor, and local politics had given color to his life. I didn't know whether Uncle Pena had been a happy man. He had always seemed that way, sitting on the steps at the farm after sauna with a bottle of Koskenkorva Vodka at his feet and Mikko in his lap, telling us salacious stories about people in town.

As I continued to stare at the canvases, I began to make out colors and shapes in the blackness. Both paintings were of tunnels that expanded into caverns. Something in one of the tunnels was strangely familiar, something in its gatelike edges, the slight lip at the mouth of the cave. Like a picture of the inside of a woman in a biology book. Of course the cave was the womb, the lighter cluster of rocks on its wall perhaps an embryo that had just begun cell division. Or maybe I was just imagining that.

The blackness of the other painting was darker, more oppressive. I looked for something familiar in it too, but in vain. In the corner of the cave it was as if some small flame burned, waiting for an opportunity to flare.

Had Meritta wanted to hide these paintings from Matti? Did something in them relate to her death? I wondered who could interpret them for me. Maybe Matti, and certainly the curator of Meritta's gallery. Looking up the number for the gallery, I called but only reached a machine that told me the gallery would reopen in mid-July.

I studied the Saastamoinen Construction bankruptcy papers until I needed to leave for the Old Mine. A local bank had granted Saastamoinen a loan on surprisingly flimsy grounds, and the fact that Saastamoinen's wife was the bank manager's sister only made it look more suspicious. No one had even begun questioning the bank manager though, leaving the investigation still wide open. Maybe I could concentrate on that instead of Meritta's murder so I wouldn't have to interrogate people I knew. After all, the bank manager hadn't moved into the area until after I left home.

The day was cloudy, the top of the Tower nearly invisible. Yet the Old Mine was swarming with tourists. Jaska was sitting at the ticket booth and apparently knew to expect me, because he simply waved me through. Then he said something to the girl sitting behind the souvenir kiosk and started walking up the stairs with me toward the restaurant and Kivinen's office.

"Didn't we sound good? And that band from Liperi I was telling you about is great too. We might get to do a single on Silent Records—just have to do another demo, but that'll take a little money. I'll find it somewhere." Jaska was having an up day again.

I nodded, hoping that some part of what he was telling me was true.

"I may have something to talk to you about tomorrow, but I have to check one thing with someone first," he said as he left me at the door of the restaurant. His face had a malicious intensity. The Old Mine staff uniform, brown jeans and a copper-colored silk shirt accented with a gold tie, made him look strangely presentable. But the smell was still Jaska, a stench of tobacco, dirty hair, and unbrushed teeth that reminded me of something I couldn't quite nail down.

"If you have something to tell me, do it now."

"Hi, Maria." Kivinen appeared at the door, which sent Jaska skittering on his way just like he had at the party the previous Friday night. "Shall we head right down?"

The entrance to the Museum of Mining tunnels had been excavated on the northwest slope of the hill. The path leading to it was overgrown with grass, but soon thousands of tourists would trample it bare.

"This part that's open to the public doesn't actually go very deep, but we can take VIPs like you down in the elevator," Kivinen said. "That's two hundred meters down."

When we entered the museum tunnel, he handed me a familiar yellow helmet. No headlamp on it this time either.

The public tunnel was a disappointment, the walls reinforced with concrete, the gravelly floor dry, and the electric lights illuminating our way all too well. At no point did we have to bend over to avoid hitting our heads. Various tools and pieces of equipment were on display and showcases embedded in the walls shared information related to mining life. In one corner was a life-size miner dummy with a drill in his hands. As we approached it, an infernal racket filled the tunnel. The dummy moved, really drilling into the wall! Fortunately, the cacophony lasted only about ten seconds.

"That startled me a little," I admitted.

There was an odd expression on Kivinen's face. "That's the idea. This job wasn't a game."

"Your father worked in the mine too, right?"

"Almost forty years. He started at sixteen and retired on disability at fifty-three. They said smoking caused his lung cancer," Kivinen said, his voice breaking.

The electric light shining from behind him cast his shadow far ahead of us, making it look strangely warped. I wondered whether sheer sentimentality could be the driving force behind this enormous undertaking after all, a desire to somehow compensate a father who had toiled his life away in the mine and to honor all the men who had sacrificed themselves. Perhaps money wasn't his only motivation.

I wasn't the slightest bit surprised by Kivinen's desire to prove himself. Plenty of my friends had the same desire, a yearning to return as conquering heroes to this oppressive little town. And when Kivinen was young, the town had been even more hierarchical than when we were in school. Even in the late seventies there had been a strict caste system. At the top were the lords of the mining company, the managers and engineers. After them came the academic professionals, the doctors, teachers, and priests. Apparently in the teachers' lounge at school, the wives of the engineers had considered themselves slightly above the rest.

On the lowest rung were the children of the miners, the untouchables. No one really expected them to succeed in school—they wouldn't even go on to high school. Clearly, expecting them to learn foreign languages was out of the question, so the Swedish teacher didn't even try. What would a wage slave do with a second language anyway?

By the end of the seventies, when the mine was forced to cut back operations and the city started looking for replacement industries, the caste system began to break down. Still, it was clear that Kivinen had accomplished a small miracle by rising from the bottom of the barrel up to a status on par with the mayor and governor.

The Museum of Mining tunnel ended at a large vault with chairs and a screen for a slideshow. Kivinen asked if I wanted to watch it, but I said no.

"Would you like to go farther down in the elevator?"

I didn't, remembering all too well the darkness and damp silence below. But I also remembered Meritta's paintings and the shades of color rising out of the black background. So I nodded yes.

"Let's take a couple of lights along. Dragging ordinary tourists down into the mine would be too cumbersome, but I have to tell you that you really can't get a feeling for it up here." With that, Kivinen led me through a heavy iron door to another vaulted chamber that ended at a yellow-walled elevator that could accommodate about ten people at a time. As we descended I could see the shaft from out the window and a rusted ladder that led up the wall.

"Emergency exit," Kivinen said. "Back in the fifties, the elevator broke about once a year, and my dad and your uncle Pena had to climb up that ladder at least twice. How is Pena doing, by the way?" he asked just as the creaky elevator jolted to a halt in the middle of the darkness.

"Worse again. He's on a respirator."

Holding the door open, Kivinen showed the way with a powerful flashlight. Reluctantly I stepped into the cone of light, and then Kivinen handed me a flashlight as well. I turned it on and with its beam scanned the black, glistening walls. I remembered what Matti had said about phosphorus. The tunnel led down, looking as if it might branch in two directions a little farther off. Pins had been driven into the walls for attaching ropes. I hoped Kivinen's flashlights had good batteries. The light of the elevator quickly fell behind as we started walking down the corridor. It wasn't going to go back up without us, was it?

Kivinen told me that we were about three hundred feet below sea level, moving north toward the sports field and the health center. This tunnel had been one of the first ore bodies they had begun mining in the 1910s. Although Kivinen spoke softly, his voice echoed off the walls. Moisture began creeping through my clothing, and I was happy I was wearing cotton pants and a long-sleeved blazer. There were no large puddles in the tunnel, so my feet stayed dry.

We came to where the tunnel branched, and Kivinen motioned to the right. "That leads to the edge of the subsidence zone. We need to stay away from there."

With that he started walking down the left tunnel until I asked a question that stopped him short. "Is that where Meritta painted?"

Kivinen's face was in shadow, but his tone was one of irritation. "Yes. She just had to barge her way into the most dangerous spot. Meritta was interested in a deep pond on the edge of the cave-in. She wanted to paint the way light moves through the water and reflects on the walls. But it was insane. No one should go down there under any circumstances."

"Then why did you let her go?"

"I didn't know she was going to go so far! I specifically told her not to! No one has been able to go there for thirty years."

There was something in the right tunnel that drew me toward it. Its opening seemed narrow, turning ever more sharply to the right. It was a place where darkness and silence lived, a place where everything in the world above ceased to exist. From somewhere in its depths came the quiet, purposeful sound of dripping water.

Kivinen's footsteps had stopped. Turning my flashlight toward him, I couldn't find him at first since he had switched off his own. A cold drop of water fell from the ceiling onto my cheek, and I shuddered. In my beam of light I saw Kivinen struggling with his own flashlight. Eventually it lit up only to go out again.

"Of course this damn thing would choose right now to act up." For the first time I heard the gliding Savo-Karelian note in his voice. "I guess I'll have to use the small one."

I turned to follow him, and a moment later the thin, flickering beam of a small flashlight appeared in front of me. This new tunnel we entered branched to the left and was narrow but level and significantly drier than the previous one. In the cold of the mine, I could feel Kivinen's warmth next to me. Being in this darkness with a perfect stranger was odd.

"Sometimes Meritta and I would meet down here," he said suddenly, illuminating a narrow bench carved into the wall. "Meritta wanted to sit there. In the dark."

"Strange thing to want," I said emphatically.

"Are you afraid of the dark?" Kivinen's voice contained a challenge, and his eyes glittered with amusement in the weak light.

"Of course not," I said and doused my flashlight. Kivinen laughed and then clicked off his own.

I was used to being able to see in the dark after a few seconds. Even on a moonless, snowless night in November you could start to make out light and shadow in the forest, the shapes of rocks and the motion of tree branches. But now—nothing. Only the weight of the rock above us, the sound of water trickling in the distance, and Kivinen's breath a few feet away. Then there was a strange scratching sound and a wild blaze from a match head that lit a candle flame.

"Meritta brought this down with her once," Kivinen said, indicating the stub of candle flickering in an old-fashioned copper holder. "I should take it away."

Marching single file behind the candle, we turned and went back up the tunnel the way we came, as silent as a funeral procession. After a while, Kivinen's dramatics started irritating me, and I turned on my flashlight. Its light was so bright that I could clearly differentiate the gray and brown colors of the rocks, the glistening of the water on the walls, the yellow grains of sand on the floor. The elevator shone like a cheerful lighthouse at the far end of the tunnel.

"When did you and Meritta last meet up?" I asked once the elevator began rattling toward the top.

"As I've said several times, our relationship ended months ago!" Kivinen said, acting put-upon. "We parted on good terms. I didn't want to lose my family, and Meritta already had a new man—Johnny Miettinen—in her sights. I guess I was a little jealous when Meritta was able to give me up so easily for Miettinen." Kivinen smiled, as if mocking himself.

Who wouldn't have chosen Johnny? Perhaps someone who valued the power of money more than anything else. But Meritta wasn't one of those people. Of course Kivinen was perfectly handsome in his own way. He had medium-brown hair cut in a jaunty, youthful style; he clearly took care of his body; and his smile seemed to stretch all the way to his toffee-colored eyes. But compared to Johnny, Kivinen was average.

Although the misty clouds hung so low they nearly touched the top of the Tower, the air outside still felt dry and crisp after the tunnels of the mine. Filling my lungs, I devoured the radiant green of the birch trees as I listened to the sounds of the city echoing from the base of the hill.

Kivinen smiled. "It always feels the same, coming up. My dad said that. Every single day the same feeling of liberation...I hope you're hungry. Let's go to the restaurant."

With that, Kivinen led us to a private room where a vaguely familiar-looking woman in a blue dress was already waiting for us.

"My wife wanted to meet you too," Kivinen said.

The woman extended her hand. "Barbro."

Apparently she had already adopted the local first-name rule too.

I had heard that Barbro Kivinen was from an old Swedish-speaking industrial family. Her demeanor was one of assured sophistication, which made me want to double-check whether I had chosen the proper fork for the shrimp cocktail. Barbro inquired about my work and education, saying that she herself had studied at the Hanken School of Economics and now acted as chairman of the board to a couple of the family's other businesses. The family's two sons were in school, one at the Helsinki School of Economics and the other in the United States, also studying business. I was telling them about Antti's postdoctoral fellowship in Chicago when the server brought the veal escalope. I declined any wine, as I was on duty and the Kivinens weren't drinking either. After the main course, Kivinen made his apologies, explaining that his next meeting was waiting, and left me with his wife to enjoy our cappuccinos.

"Cappuccino in Arpikylä. Unbelievable," I said, smiling at Barbro. "Fifteen years ago you couldn't even get artificial sweetener in your coffee here. So how have you been settling in?"

"I have to admit it is quite strange, having lived my whole life in Helsinki. I do visit there almost weekly though. Our son Mikael lives in our apartment downtown, so I always have a place to stay. Especially last winter I found myself longing for the theater and the opera, and decent places to eat lunch."

"Not Tokmanni?"

Barbro laughed. She knew what I meant. That spring a new discount big-box store had come to the county. Tokmanni was a sort of doggerel of the storied Stockmann department store and its café that stood at the center of cultural life in Helsinki. Somehow this captured perfectly the difference between Helsinki and Arpikylä.

The foam decorating the cappuccino left a mustache on my upper lip, which I tried to lick off quickly. Why wasn't Barbro Kivinen having the same problem?

"But life here is just as dramatic as in a big city, even without any murders," Mrs. Kivinen continued. "How is the investigation progressing, by the way?"

"Bit by bit. We still don't really know whether it was an accident or a homicide."

"I met Ms. Flöjt several times, since she painted at the mine quite often. A very unique woman, very determined." Barbro gave a tight-lipped smile, and I wondered whether her husband had been able to keep his relationship with Meritta a secret after all. I was sure that Barbro Kivinen was a determined woman too. But would she be prepared to murder to keep her husband to herself?

After coffee I wandered over to the ticket booth, but there was no sign of Jaska, so I stopped to look at souvenirs—forged copper miniatures of the Tower and small copper hearts. Where had I seen a copper heart like that?

On impulse, I picked up the dime-size earring, turning it over in my palm. Its color was warm, almost the same color as my hair.

"Copper is the metal of love," the salesgirl said. "The hooks are gold though, so they won't turn your ears green. Genuine Arpikylä artisan craftsmanship."

I decided to buy a pair of earrings and send one to Antti. Maybe it was sappy, but I didn't care.

By the time I left work for Joensuu, it had started to rain. The Lada's windshield wipers worked well enough, but the back window fogged up almost instantly. After trying the heater, I finally opened the front windows and within a few miles I could see behind me again.

I had always hated the Joensuu Central Hospital. Whereas the Arpikylä Tower watched over the surrounding landscape mysterious and castle-like, this building was simply cold and sterile. When I was fourteen, I had my tonsils removed, but the wound refused to heal. I lay in a bed on the eighth floor of the hospital for nearly two weeks before the doctors managed to patch my throat back together properly. The taste of blood in my mouth still unnerved me, making me imagine that my scars had reopened and I would have to be hooked up to all those tubes again.

Uncle Pena was lying in his bed with his eyes closed. He looked completely different from how I remembered him. My dad was waiting for me, but Mom had already left to see her baby grandson. Pena's room was filled with various machines, one of which monitored his heart. The wave pattern was beautifully regular. An oxygen machine pumped air into his lungs and a tube connected to his arm provided a nutrient solution. Presumably the blanket concealed a catheter. The paralyzed side of his mouth was strangely twisted.

Looking at my uncle, suddenly I had an almost uncontrollable desire to rip out all the tubes and end his life once and for all. Maybe that's what he wanted. But I had seen the bright expression in his unparalyzed eye when he had been conscious and had seen how his healthy hand moved as if in a petting motion when I talked to him about his cat. How could I know for sure what he wanted?

"Just before you came he was awake for a few minutes," my father said.

"Did you tell him that Mikko caught two mice?"

"No, I forgot. Look at that bouquet of flowers. From the town council."

The white roses and blue irises were elegantly arranged, vaguely reminiscent of a Finnish flag dotted with splashes of bright yellow. It would have been perfect as a funeral arrangement; all it needed was a ribbon with an appropriate patriotic line from "Oh Dear Finland, Precious Fatherland." The vase was too small for the bouquet, making it look as though it might tip off the narrow table onto the floor.

"That reminds me. Who will take Meritta's seat on the city council? Do you know?" I asked.

My father's brow furrowed. "As I remember, the Greens only had three candidates in that race, including Meritta, who received almost all the votes for the party. The others I remember were Matti Virtanen and a recent high school graduate who doesn't even live in town anymore. I think he moved to Helsinki. So I guess it would be Matti, seeing as he's the only person on the Green party list in town."

I didn't think a seat on the town council could be sufficient incentive to murder someone, and imagining Matti wanting it that badly was beyond impossible. But now I had one more important reason for interviewing the Virtanens. I really couldn't put it off past tomorrow.

We waited for a while, but Uncle Pena didn't wake up. A nurse came by on her rounds and assured us all was well, so well in fact that they were even considering taking him off assisted breathing. She looked at me a little funny when I asked her to tell him about the mice Mikko had caught, but she promised she would.

"Pena and Meritta did have some scheme in the works before his stroke," my dad said thoughtfully as we drove toward my sister's house. "I don't know whether Meritta was trying to get the Dems on board with one of her environmental issues or what, but they were talking a lot. Sometimes I would even see them at the Copper Cup together."

"Meritta was working on a series of paintings of the mine, so maybe she wanted Pena to tell her about what it was like to work down there," I suggested.

"Maybe. I think Pena was a little infatuated with her too. I'm sure that did him good. He was always a little afraid of women. Our eternal bachelor."

I had always gotten along great with my uncle, but growing up Eeva and Helena were a little shy around him. Perhaps Uncle Pena had put them in the "women" category but hadn't done the same with me. I had always been willing to cut hay and listen to his stories even longer than my aunt's sons who were about the same age as me.

At my sister's place I played cars with Saku for an hour until he started getting hungry. While the others tried to feed him—it seemed as though food ended up everywhere but in the little man's stomach—I tried to call Koivu. At his home no one answered, and the police station said he was at the hospital questioning Somalis and skinheads. Judging from that, Anita's birthday probably hadn't panned out too well. For a second I considered whether I could stand going back to the antiseptic-smelling hospital, but I decided I couldn't bother Koivu while he was doing work.

As I drove back through the rain-drenched forests, I thought of Uncle Pena. What if I tried to smuggle Mikko into the hospital? Maybe feeling his cat's smooth coat one more time would do him good. Bryan Adams' voice pouring out of the radio as he bleated about forgiveness didn't do anything to improve my mood.

The single, small copper heart dangling from my earlobe was strangely heavy. I had mailed Antti's heart immediately, knowing I would hesitate if I didn't act on my romantic impulse right then. Touching my own heart earring, I remembered where I had seen one just like it—on Meritta's ear. But one of her earrings was also missing. Had the killer taken it?

10

As I went out to retrieve the newspaper from the mailbox, I discovered a giant puddle at the foot of the front stairs when my foot squelched into an ankle-deep mixture of mud and water. It had been raining all night. After my morning coffee, I pulled on some rubber boots and set out into the yard to see whether I could do anything about the new pond in front of the house. With the heel of my boot, I started scraping a shallow trench in the dirt to the yard drain thirty feet away.

Mikko appeared on the steps as if pondering whether to go out in the rain at all. In the end, he jumped off the side of the stairs and in a streak of gray bounded under the sauna, where apparently a family of voles had nested.

I watched with pleasure as muddy brown water began trickling down the waterway I made, first slowly and then flowing in a little stream, quickly filling the entire trench and gurgling happily down the drain. I cleared the worst of the stones from the mouth of the channel, and when I came back outside after grabbing my purse, the puddle was noticeably smaller.

At the police station a report on drunk driving arrests that I had asked Järvi to write up the week before Meritta's murder was waiting on my desk. Glancing over it for a while, I discovered that his calculations were completely off. According to Järvi, three plus twelve was eighteen.

I hollered for him to come in from the break room. "This whole statistics section is full of mistakes. Which of these is right, the counts or the totals? They don't match." My good mood from successfully draining the pond was gone. And, of course, I knew pointing out the problems in the report wasn't going to help my reputation as a nagging bitch.

Järvi ran his eyes over the table of numbers, his ears growing red. Finally he had to confess to his poor addition skills.

"Redo this table, and in the meantime I'll read the text," I said, trying to sound conciliatory. "We need to send these papers to the county by the end of the day."

Järvi closed the door with exaggerated caution, so as to clearly demonstrate what he thought of me. I sighed. All these statistics and reports were nothing but pointless bureaucracy, which seemed to be getting worse every year. The new statistical software that the police district ordered was a bear too, and it was probably the original source of the calculation errors. But getting money for machines was easier than securing funds to hire additional manpower.

I had just finished slogging my way, with much sighing, through Järvi's report when he appeared at my door again.

"Um, Maria..." he began, as if expecting to get yelled at. "Our guys just called from the Sump. They found...well...a body. Floating in the pond."

"What the hell?" I was halfway through the door before he even finished his sentence. "Where are Lasarov and Antikainen? Call county forensics and Koivu and send Car 2 over. I'm driving out."

As I backed our other cruiser out of the parking lot without looking where I was going—luckily the street was empty—Järvi ran up with a phone in his hand.

"Did they say who it is?" I asked him.

"No. Some jogger reported it. She ran to the nearest house to make the call and then collapsed. Antikainen left to take her to the health center and question her on the way. All she was able to get out was that someone was floating in the pond." Järvi's voice was shaking, but I knew it wasn't from excitement. He was afraid. He knew the whole city. Whoever had died would at least be an acquaintance...

I drove the Saab as far as I could to the end of the road. The tailing pond at the base of the Sump shone a deep burgundy. At its edge a body lay oddly sprawled, half in the water and half out. I hoped the person was just passed out drunk, maybe after deciding to go for a swim. But as I ran down the loose wall of yellow sand, I knew that hope was in vain. The jogger had probably already checked to see if the person was alive.

I didn't want to see who was lying at the edge of the wine-colored pond. Johnny? Ella? Kaisa? Forcing myself to approach the heap sprawled on the ground, I looked at the face, its temple a bloody mess. A trail of blood ran into the water as if it were giving the entire pond its crimson cast.

Jaska Korhonen was never going to be a big rock star. But the tabloids would take note of his death, and maybe *Sound* would give him a few lines too. Jaska's never-say-die rocker's uniform looked tragicomical, the leather jacket sopping wet, his sneakers covered in the copper sand of the mine hill. There was dirt under the nails of his right hand, which were significantly longer than those on the left. A guitarist's hands.

Beside me, Järvi's breath was raspy. "This isn't going to be easy for Meeri. First a daughter and now her only son...Should we check to see if he's maybe still alive?"

"He's been here all night. He's soaked through. But yeah, check his pulse. Carefully."

But of course there was nothing to feel for. As Järvi checked the wrist, I saw a tear drip from his cheek onto the sleeve of Jaska's jacket.

"Rope off the area," I said, avoiding looking at Järvi again. Fortunately Officer Lasarov and Detective Antikainen turned up and started the routine. Unsolicited, Lasarov said he would go visit Jaska's mother.

Järvi and Antikainen set up barricades and tape around the pond. While they worked, I looked out past the hole where the second mine tower had once stood beside the lake and shivered. Goddamn it, Jaska. You knew something. Why the hell didn't you tell me? You just had to go playing Marlowe. But Jaska wasn't cut out for that sort of thing. He would have been as bad a private investigator as he was a guitarist. Even after all these years, he still couldn't play anything with more than three chords.

Then the tears came. I tried to screw up my face to stop them, but it was no use. I didn't want my colleagues to see me crying, but I couldn't leave. I was determined to wait for Detective Sergeant Järvisalo and Koivu so we could decide what to do next.

"Um...Should we look for footprints or something," Antikainen suggested hopefully.

"He's probably been here all night. The rain will have washed the sand clean."

"Was he killed here?" Antikainen asked.

"It's almost like the killer was trying to sink the poor guy to the bottom of the pond," Järvi said with a sniff. "Why didn't the bastard finish the job?"

Then Hopponen yelled from the direction of the parked cars. "The county is halfway here. They want to know if they can get all way to the pond in their van."

"The whole damn wall of sand would give way. Of course not!" I yelled back.

As if to emphasize my point, Hopponen's feet suddenly slipped on the edge, sending yellow sand pouring down the slope.

When we were kids, Jaska and I used to play cops and robbers here with the other kids in our class. A few years later we smoked our first nauseating Marlboros in the pits of the Sump. The sand still smelled of copper and sulfur. Walking farther along the edge of the pond, I stopped and squatted to pick up some pebbles. Polished from the rain that had washed away the dull yellow dust, they shown with deeply saturated reds and greens. I wished I could have sat down in the sand and spent the rest of the day just looking at the vibrant rocks and the Tower, made darker by the rain. Anything to forget that Jaska lay dead a hundred feet away.

Why hadn't I gone with him to the Copper Cup the other night? Why hadn't I asked him yesterday what he was implying when he said he needed to check on something? Jaska had said he needed money for his band's second demo tape. Maybe he had been trying to blackmail someone? If so, he failed miserably at that too.

I threw one of the phosphorus green stones into the red water, and it plopped into the middle of the pond, sending ripples in every direction. I watched as the tiny ripples gradually reached the opposite shore where Jaska lay, kissing his outstretched hand.

"What are you playing with, Kallio?" Hopponen yelled down to me from on top of the sandy ledge. I was squatting by the pond, sifting pebbles through my fingers, when Lasarov began striding toward me taking long, sliding steps down the slope. But the wet sand gave way more than he expected and he slid the rest of the way down on his rear end, almost landing in my lap. But when I saw his face, any amusement I might have felt evaporated instantly. He shouldn't have gone to Jaska's house alone. A support person should always go with an officer delivering news of a death, but that practice hadn't reached Arpikylä yet.

"I just pray to God I don't have to go there for a third time," Lasarov said when I asked how it had gone. "Luckily Jaana, the youngest daughter, was there, so Jaska's mom doesn't have to be alone. And my wife promised to take them dinner."

I wanted to comfort Lasarov with a hug, but all I could do was pat him on the shoulder.

"Thanks for going."

"This was in Jaska's room," Lasarov said, digging from his pocket a wrinkled envelope originally sent from the Arpikylä Employment Center. Jaska had closed the envelope shut again with masking tape and scrawled "Maria Kallio" on the front.

Feeling something hard inside the envelope, I tore it open. A small copper key fell into my hand. Just a key, no chain of any kind. It looked like a key to a box or a very old safety-deposit box.

Inside the envelope was also a scrap of paper.

> Hi, Maria. If you're reading this, something happened to me. It's Meritta's. She said she didn't dare keep it herself so she gave it to me. It's supposed to be valuable. Jaska.

The idiot had known he was in danger! Why the hell couldn't he have just told me what he knew? Could trying to extract money from someone have been that important to him?

"Was Jaska's mother able to shed any light on where he was yesterday?" I asked Lasarov.

"I didn't think to ask…Maybe I can go back later and talk to Jaana. She's been here since Meritta died."

I nodded. "Try to get a hold of Antikainen to see if he has a statement from the jogger yet."

From up above the pond came the hum of a car engine, which turned into a desperate whine as the vehicle became stuck in the loose sand. The ambulance following the county forensics team was more careful. Eventually Koivu, a county crime scene technician, and Dr. Turunen all climbed out to push the van free. Hopponen stood by and shouted advice. Was Järvisalo sitting comfortably in the front passenger seat thinking bosses didn't need to exert themselves?

Once they dislodged the vehicle, everyone started down the slope, but I still didn't see Järvisalo. I walked back along the edge of the pond toward Jaska to meet them. My shoes were yellow and wet from the sand, and I wished I were still wearing my rubber boots.

"Järvisalo is in Helsinki for a meeting," Koivu explained.

"So are you in charge now?"

"Don't look at me!" Koivu blurted out with surprising irritation. Then he apologized. "The last time I had a good night's sleep was at your place. So let's run through the routine. The deceased is Flöjt's brother, right?"

After recounting my discussion with Jaska the previous day, I showed Koivu the key and note. He shook his head.

"Do you want to hear how he got found?" Detective Antikainen appeared from out of nowhere munching on a ham sandwich. "Kaisa Miettinen cuts through here almost every day on her morning run and saw a strange shadow in the pond. She went down to have a look and found Korhonen. Brave girl. Then she ran back to a friend's house in town and called me. She even came with me to show where the body was, even though it was pretty hard on her...So then I took her to the health center so she could calm down."

"Is she alright?"

"Yeah. I drove her home. That's what took me so long. She said she checked his pulse but didn't touch anything else. Smart girl. I guessed she wouldn't want any publicity for finding a dead body, which is why I didn't tell Järvi right away who had found him," Antikainen said, obviously pleased with himself.

"So she came back from Helsinki yesterday..." I said thoughtfully. I had checked and verified that Kaisa really had flown to Helsinki the night before the break-in at Meritta's house. So she couldn't have been the intruder, but the intruder didn't necessarily have to be the same person as the murderer. Jaska had wanted to speak with someone yesterday. What if Jaska had found what he was looking for and the person he needed to talk to was Kaisa? Trying to throw investigators off by finding the body was a common killer's trick. But why would Kaisa have murdered Jaska?

I looked around. The forensic techs and Dr. Turunen were deep into their work. Just then one of the technicians motioned for Antikainen to come over. Seizing the opportunity, I grabbed Koivu by the waist and pulled him toward me. So what if someone saw? I didn't care how it looked. I just needed a hug. Swinging his right arm over my shoulder, he turned his head to look me squarely in the eye. When his image started to blur, I pulled a handkerchief out of my jacket pocket and wiped my tears, presumably also smearing mascara on my cheeks.

"I didn't spend last night at home," Koivu whispered into my hair. "Anita got mad about the nightgown and threw me out. I think that's the end of the road for us." Koivu showed me his left hand. On his fourth finger all that remained was a white stripe where his gold engagement band had blocked the sun.

"Was it really about a scrap of cloth or your stance on Somali refugees?"

"What does it matter?" Koivu shook his head, sending a drop of rain down the tip of his nose. "I'll have to start looking for a new apartment. I'm not sure why I'd bother staying in Joensuu after this though…" When Dr. Turunen started trudging toward us, Koivu removed his arm from my shoulder.

"Our friend's been dead for almost ten hours. Someone hit him on the head, possibly with a tire iron. I'll have a closer look at the wound back at the lab. He didn't die immediately, since there was so much blood. It appears he held on for quite a while."

"Conscious?" I asked, alarmed.

"Not after an impact like that. The rigor mortis is a little strange. He may have been carried after the blow. Forensics doubts he was killed here."

Later, as we were sitting in the break room back at the police station having a meeting, the head forensic technician confirmed as much. The dirt on the soles of Jaska's shoes was different from the sand around the pond, which indicated he had likely been dragged down from the roadside. Unfortunately the rain had washed away all the footprints, but forensics decided to continue their search after lunch.

Koivu went out with Lasarov to eat and then visit Jaska's house again. I wasn't hungry. I stared at the key, shining copper on top of the green plastic writing pad on my desk. Had Meritta really given Jaska the key or did Jaska find it in Meritta's purse? I remembered the burglar and his smell: grime, sweat, tobacco. Jaska's smell. That had to be it. But how did Jaska get his hands on the purse? Did he murder his sister? And then who killed Jaska? And if Jaska found what he was looking for at Meritta's house, why did he leave me the key? And what lock did it fit?

With an infuriatingly shrill explosion of sound, the phone rang.

"Tuija Miettinen here. People are saying around town that a body turned up in the Sump. It isn't Johnny, is it?"

"Is Johnny missing?"

"He was supposed to come fix Tuomas' bike this morning, but by the time I left at noon, he still hadn't showed up."

"Don't worry; it isn't Johnny."

Tuija's sigh sounded relieved, despite her petulant tone.

"Well, good. He isn't much of a husband, but I wouldn't want my children losing their father."

"Should I ask him to call if he shows up?"

"Don't you know where he is either?" Tuija hissed and hung up.

I was so taken aback that, for a second, setting down the phone didn't occur to me. What did Tuija mean? Did she really think there was something between Johnny and me? Hopefully not. The last thing I wanted was rumors circulating in town that Johnny Miettinen murdered Meritta and then got off because he was having an affair with the summer sheriff.

Meritta's key felt heavy and hot in my hand. I remembered the lock on the Tower, but that was an ordinary ABLOY cylinder type. Going to the Flöjts' home would probably be best, and maybe Aniliina and her father would be there. Since that was where the burglar had been, the key probably fit some lock at Meritta's house. Damn Jaska! He could have left a better explanation about the key. Or maybe he hadn't known?

Outside, the rain had picked up again with heavy drops creating furrows in the gravel path to the parking lot from the station. Just the thirty-foot walk to my heap of a Lada left me soaked. Driving to Meritta's house, I passed the Sump again. You would have thought the incessant rain would somehow dilute the color of the pond, but it glowed just as deep a burgundy as ever. Oddly, Jaska's hand hadn't been dyed purple by soaking in the water.

The Sump's vibrant colors were strange given how dead and denuded the ground there was. The mining company had extracted the minerals from the bedrock, hollowing out the city's foundation, and chewing up and spitting out its inhabitants in the process. After the copper seams tapered off, the company calmly withdrew, leaving behind a ghost town every person under the age of thirty wanted to escape. Only the elderly and people like Jaska nursing empty dreams chose to remain on the fringes of this spot of sinking earth. Fortunately people like Meritta, Matti, and Seppo Kivinen had returned to revive the land left scarred by the mining company.

No one came to open the door at the Flöjts', but that was probably because of the music blaring inside, drowning out any other sound. The front door was unlocked, so I slipped inside.

In the studio I found Aniliina and an almost-bald man sitting curled up on the floor and staring out one of the large windows at the rain, which was beating down as if it were trying to get in. Meritta's stereo was turned up all the way, filling my ears with a cello lament, which was then joined by a mournful bass vocalist. "*L'amour per me non fa...*" or something like that, the whole thing sounding vaguely familiar. Aniliina was almost hidden under her big shirt. Perhaps sensing the vibration of my steps on the floor, the man turned toward me.

In terms of looks, Aniliina clearly took after her father, although his face had more meat on it and his lips were different. A remote control silenced the music, making Aniliina take notice of my arrival too. I introduced myself to Mårten Flöjt, and Aniliina said she would make some tea.

"Thank you for taking Ani into your home the night of the break-in," Mårten Flöjt said once we were alone. "I couldn't come any sooner because the orchestra was in the middle of recording *Don Carlos* and I happen to be the solo cellist."

"Was that it just now?" I asked, pleased that I could tell the difference between a cello and a bass violin.

"Yes, that was me with Jaakko Ryhänen. That's the master tape. Philippe II's aria."

At some point during my teenage years, my parents had dragged me to the Savonlinna Opera Festival to listen to Verdi's *Don Carlos*. To my horror, I had found that I liked opera. Perhaps that was why the aria sounded so familiar.

"Did you come because of Jari?" Mårten Flöjt asked.

I was relieved that they had already heard about Jaska, even though I had prepared myself on the drive over to be the bearer of bad news.

Then I explained the story of the key, but Mårten said he didn't really know the house.

"Meritta and I were still good friends, but I never visited much. Aniliina preferred to come to Helsinki to see me."

"How has she taken Jaska's death?"

"Right when she heard, she threw up. Since then she's mostly just been quiet. We've been listening to music. One of Ani and Meritta's friends is coming to visit tonight, someone named Kaisa. Ani doesn't want to see her grandma or Aunt Jaana though."

"When does Aniliina's therapist get back from vacation?"

"She said sometime in early August."

Almost another month. I had the feeling Aniliina was going to need serious professional help. Anyone who lost two close relatives to violent deaths would, let alone a mentally ill teenager. As Mårten and I talked about his daughter, I was relieved to see that he seemed to grasp the seriousness of the situation.

Then Aniliina reappeared with the teacups, along with what looked like fresh cardamom *pulla* on a tray. I realized I probably should eat something. Aniliina tasted the *pulla* too, slowly and birdlike, just a crumb at a time, chewing each little morsel a ridiculously long time. She drank only a small sip of tea. In a hushed tone she asked me about my uncle's cat.

After tea, we started looking for which lock might fit the key. A few of Meritta's paint boxes looked promising, but upon closer inspection, the color of the lock made it seem doubtful the key would fit. None of the locks were made of the same gleaming copper as the key. And besides, most of the paint boxes were already open.

"There's all kinds of junk in the basement storage room. You could go look there," Aniliina suggested.

The storage room was mostly filled with cardboard boxes stuffed with fabric, which I shoved aside trying to find something more substantial. Finally on the back wall I came across an old cracked-and-peeling chest of drawers with keyholes that were obviously copper, despite a patina of age. I was already squatting, so I tried the bottom drawer first—no luck. The top one was already open, and inside it I found a smaller compartment like many old chests of drawers typically have. The keyhole looked about the right size. My hands were sweating as I tried to shove the key into the lock.

Damn it! Just a tad too small, and one of the grooves was completely wrong. Sneezing from the dust, I finished by rummaging through the bike shed in the yard, which also turned up nothing.

"Is there any other place Meritta would have stored something important?" I asked Aniliina after returning inside.

"I don't think so. Or, wait, she did go to the art school when she was working on silk or teaching oil-painting classes. And she and Matti met there to plan their art camp. She probably left stuff there. There's all kinds of boxes and cabinets at the art school."

"Did Meritta have keys for the school?"

Aniliina grabbed the keys from the entryway and handed them to me. Then she said she was going out for a run.

"Don't be crazy! Not in that rain you aren't!" her father yelled.

"Just a couple of kilometers. Running helps you calm down, doesn't it, Maria?"

Over our morning coffee out at the farm we had talked a lot about sports. I couldn't help but say yes, even though I knew that an anorexic shouldn't be allowed to burn off the one piece of *pulla* she had allowed herself to eat. Mårten had no interest in dealing with a temper tantrum either, so he just shook his head when Aniliina appeared in the studio in her jogging clothes.

"Why did you break up?" I asked after Aniliina had rushed out the door. Mårten looked at me thoughtfully, and I realized how intrusive my question sounded. The chances that the Flöjts' divorce had anything to do with Meritta's murder were slim. I just wanted to know as much about Meritta as possible. After considering for a moment, Mårten answered.

"Sometimes a marriage between two people who put their work ahead of everything else works. Sometimes it doesn't. We belonged to the latter group. In a way, neither of us should ever have gotten married and had a child, although we were both overjoyed about Aniliina. Things just started falling apart. We never had time to spend together, and we were always fighting about housework and childcare. Eventually, Meritta decided to move here, both to paint the mine and because her mother volunteered to nanny. Of course, I couldn't leave my work in Helsinki."

Mårten stared out, watching the water cascade off the eaves. Birch leaves torn from the trees floated in rivulets in the yard.

"And Meritta did want to see other men, but she didn't want to cheat on me. I imagine you know Meritta's reputation as a man-eater. She did change partners frequently, but as I understand it, she only ever had one relationship at a time." Mårten Flöjt's narrow fingers ran through nonexistent hair; only a few dark locks remained above his ears. "She was a unique woman. So absolute about so many things. She always aroused strong emotions in people. Somehow it's easy believing that someone could have murdered her."

Suddenly the door opened with a clatter and Aniliina staggered in, complaining of dizziness. Although her breathing indicated she had been running, her face lacked any hint of color. Her pulse was strangely slow and uneven. As Mårten carried her to bed and stripped off her wet clothing, I cursed the stupidity of two adults allowing a girl like her to go out at all. Running to the kitchen, I found homemade apple juice in the refrigerator, into which I dissolved a couple of tablespoons of honey. Aniliina needed calories.

I forced her to drink the liquid even though she resisted. In the meantime, Mårten tried to reach the physician who had treated her at Joensuu Hospital. She was in serious danger of dehydration, which I had heard could be deadly for anorexics who exercise too much.

"I don't want to go back to the hospital," she croaked after recovering a bit. "It's a prison there. They won't even let you go outside and they threaten to feed you with a tube if you won't eat. The nurses even come into the bathroom with you to watch you so you don't throw up!"

"You're in really bad shape, Ani. You either go back to the hospital or you start eating!"

"I don't want to turn into a fat-ass cow like Mom!" Aniliina's cries were furious again, as if we were trying to cut her in half. I had no way to calm her down, and I couldn't even decipher the meaning behind all the things she was crying about. Then her father came into the room with a glass of water and two pills. Aniliina looked at him skeptically but swallowed the pills anyway.

"Those sleeping pills aren't going to solve anything," Mårten said to me after Aniliina had finally nodded off. "I don't want to take her to the hospital, but at this rate she's going to kill herself."

"One of my friends was a patient at a Helsinki University clinic that specializes in eating disorders. She talked a lot afterward about how good their therapists were. I'll call her today to find out more. We'll figure something out."

With that I started making my way to the art school. My appetite had come back now, so on the way into town I stopped at a grocery store and bought some cold smoked salmon and pasta salad. Then I went to the police station break room to wolf them down. Detective Antikainen peeked his head in and then came to sit with me over coffee.

"County forensics just called," he said. "They're pretty pissed that whoever killed Flöjt and Korhonen was smart enough not to leave any prints."

"People watch too much TV nowadays."

"There should be a law that cop shows have to do things wrong so we can bust murderers easier. They do have the prints from the piece of jewelry we found in the Tower though. They say they found a match on a pocket mirror that Koivu brought in, but he never said who it belonged to. You don't happen to know, do you?"

I fought hard not to blush and reveal that I knew, but to no avail.

"I was betting they were Johnny Miettinen's. You and Koivu did almost arrest him on Sunday. Shouldn't we ask Forensics to get official prints? He was dating our first vic, after all." There was a malicious note in Antikainen's tone. Of course he remembered Johnny saying in his first interview that he left the Old Mine gala with me. This was unfolding in exactly the way I feared it might.

"Go and get his prints yourself. But maybe you should ask Sergeant Järvisalo first."

"But Miettinen is missing. His wife hasn't seen him, or his parents, which is where he was supposed to stay last night."

To my surprise I managed to stay calm despite my vivid memory of the warning we had given Johnny Sunday night to stay put. So the little shit had skipped town. Was Johnny the one Jaska had intended to talk to?

Detective Järvi blew into the break room with new information about Jaska's whereabouts the day before. After work had ended at six, he stopped by home to eat and then had gone out at around eight o'clock. From eight thirty to eleven thirty he had been sitting in the Matador, where, according to the waitresses and the other customers, he had drunk astonishingly little, only two pints in three hours. I imagined that would barely touch

Jaska's liver, and indeed according to our blood test, his BAC had been only 0.06. So Jaska had wanted to stay relatively sober.

At around eleven thirty he had left, cursing the rain and the umbrella he had forgotten at home. One of the guys at the Matador was sure that Jaska had a meeting with someone. When he left he seemed in good spirits, even excited.

I could imagine. Of course he was probably thinking of the money he was going to get from whomever he was hustling. And then the demo tape he would make, the record deal, the fame…In a teenage boy these periodic paroxysms of enthusiasm for future glory aroused feelings of sympathy, but in a thirty-something who had failed too many times to count, they were just pathetic.

No one had seen Jaska after the Matador. Arpikylä had been sleeping soundly on a rainy Wednesday night. Even in the houses that overlooked the Sump, no one had noticed anything. The curtain of rain had obscured everything from view.

11

The art school was just down the street from the police station. Taking a pair of rubber boots three sizes too large and a raincoat that reached to my knees, I decided to walk. The pelting downpour had made the summer day nearly dark. Even the Tower was concealed behind sheets of rain, its existence attested only by the red light atop the radio tower sending its warning message to low-flying planes with three quick flashes.

Previously the art academy had been a regular duplex house. Now the door was painted in a rainbow that continued along the exterior wall, and the gutters were painted bright red. The door squeaked as I stepped inside. The cabinet-filled entryway was dark, but somewhere farther inside a light shone. After shaking off most of the rain, I walked in.

"Don't come any closer or I'll stick this in your throat!"

Someone jabbed a dangerous-looking palette knife toward me from where they stood backlit by the doorway down the corridor. My heart did a backflip. Had the burglar somehow happened to come in just before me?

"I have a phone in my other hand, and I'm calling the police," the voice continued. It sounded familiar. Grabbing the wrist of the knife-wielding hand and bringing my assailant closer, I burst into laughter when I saw Matti trembling with fright at the end of the arm.

"You shouldn't play with knives, Matti."

"Maria!" Matti looked embarrassed. "I thought that…Never mind."

"Who did you think I was?"

Matti thrust the palette knife back into a box but didn't turn back to look at me.

"I heard about the prowler at Meritta's house. I thought maybe he had her keys and was coming here now. Or—Or maybe I thought it was Meritta herself."

"You believe in ghosts?"

"You never know. If anyone was going to come back to haunt the living, it would be Meritta."

"I guess some traditions do believe that the souls of the murdered can't rest until their killers have been punished. But why would Meritta bother you…because your fingerprints are on the brooch we found in the Tower after her death? And Ella's folk costume happened to have the same brooch."

Matti still wasn't looking at me as he turned on a faucet and started rinsing brushes. His pink-and-violet-striped Marimekko shirt was stained with paint, and he was wearing dark-blue corduroy work trousers. Did he have to dress like the stereotype of an artist all the time? Where was his beret? Brownish water ran from the brushes along the edge of the counter onto Matti's moccasins, but he didn't seem to notice.

"I don't know anything about a brooch," he said finally. "And what do you mean about my fingerprints? I've never had my fingerprints taken."

"Did you go home with Ella after we split up? Or did you go back to the Old Mine, perhaps in search of Ella's missing brooch?"

"What do you mean? Of course I went home with Ella!" Matti spun to face me, the paintbrushes splashing water across the floor. "Did you just come here to harass me? Do me a favor and get lost. I have work to do. All the arrangements for the art camp fall on me now that Meritta isn't around anymore."

"I have work to do too. How did Ella's brooch end up on top of the Tower?"

"We all went up to the view deck at the beginning of the party. She must have dropped it then."

"She was wearing it after that. I remember."

"Why don't you ask Ella! I wasn't watching her all night. Ella has keys to the Tower. She could have climbed up any time she wanted."

Now there was no longer any way to avoid talking to Ella. Better me than Järvisalo or Koivu though. But for now I needed to inspect the locks on all the storage boxes and cabinets at the art academy. I didn't want to do it with Matti present though. What if I found something he didn't want me to see and he started waving the palette knife around again?

"I have to ask you to leave now, Matti. I need to search the premises, and you're in my way."

"Do you have some sort of warrant?"

"No, but it will only take one phone call to get one," I lied.

"Wait ten minutes and I'll be done cleaning up."

So I sat down at a drawing desk and looked around. The room we were in had once been a spacious kitchen, and the sink was surrounded by cabinets with no locks on the drawers. At least in this room I couldn't see anywhere that would have fit Meritta's key.

I'd have to check the local banks in case Meritta had a safety-deposit box. The key didn't look like a safety-deposit box key, but it could belong to a smaller container that Meritta might have hidden inside of one. And, of course, I would have to visit Jaska's house. Maybe Meritta gave him more than just the key for safekeeping. I wondered a little about the likelihood of Meritta trusting Jaska with anything important to her. But maybe she hadn't trusted him. Maybe the key was stolen from Meritta's purse, and for some reason or another Jaska had known it was important. Why hadn't he left any clues in the envelope? He must have known something about the key because he appeared to have tried to use it for blackmail.

Matti was finished washing and drying and was now wiping his round eyeglasses with a checkered handkerchief. He opened his mouth a couple of times as if to say something before deciding against it. Finally he made up his mind to speak up.

"I'll admit that I know Ella and Meritta were having some sort of disagreement. I imagine it had something to do with the grant money for the art camp. Ella thought Meritta was using it for things other than what it was intended for, which was paying for materials and hiring instructors. Eventually the city auditors were going to end up getting involved, and then Ella would be in trouble."

"Who was organizing the art camp, officially?"

"The Aprikylä Artists' Association. The same group that runs this school. I'm the board president, and Meritta was the treasurer. The city has been quite generous in funding us, and Ella administers the grant. But she wouldn't have murdered anyone over that!"

"So you haven't talked to Ella about this?"

"No. This is the first I'm hearing about the brooch." I could tell from Matti's voice that he was lying, and I remembered Ella's bitter words about Matti hanging around in bars with Meritta. Had Ella been jealous?

"What was your relationship with Meritta?"

"Coworker. Colleague. Yes, we spent a lot of time together. Finding kindred spirits isn't easy in this town, and we'd known each other for twenty years after all. There was never anything romantic between us though. If you believe all the gossip and newspaper stories, you probably have completely the wrong idea about Meritta. She might have liked sex, but she didn't try to seduce every man she met walking down the street. Just being friends with her felt completely natural."

This time I believed Matti was telling the truth. But had Ella thought the same way?

"So will you inherit Meritta's city council seat?"

Staring at me in puzzlement, Matti shook his head. "More like it's being forced on me. The third member of our party list has already moved away, so I have to take it. But you can't think I'd kill my friend for that. I don't even want to be on the city council!"

"Of course I don't think that."

But Matti continued as if he hadn't heard me. "City politics around here is absurd. They spend hours fighting over dog-license fees, but big land deals go through without comment. Or they would have if it hadn't been for Meritta. But one person can't accomplish anything there since everything is arranged behind closed doors. And I don't have the energy to bang my head against the wall like Meritta." Matti's tone left no doubt what a waste of time he thought being on the city council was going to be.

I considered asking Matti about Meritta's mine paintings but decided to let it be. Best to talk to Ella first. Without prying anymore, I refrained from asking any more questions and Matti obediently exited the building. From the window I watched as he walked toward the center of town in the rain without an umbrella. Only then did I realize he hadn't asked about Jaska. Was he a broken link in the Arpikylä rumor chain?

Before moving on to the other rooms, I checked the kitchen once more thoroughly. The art school was out for summer break, so the whole place was filled with finished works from the previous spring: vernal watercolors, plaster sculptures, photographs…The most daring pieces were usually made by children. The school also had classes for adults, but their work seemed boxed in, as if evidence of how successful the public school art teachers had been administering low grades for anything with originality. Since everyone knows dogs don't have green tails. For a while I looked at the drawings, enjoying the stacks of rocks collected from the Sump that lay on the floor of one room, marveling at an excellent series of pictures of a field of fireweed in various stages of flowering. In my day there hadn't been anything like this for kids in Arpikylä. The sports clubs and marching band were the only games in town back then.

Good Lord…I was supposed to be looking for a lock that matched Meritta's key.

The house was a good two thousand square feet, and I rummaged through every cabinet and drawer in the place, peering behind rolls of paper and pots of paint, even opening a medicine cabinet that turned out to be empty. Nothing. Finally in the old bedroom that apparently now served as the teachers' lounge, I found a cabinet labeled M. Flöjt. In it hung a towel and a couple of frocks, but at the base of the cabinet was a locked container about the size of a shoebox. With an exclamation, I picked it up.

The box was already open, and nothing was inside. Had the burglar beat me to it after all? Just in case, I pushed the key into the lock. It didn't fit.

Then for good measure I searched the pockets of the frocks, but all I found were soiled handkerchiefs. Why couldn't people keep diaries anymore? Then I could just read all of Meritta's secrets.

I felt miserable. This was already the second dead-end of the day, and I still had to go talk to Ella. Back at the police station, I called all the banks in town. Meritta didn't have a safety-deposit box at any of them. The same bank manager whose slack lending practices had amazed me in the Saastamoinen Construction bankruptcy fraud case began voluntarily opening up to me about Meritta's financial matters and even seemed offended when I told him I didn't need to know any more.

"With your predecessor I was just in the habit of cooperating and not being too uptight about privacy, since Jussi is a relative and all…"

"What? You're related?"

"Sure. Our wives are sisters."

As the handset clicked into place, I completely forgot about Meritta. No wonder Sheriff Jussi wanted out of town while the indictments were being filed for the Saastamoinen fraud case. Jussi's wife was the bank manager's sister-in-law. And Saastamoinen's wife was the bank manager's sister. No doubt Jussi and Saastamoinen had spent many a pleasant evening at the bank's corporate cabin retreat. And I wondered which building company Jussi had hired to build his new house last year. That rat bastard!

And now I was left to clean up their mess. Or had Jussi thought I was just a dewy-eyed little girl who probably wouldn't figure it out? Or perhaps an old townie who would understand this was how business got done in small towns and would leave well enough alone. I kicked the trash can, which, of course, was full, and sent its contents flying across the carpet in my office.

Getting down on all fours, I started cleaning up my mess. Jussi's idiocy wasn't the cleaner's fault, after all. I stuck my tongue out at President Ahtisaari, but he didn't look amused.

Then I read white-collar crime laws until I had calmed down enough to call Ella. I caught her as she was just leaving work.

"Drop by here on the way for some coffee," I said. "I have some ice cream hidden in the back of the freezer too."

Ella sounded reluctant but promised to come. I figured she would be here by car in five minutes. In the meantime I dished up servings of mint chocolate chip ice cream to let soften a little before she arrived and then sat down in an armchair next to my coffee table to wait. This was just going to be two friends getting together for a gab session, even though we were in my office.

When she arrived, Ella looked stressed and somehow heavier than normal. Eventually I realized the reason: usually she wore loose-fitting, colorful clothing, but now she was dressed in a black velvet jacket two sizes too small, which looked like it was from Matti's wardrobe.

I poured her coffee before asking if she had heard about Jaska.

"No. What? Did Jaska kill Meritta?"

"Probably not, because last night someone killed him too."

Ella's spoonful of ice cream clattered to the table, her mouth twisting into an amused expression that reminded me of when we were children. Once Ella had explained to me in horror that whenever she heard something truly shocking, her first reaction was always to laugh. Together we had tried to work on controlling her odd reactions, with me conjuring up the most horrible things I could think of, such as, "An atomic bomb just hit Joensuu." But that had only caused even wilder fits of laughter.

"Killed? How?"

"The investigation is ongoing." I didn't know how to beat around the bush any longer, so I got to the point. "Ella, about your Kalevala brooch. The one we found on the Tower after Meritta's death was yours, wasn't it? It wasn't in the washing machine at all."

"I don't know where it is. I lost it somewhere that night."

"We found three sets of fingerprints on it. One set was Meritta's and another was Matti's. The third set, the most prominent, must be yours."

"Have you been talking with Matti?" Ella's face was redder than usual and she was fidgeting with the buttons of her black coat. Unbuttoned it revealed an oddly cutesy slate-blue flowery blouse.

"I did see Matti a couple of hours ago at the art school."

"What did he say?"

"That you and Meritta had been fighting about the grant for the art camp. Apparently Meritta had misappropriated some of the funds."

Ella took a long sip of her coffee and then another. The look on her face was the same expression she wore back in high school Swedish class when our teacher had asked her to conjugate an irregular verb: she seemed to be thinking very hard. I let her ponder in peace because I remembered that hurrying her was never a way to get a sensible answer. Of course, I was hoping that she would laugh and say it had just been some trivial thing.

"So Matti told you that," she finally said slowly. "He's right. Meritta had inadvertently spent part of the materials budget on her own supplies. But arts and culture organizations don't have room to make mistakes like that. The city leadership watches our money like hawks, more than any other area. And it would have looked even uglier with Meritta on the city council. She was one of the people who authorized the money she misused. I can't believe Matti would tell you, that he would be willing to sully Meritta's reputation…"

Ella didn't seem to approve of what Matti had done. She was one of those people who never talked behind someone else's back; she was more likely to read you the riot act to your face. Perhaps talking about the peccadillos of the dead felt like betrayal to her.

"We'll be able to fix it though. We'll find the money somewhere," Ella said, more to herself than to me.

"So you didn't go back to the Old Mine that night to meet Meritta or look for your brooch?"

Ella fixed me far too firmly in her gaze. "I did not go back to the Old Mine that night to meet Meritta or look for my brooch," she repeated. Breaking eye contact, she went on. "Maybe Meritta found the brooch somewhere, remembered that it was mine, and picked it up. Maybe it slipped out of her pocket when she…fell."

"That may be," I said soothingly and poured us more coffee. The ice cream had melted in our bowls into green-and-brown puddles, which no longer looked particularly appetizing. Something was clearly wrong with Ella and Matti. I wanted to see the grant files for the art camp. Was Meritta planning to dump the blame on Ella if her malfeasance came out? How much money were we talking about?

"You said yourself you got your job when you finally had the sense to join the right political party. You said so yourself. Are you going to have trouble now that Matti is representing the Greens on the city council?"

"Some eyebrows did go up when Matti ran on the Green ticket. Maybe because he was in a different party than me, they wondered why he couldn't keep his ball and chain in line. But Matti is about as Green as a mink farmer. Meritta talked him into running."

Now Ella was starting to sound like herself again. I did what I could to turn the conversation in a lighter direction as well. Only when Ella said she needed to head home to make dinner for the kids did I finally dare to ask the critical question.

"You and Matti spent last night at home in bed together, right?"

For a second Ella looked at me in confusion, and then her mouth fell open. "Yes, we did. But we don't have any witnesses. Our kids were fast asleep!"

She slammed the door hard as she left.

Going to the break room to rinse our dishes, I found Lasarov and Hopponen gossiping. Lasarov was saying that Jaska's mother was at home with a nurse and that both she and her daughter had needed sedatives. I felt like a heel for thinking about going to their house to rummage through their closets. But I had to. When I returned to my office to straighten up before leaving, the phone rang.

"Hey, it's Koivu. I'm on my way back to Joensuu. There's a suicide I need to check out. Hanging, apparently."

Koivu's voice was pained, and I wondered how long he was going to be able to stay on his feet with no sleep and a broken heart. Still, we talked shop for a few minutes.

"The Virtanens admit that the brooch is theirs. But don't tell Järvisalo yet. And where are you sleeping?"

"We do have hotels in Joensuu."

Seldom had I heard such obvious bitterness in Koivu's voice.

Earlier in the morning, I had parked my car out in the rain. Now when I turned the ignition key, it wouldn't even click. I swore. Old Soviet cars had a habit of acting up in rainy weather, and I knew I wasn't going to get it started until the moisture that had penetrated the electrical system dried out. I felt like kicking the miserable piece of junk. There was nothing to do but get my keys to the sheriff's Saab from inside and haul it out of the back of the station's garage.

As I drove down the hill to Jaska's mother's house, I remembered how a mere two days before I'd gone down this same road looking for Jaska himself. Why had I let the sentimental human side of me push aside the police officer that night? I shouldn't have let Jaska off the hook. Even though self-recrimination wasn't going to bring him back to life, I indulged it. Maybe next time I wouldn't make the same mistake.

Jaana came to the door, her speech unnaturally calm and slightly unclear. Probably the sedatives. "Mom is sleeping. Did you want to talk to her?"

"No, I just want to look around Jaska's room a bit. I don't have a warrant, but will you give me permission?"

"You can do whatever you want if it will stop all this dying. It's there, on the left."

Jaska and his mother lived in a cramped two-bedroom apartment. The larger bedroom, next to the bathroom, was his. The door beyond the kitchen was shut, and the living room was overflowing with flowers.

A concert poster from his previous band hung on his door. In it Jaska glared angrily at the world, ever the defiant metal-head. Opening the door, I stepped into the stuffy stench of years of cigarette smoke. Was this really the bedroom of a thirty-year-old man? If I hadn't known, I would have guessed the occupant was about fifteen.

The walls were plastered with posters of rock bands, motorcycles, and, especially, half-naked women—there were several posters of voluptuous blondes with their butts sticking out smiling on sandy beaches, and one of Madonna groping her crotch. Someone had obviously cleaned recently, but the stench of old ashtrays lingered. Jaska's lesser electric guitar rested on the bed, his better one leaned against the wall in its case. The amplifier was stuffed between the chair and the desk. The bookshelf was crammed full of pornographic magazines, Jerry Cottons, and Stephen King. In contrast, all of the sheet music was neatly arranged in binders. On the spines Jaska had written in wide capital letters their contents: RAINBOW, RAMONES, ROLLING STONES…The best-kept binder said JASKA.

I opened it, finding dozens of handwritten songs, some on staffs drawn in pencil on graph paper and some just words and chords. Mostly three-chord songs utilizing a twenty-word English vocabulary. *Rock, baby, fuck.* Tears started dripping from my eyes onto Jaska's papers, one drop smearing the words in the second verse of a song called "Avenger." For the first two years of high school, Jaska had sat behind me, mostly sleeping but sometimes working on his music. Whenever he finished a song, he would tap me on the shoulder enthusiastically and ask me to give him feedback. If the song was bad, I talked it up and just corrected the spelling. If the song was even a little good, I made suggestions for improvements. I don't think my help made Jaska's work much better, since I knew even less about writing music than he did.

On the shelf was also an old box that said BAND PHOTOS. I grabbed a few at random. And there we were, Rat Poison fifteen years before, all of us wearing black leather jackets and white T-shirts, with our hair done up. Jaska was trying to look as if he knew how to play the guitar and jump a hurdle at the same time, and I was pretending to vomit. I had heard the drummer, who was also in our class, now worked as the principal of an elementary school in Kuopio and that our backup guitarist was an unemployed electrician in Tampere.

Jaska's stereo adorned the desk. I had to restrain myself from rummaging through his record collection. Instead I examined the dresser and closets. In the dresser drawers I found some hardercore porn and various articles of clothing. Running my hand between them, I didn't find any boxes or other containers the key could have fit.

In the closet hung two pairs of jeans, two dress shirts, and the dark-blue suit purchased in honor of his graduation, which he clearly had not worn since. On the top shelf was a pair of soccer cleats. I peeked behind them. Nothing but dust bunnies. There wasn't anything under the bed either.

I sat down on Jaska's bed to think. Why had he left me a key but no idea what to do with it? I reread the note that came with it searching for a hidden message, but there was none. Neither the first, second, nor third letters spelled anything significant. I could have easily imagined Jaska doing something like that. He hadn't used the old lemon juice trick from *The Famous Five* had he? Grabbing a lighter from the desk, I held the flame carefully under the paper. No brown letters appeared. And the envelope? Was it a hint about the employment center? Why would Meritta have hidden something there?

Bah. My mind was running in circles. Why wasn't I Lord Peter Wimsey? The riddle of the key would be clear as day to a detective like him. Shoving the cursed letter back in my pocket,

I decided to leave this mausoleum to my dead friend's shattered dreams before I started bawling again.

I didn't want to go home and be sad and alone yet though. And I wasn't going to be able to deal with my parents or their questions about the progress of the investigation right now. Glancing at the weight room schedule I had in my purse, I noticed that every Thursday night from seven to nine was ladies' night. That was perfect. Maybe enough sweat would wash some of my grief and guilt away.

12

The weight room was empty except for two women who were apparently trying to figure out a new core-strengthening routine from a piece of paper. I spent about ten minutes jumping rope to get my muscles warmed up. In Arpikylä we didn't bother with froufrou things like stationary bikes or stair-steppers. Lacking proper air circulation, the low-ceilinged basement room was dogged by the stench of wet sneakers and an occasional sickeningly sweet puff of perfume from one of the *Abs of Steel* ladies. The room had no windows to open, and the only light came from bulbs in metal cages.

So not a very pleasant environment for self-therapy, but I knew I just needed to exert some energy. Loading a bar with a moderate amount of weight, I started a bench press set.

If our original plans held, Antti would be returning to Finland in seven weeks. My job would finish at the end of October, and Antti had promised to stay with me at the farm until then. His teaching semester at Helsinki University wouldn't start until early November.

Grimacing, I pushed out five more reps than usual. I probably needed to start actively looking for work now during the summer. Antti still had a couple of years left on his assistantship at the university, so presumably I needed to find a job somewhere in the metro area.

Then a strange thought crept into my mind, and for the first time in my life I managed to think it all the way through: What if I got pregnant? The bar almost fell out of my hands when I realized what I had just considered.

A baby? Back in my twenties I was absolutely sure I would never get married and have kids. I was also just as sure that I would never own a suit or listen to classical music. Well, just so long as I didn't own a set of curlers, at least some of my principles remained intact.

From the bench press I moved to the rowing machine. I couldn't deny a little curiosity about how it would feel being pregnant and giving birth. But it would be a lifelong commitment. I could always get away from a spouse or a job, but a child would be mine for the rest of my life. Stupider people had survived it though, so why not Antti and me?

A tall, blonde figure opened the door. After sniffing the sweaty air for a second, she looked around for something heavy and propped open the door. Small doses of fresh air smelling of rain flowed in.

Kaisa was clearly accustomed to dealing with the unpleasant weight room. Why on earth did she accept such miserable conditions? Even though she detested the media clamor, she was a determined woman, not some shrinking violet. There were rumors that Kivinen was building her a winter practice facility in the Old Mine's ore-milling building. Maybe that would also include a decent gym.

Kaisa said hi as she marched past toward the leg machines. Her face was already sweaty, her shirt plastered to her beautifully shaped back. Her frizzy hair was pulled back in a ponytail at her neck. I wanted to chat with her about the details of how she had found Jaska's body. She seemed calm. Apparently she had pulled herself together since the shock of the morning. But the focused way she started her workout made me decide she probably wanted to be left alone.

While I worked on the leg press, I admired Kaisa's flawless technique. She probably would have done nicely in competitive weight-lifting too. Her loads were twice as heavy as mine. That was one damn strong woman. Dropping 110 pounds of Meritta off the Tower would have been a piece of cake. Jaska wouldn't have stood a chance either.

The more heavily perfumed of the two aerobics women went and exchanged a few words with Kaisa before disappearing with the other aerobics woman into the dressing room, leaving us alone. Even though we were working on opposite sides of the room, some energy field seemed to run between us. We each seemed to be waiting for the other to break the silence.

When I went to get a drink from the fountain, which was almost right next to her, Kaisa lifted her eyes from her toes.

"You lift pretty regular, don't you?"

"No pain, no gain, right? Congratulations on your win, by the way. You must have really good concentration to stay focused with everything that's been going on."

Kaisa smiled modestly and wiped the sweat from her neck. "I'll admit I was relieved to get away from home for a while and think about something besides Meritta. Not that the reporters let me forget. And then this morning...Look, I gotta finish my workout. I can't afford to compromise my training now. If you ain't in a hurry, come to my place after we're done. I got something I need to talk about."

Of course that was fine with me since I had questions for Kaisa too. Maybe she would know about Meritta's key and the mystery of the mine paintings. And I guess I would have to ask about Meritta and Johnny too, even though I remembered Kaisa's pained expression last Friday night at the opening gala. And where the hell had Johnny disappeared to? If he was trying to escape a murder conviction, he would be running for the rest of his life. But did Johnny have it in him to commit a double murder? Would he really have beaten an old friend's brains in, in cold blood?

Kaisa finished her workout with a full half hour of careful stretching. After watching for a second, I started mimicking her movements. It helped. That plus a hot shower afterward left me feeling relatively relaxed.

Even though the trip was only a few hundred yards, we went to Kaisa's place together in my car. Kaisa lived in a fairly new row house smack dab between the sports field and the swimming pool. The first thing she did after walking into the house was dump the entire contents of her large gym bag into the washing machine. Then, from a pitcher in the refrigerator, she poured us glasses of a green sports drink that tasted like salty sweat.

"Are you hungry? I usually don't eat until after my workout and I have an extra steak in the fridge. It was supposed to be for Johnny, but he decided to go home."

"Was Johnny here today!"

Kaisa's surprised look made me realize I was shouting.

"Yeah. Last night sometime around one he came knocking on the window, wet to the bone. He said he didn't have nowhere to go."

Kaisa sprinkled pink peppercorns and garlic powder on the beef tenderloins.

"Where is he now?"

"He left while I was out running. The note said he would be back in the afternoon, but I haven't seen him since."

"Why couldn't he go to his parents' house?"

"His dad accused him of murdering Meritta." Kaisa dropped the steaks into a glowing-hot pan, poured a little olive oil over them and switched on the range hood fan. "They had a fight. And Johnny couldn't go to Tuija's house for obvious reasons."

"So you and Johnny are pretty close?"

Kaisa put some whole-wheat pasta on to boil and started mixing a salad. As she sliced tomatoes, she continued. "I don't have any siblings. Johnny is the youngest in his family, and I guess he thinks of me as his little sister."

Adding chopped chives to the tomato and lettuce salad, Kaisa began to set the table. Somehow talking before dinner about finding a dead body seemed tactless, but tact had never been one of my strong points.

"How are you holding up, Kaisa? I'd think you've probably had enough pressure already without getting mixed up in two murders."

"You're telling me. The European Championships are in four weeks. I know everyone is expecting me to win a gold medal. I'm expecting it too. There ain't no point trying to hide it. That's why I want all this to get resolved as fast as possible. I just didn't know how to talk to Detective Antikainen. He tried to be friendly, but it was like he wasn't treating me like a person or something."

"Giving you a ride was probably the high point of Antikainen's summer. What did you want to talk about?"

"Those are going to take a little while to cook, so let's start the salad. Mineral water?"

With that, Kaisa piled a large heap of salad onto my plate, and I suddenly realized how hungry I was. Lunch had been scanty, and I hadn't really eaten any of my ice cream with Ella. Kaisa ate as intently as she threw a javelin. Apparently eating right was an essential part of the training program for winning gold medals.

Over the steak and pasta we talked about cooking and sports. I let Kaisa set the pace of the conversation, since this wasn't a formal interrogation. For dessert, Kaisa produced a sack of early strawberries from the pantry and suggested that we go sit in the living room.

The room appeared normal. Table, sofa set, TV, houseplants. Then my eyes landed on a birch cabinet on the right full of trophies, vases, and medals. In the middle of it all hung Kaisa's World Championships silver and next to it a picture taken at the podium. Kaisa was hugging the winner, Trine Hattestad, and smiling widely.

Folding her long legs under her on the sofa, Kaisa poured the contents of the bag of strawberries into an Alvar Aalto vase she had grabbed from the shelf and started to talk.

"I ain't never seen a dead person before. For the past few days I've been wondering what Meritta looked like. Was she still like herself? The strangest thing this morning was that the thing lying by the pond was obviously Jaska Korhonen and also just a body, like he was no one. Did that happen with Meritta too?"

A drop of red strawberry juice ran down the corner of Kaisa's mouth toward her neck.

She continued without waiting for an answer. "At first I thought I was seeing things, that I'd been thinking too much about Meritta. But I had to go see what was wrong with him. Fifteen feet away I realized he must be dead. I saw blood in his hair and started looking where he could have fallen from and hurt himself. But there ain't anywhere in the Sump with rocks big enough to trip on and hit your head that bad. It's all sand. Then I forced myself to check his pulse. And then I ran. I didn't really come to my senses until I was in the health center and they were starting to stick me with something. I don't dare take anything without talking with the Olympic team's doctor so I don't get accused of doping." She paused. "So how did Jaska die?"

"We're still waiting for Forensics and Pathology to finish their investigations. But I think Jaska knew who killed Meritta and was trying to blackmail him."

I also folded my feet under me on my chair and gazed out the window. A fat grayish-brown cat was stalking a wagtail sitting in a tree in the yard. Suddenly the bird made a kamikaze dive straight at the cat and then wheeled back to the tree chirping exultantly. The cat was furious. I missed Einstein, who was just as helpless in the face of wagtail cunning.

"You said Johnny was soaking wet when he came here last night. Did he tell you where he had been?"

I could see from Kaisa's expression she understood what I was really asking.

"No. But he was obviously upset. And there was…sand. On his clothes. Yellow sand. Like up the hill at the mine…and in the Sump."

I knew Kaisa would have preferred not to say those words. We were in the same boat: she didn't want to give evidence against Johnny, and I didn't want to arrest Johnny. But neither of us was going to protect a murderer either.

"You asked at the Old Mine party whether Meritta and Johnny were in a relationship. Did you know then that Johnny lied to you when he said no?"

"I guessed."

"Were you jealous of Meritta and Johnny's relationship? You are in love with Johnny, aren't you, Kaisa?" I said it as calmly and gently as the best psychologist-detective would have.

Rising from the couch, Kaisa turned toward the trophy case, away from me. Her tank top revealed stunning upper back musculature, which her loose blonde locks tumbled toward.

"Yes, I was jealous," she said quietly. "But not of Johnny. Meritta was the one I was in love with."

I felt like a complete idiot. Even though I was infatuated with Johnny, did I have to assume everyone else was too?

"Did Meritta know?"

"Oh, did I tell her that I'm a lesbo?" Kaisa said even more quietly. She turned back to look at me, as if searching for disgust in my expression.

"So what, Kaisa? Is that something you're supposed to hide?"

"Maybe not in Helsinki. But think about here…"

I did. As far as sexual mores went, my hometown seemed still to be living in the 1950s. Not one single openly gay person lived in the city. And the only guy who had ever brought his boyfriend home to meet his parents received a beating in the Copper Cup. Presumably our Christian member of Parliament, who had wished every homosexual in the world a pleasant journey to hell, wouldn't be too thrilled about taking her picture with Kaisa after her sexual orientation became public.

"And that's not all. I'm an athlete. Chasing an Olympic medal. You've read the newspapers…You know how they write about me. You know the kinds of words the announcers use on TV. Shot-putters are 'robust girls' and stuff like that. What would they say about a lesbian javelin thrower? And you've seen my sponsor's advertising campaign. All that stuff about my javelin speeding through the air like a call to my one true love. I don't think they'd like it all that much if my one true love was a woman. I ain't the only queer athlete though. But no one wants to see us."

"But it shouldn't be that way!"

"Well, yeah. But am I supposed to change it?" Kaisa sat back on the couch and shoved five strawberries into her mouth at once. "Meritta said exactly the same thing. She thought me coming out of the closet would be great. That's what she said."

"What did Meritta say when you told her you were in love with her?"

Tears welled up in Kaisa's eyes and she wiped her cheek with her hand, leaving a strawberry streak.

"Well, she—she wasn't no more shocked than you. She said she liked me a lot and that she had never thought about being with a woman, but that she didn't find me unattractive either. She had a rule of only one lover at a time. She had to finish one relationship before she even started planning the next, and she was already taken because she was dating Johnny. She didn't tell me it was him, but I was pretty sure."

I nodded. Mårten Flöjt had said the same thing. But could Meritta have considered making an exception in Kaisa's case? Could she have been telling Johnny on the Tower Friday night?

"And so I was just waiting for Johnny and Meritta to get tired of each other," Kaisa said bitterly. "I hoped Meritta would finally allow me to be my real self. I ain't even ever dated anyone. Not really. The boys around here always treated me so weird. They might have liked me but they always had to put me down. Maybe a woman throwing javelin is so frightening they had to keep me in my place by feeling me up and calling me a whore," Kaisa said, grimacing.

I grimaced back. "Yeah, I know the type."

I was happy she was still confiding in me even though I had been so dense as to assume she was infatuated with her cousin.

"I don't even know no other women like me," Kaisa continued. "Last summer there was this one Estonian hurdler, but she's in Estonia."

"I know other lesbians. And gay men and bisexuals. You're not the only one in the world, even if it might feel that way in Arpikylä. When I lived here I thought I was the only girl in the world who didn't want to squeeze herself into the traditional woman's role."

Next to Kaisa, I almost felt old.

"Sometimes I wish I was as bold as Meritta. Then I could just tell the nosy reporters that there ain't never going to be no boyfriend. Girlfriend, maybe." Kaisa tried to laugh.

I didn't believe that Kaisa killed Meritta, even though I knew that plenty of people would think she had the strongest motive. I wondered whether I would bother telling even Koivu about our conversation, despite the fact that he wasn't the gossiping type. Kaisa had the right to decide for herself how much other people knew about her love life.

The rain, which had let up momentarily, began pattering against the window again, and I realized it was about time to go home and say hello to Mikko. As I left, I hugged Kaisa. She was just as warm and firm as her cousin.

"Kaisa, promise me one thing," I said at the door.

"What?"

"When the reporters ask what your goal is in competitions, don't say you're going to try your best and see if that's good enough."

Kaisa grinned and promised she wouldn't.

With that, I started to drive back toward the farm. The roads were slick and visibility was poor. The gas pedal on the department Saab was much more sensitive than the Lada's, and I inadvertently found myself going forty-five in a thirty-five zone. So I was a little astonished when someone careened past me going almost twice as fast. Most people tended to let the needle climb a little on the straightaway near the railway bridge, but the dark-red Volvo speeding ahead of me was going entirely too fast and swaying alarmingly from lane to lane.

Just then the voice of the county dispatcher came over the radio: "Arpikylä patrol, what's your twenty?"

Timonen's voice crackled in reply, reporting he was on the other side of town.

"We have a report of a drunk driver. He left the Copper Cup in a dark-red Volvo heading toward Joensuu. The bar confirms he had three stouts with dinner and then five shots of brandy for the road."

"License number?" Timonen asked.

I quickly accelerated to catch up with the Volvo.

"Sheriff Kallio here. I think he's right in front of me. I'll try to pull him over," I said into the radio.

"It's Veikko Holopainen. He's probably on his way home," Timonen said, adding that he was also heading home.

Switching on my siren, I swore when I realized I was going too fast to get my light out on top of the car.

At the next intersection I made up for lost ground, shortening the distance between us. From the top of a hill, I saw an eastbound car nearly broadside the Volvo. Damn, I had to get him stopped before he caused an accident!

On the straight stretch following the intersection, I sped up even more, pushing eighty miles per hour. Thankfully the Saab purred nicely; Uncle Pena's Lada wouldn't have stood a chance. As I caught up to the Volvo, I saw there was only the driver inside. The car continued veering back and forth, nearly going into the ditch before swinging back across the center line. Trying to pass would be risky. Flashing my headlights, I turned on the emergency blinkers as well. Nothing helped. The Volvo just kept zigzagging its way toward Joensuu.

I was endangering my own life right now too. Should I just let the Volvo go? I decided to try one more time. On the next long straightaway, I pulled up alongside and laid on the horn. The driver, a pudgy middle-aged man, shook his fist at me through the window. That gesture cost him though, because the car then veered toward the edge of the road and began sliding in the gravel on the shoulder.

In my rearview mirror I saw it come to rest in the ditch. I slammed on the brakes, furious and scared, hoping the goddamn idiot wasn't a bloody pulp. Not seeing any other traffic on the road, I made a U-turn.

The driver was lucky: his car's brakes worked well and the rain-soaked gravel had softened the impact. He sat buckled in his seatbelt with a bump on his head and cursing a blue streak. When I opened the driver's-side door, the stench of cheap cognac rolled out.

"What do you mean driving like that, you stupid bitch!"

"I'm a police officer, sir. Didn't you hear the siren? You seem to be intoxicated."

"The fuck you're a cop!" he yelled angrily, eyeing my messy hair, tennis shoes, and jeans.

Suddenly his right fist approached my face, but he was so drunk I was able to lightly brush it aside. I guessed he was at about twice the legal limit. Flashing my badge silenced him temporarily. I still wished the boys would show up though.

A white Mazda stopped, and the man driving asked if we needed any help. Curious little eyes peered at us from his backseat. He seemed a little disappointed to hear that a patrol car was already on its way.

After the Mazda left, my reckless driver was suddenly in a talkative mood.

"I do recognize you. I was just fooling. You're Toivo Kallio's oldest daughter. I'm Veikko Holopainen. Your uncle is on the city council with me. He's a good man, even if he is in the wrong party. Listen, don't…I was just celebrating a little, but I would've gotten home just fine if you wouldn't have come along distracting me with your siren."

"We'll see what the breath test says."

"I don't have time to sit around here waiting for some stupid breath test!"

With that, Holopainen tried to restart his car, but no matter how hard he pressed on the gas trying to rock the car loose, the Volvo wasn't budging.

"Listen, girlie. I'll give you a thousand marks if you help me out of this. You come drive and I'll push."

With impeccable timing, the cruiser pulled up, this time without needlessly running its siren. Timonen and Hopponen, who was having another long day, handled the field sobriety test. The Breathalyzer showed 0.16 percent.

"A blood test it is then. Looks like Holopainen's license is going on ice again," Timonen said after they were done.

"Come on, boys. This bitch forced me off the road. Nothing bad would've happened if it weren't for her. I could drive home with my eyes closed. I am on the city council, you know." And then, in a more threatening tone, he said, "Your badges are going on ice if you lay a finger on me."

And so on. Bluster and threats. I always hated don't-you-know-who-I-am types, so this only made me feel increasingly bitter toward him.

While Officer Hopponen attempted to get His Eminence into the back of the police cruiser amicably, I gave Timonen an account of the chase.

As I talked, he alternately grinned and shook his head.

"When we had his license last summer, he demanded that the city pay him for taxi rides to council meetings because he supposedly didn't dare drive with his wife. That next intersection is where you turn to get to his place. It's a pretty big spread, and they milk about a hundred head. He has a bit of a bad habit of trying to use his money to get out of stuff like this."

"I noticed. He offered me a thousand marks if I'd help him out of that ditch."

Holopainen screamed from the backseat of the patrol car. "Stop making up stories, you fucking whore! You don't have any witnesses!"

That's when Hopponen raised his hand to strike him down.

"Don't! He isn't worth it, pard," Timonen said, which was enough to stop Hopponen's fist.

"We'll just add that to the report and you can have a charge of attempting to bribe an officer of the law to deal with too," Hopponen grumbled.

I was almost amused. Maybe I was finally part of the club now.

As I was leaving for home, I heard Holopainen complaining about his car, worried that the Russkies would come during the night to pinch it.

After driving half a mile, I realized I was shaking. This was what I had imagined I was coming here to do, chase drunk farmers, which apparently also involved risking my life. My hands were shaking so much I had to stop at the edge of a field to calm down. It felt so strange to still be alive when Jaska was dead. Getting out of the car, I let the rain wash over me. I wished I didn't have to spend the night at home alone. What I wanted was to make love to Antti. Could anything else make me feel that alive?

When I finally arrived at the farm, Mikko was standing at the door waiting for me. Taking him in my arms, I rubbed my face against his warm coat, and he started to purr.

Although it was only Thursday, I opened Uncle Pena's liquor cabinet and poured myself a triple shot of whiskey in a teacup. Mikko didn't like the smell and slipped out of my arms. After drinking half, I went into the bedroom. The face that looked back at me in the mirror on the dresser was dark and lined, and the three gray hairs at my temple were more prominent than usual. Pouring myself a little more whiskey, I dug Antti's old letters out of the dresser drawer and curled up on the bed to reread them. After a minute, Mikko, bless his feline heart, jumped on the bed too and curled up at my feet. Once I had read through all the letters, I shoved them under my pillow and dragged Mikko under my arm like a teddy bear. But that only helped a little.

13

My head ached. We were gathered in the police station break room with Detective Sergeant Järvisalo, who was explaining his theory about Jaska's and Meritta's murders. There wasn't much to explain because Järvisalo still didn't have any solid evidence regarding who was behind the killings. Even so, he suspected Kivinen or Johnny. At least Officer Järvi had known about Meritta and Kivinen's relationship and mentioned there were whispers about it circulating around town. I still wondered how much Barbro Kivinen had known. Sergeant Järvisalo said he was going to go talk to Kivinen himself.

"I really hope it isn't him," Antikainen said. "What would happen to the Old Mine if it was?" He seemed genuinely concerned.

"I don't think any jobs depend on him. His old lady will just take the reins if we have to lock him up. My understanding is that at least half of the shares of the company are in her name anyway," Sergeant Järvisalo said. "Should we talk to the wife too then? Maybe she did know about her husband's affair with Flöjt." I noticed the detective sergeant's eyes turn imploringly to me again. "Maria, could you and Koivu interview his wife?"

"I do have some other…Oh, well, let's call and see if she's around." I hated having Järvisalo boss me around, but my curiosity won out.

Kivinen's secretary informed us that Mrs. Kivinen would be returning on the afternoon flight from Helsinki, so I asked her to arrange a meeting for us at one thirty.

Then Koivu left with Järvisalo to interview Seppo Kivinen and I dove into my pile of paperwork again. Then as if I didn't have enough on my plate, our clerk dropped another heap of identity cards and drivers' licenses on my desk to be signed. These new licenses weren't nearly as easy to forge as the ones we had when I was growing up.

During our freshman year of high school, Jaska and I and a couple of other kids cooked ourselves up some fake IDs by using the discarded IDs of older friends who had just received their drivers' licenses and so didn't have a use for their old ones anymore. Slicing their pictures out with razor blades, we glued ours in. No one was going to take a close look at the stamp on the picture. In place of the sheriff's official seal we used a hand stamp with the Arpikylä A's logo usually employed for marking who had paid to get into a game. After adding some self-laminating plastic, we were able to use them to breeze into any tavern in Joensuu or Kuopio.

I didn't know until I enrolled in the police academy that we had committed felony forgery that could have cost me not only my spot in the academy but also my right to act as a judge or attorney after law school. That night I ran home and burned that memento from my younger years. That isn't the only law I've ever broken in my life though. Speeding, smoking weed, providing alcohol to a minor, and riding a bicycle at night without proper illumination come to mind. But my terrible criminal past came in handy now that it was my turn to check identity documents. Since I knew all the other common tricks too, I paid special attention to the IDs of anyone who looked suspiciously underage.

I called the Joensuu Central Hospital again to ask about Uncle Pena's prognosis. The doctor who came to the phone was a young guy I had talked to a few times before. He was a big cat lover and was always happy to pass along my reports about Mikko's adventures. He told me that Pena's condition was stable again and that he had even been able to eat a little with his healthy hand.

"We've been noticing around the ward that he always seems to have his attacks when local talk radio is on. The last time they were saying something about an artist who got murdered out your way."

"Oh, no! Yeah, he knew the woman who was murdered really well. Her name was Meritta Flöjt. And what about the time before that?"

"The nurse had turned the radio on because she knew they would be talking about the opening ceremonies for the Old Mine. We all knew your uncle was instrumental in getting that whole thing started."

"Keep the radio off for a couple days. There was another murder here yesterday."

Of course it was natural for Uncle Pena to be shaken up hearing about the opening of the mine attractions and Meritta's murder. He definitely would have wanted to be present at the gala, and according to what everyone said, he had known Meritta quite well. But could there be something else to it too? What had caused his first stroke?

I was expecting to eat with Koivu, but there was no sign of him or Detective Sergeant Järvisalo. Perhaps Kivinen had been equally as hospitable to them as he was to me and treated them to lunch. The hunger that usually hit me after drinking too much whiskey was starting to get in the way of work. I didn't feel like calling Ella, so I tramped off toward the city building cafeteria to eat by myself.

At the cafeteria, I lucked out: they were serving a greasy hash of the week's leftovers. To each her own. I piled a small mountain of it onto my plate, along with some salad. I grabbed two glasses of nonalcoholic home brew and looked for a spot with some HP brown sauce on a table. Then I noticed Tuija Miettinen with a bowl of soup at the corner table by the window. Raising her head, she saw me and waved me over. Since her table did have a bottle of chili sauce, I decided to join her.

"Have you heard anything from Johnny?" she asked before I had even sat down.

"Not for several days. Why?"

"He had a fight with his dad Wednesday night and ended up knocking out two of his teeth." Tuija's gray eyes looked almost black, and the fourth finger of her left hand had the same flattened, white strip of skin as Koivu's.

"That sounds like a matter for the police. Tell Mr. Miettinen to file a report."

As far as I knew, Johnny had been at Kaisa's house Wednesday night. After that we didn't have any more sightings of him.

"What were they fighting about?" I asked, curious to hear if the story was the same one Johnny had fed to Kaisa.

"Oh, I can fix his teeth. Johnny can pay for it. And they've always fought. Johnny may have been getting rougher lately though." Tuija's voice was expressionless, but if she kept squeezing her soupspoon the way she was, it was going to start bending.

"I don't want to tell my children that their father is a murderer," she suddenly hissed.

"So you believe Johnny did it?"

Slamming her spoon down, she leaned over the table closer to me so that her straight, dark hair almost touched my half-empty plate of hash. "I wasn't even really asleep when Johnny came to get his bike," she croaked. "I wondered what he could be up to. We have a pretty good set of binoculars, so I grabbed them and watched what he was doing. Sometimes he disappeared into the trees, but I always found him again. His dark-red jacket was easy to spot against the yellow sand. He was riding the bike up the back way to the Old Mine at three thirty on the night of the murder."

"Why didn't you tell me this before?" I shouted, and half the cafeteria turned to look at us.

"He's the father of my children!" Tuija said, keeping her voice low. "And he wasn't the only one I saw. A little before him, Ella Virtanen came down the hill from the direction of the Old Mine. I don't think she and Johnny noticed each other though."

So here we were. The best thing would be to send Tuija to talk to Detective Sergeant Järvisalo, who would certainly put out a warrant for Johnny's arrest on the spot. Johnny and Ella had both lied. But was Tuija telling the whole truth?

"And what about you? Did you go back to sleep? Or did you go up the hill too?"

"Of course that's what you want, isn't it?" Tuija's voice was still quiet but full of rage. "I'm sorry, Maria, but I did go to sleep. I don't care nearly enough about that man anymore to go to the trouble of killing someone over him."

Tuija stood up, grabbing her tray.

"You have to tell this to Sergeant Järvisalo too!" I yelled after her.

Absentmindedly, I bolted down the last of my hash, which I had doused with far too much chili sauce. So here I was. Back in my old hometown to arrest my teenage crush for two murders, one of which I might have been able to prevent.

I almost marched straight over to the state liquor store for a new bottle of whiskey. I didn't do it though and instead went back to the police station, where I found Koivu sitting in the break room eating something he claimed was microwave pizza.

"Didn't Kivinen feed you guys?"

"He was pissed because we've been hanging his dirty laundry around town. He claims the relationship with Flöjt ended out of mutual consent and without any bitterness. His wife doesn't know anything about it. Or so he says. But he doesn't have an alibi for either night of the murders. They sleep in different rooms, and his wife was already asleep last Friday when Kivinen came home from the Old Mine. They were both supposedly sleeping on Wednesday night too. It was pretty hard getting anything out of him. Järvisalo was being kind of a pushover. Stars in his eyes."

"Järvisalo's the bootlicker type?"

"Not compared to our old boss down in the city. But yeah, he's afraid of anyone he thinks is bigger than him. I guess the governor told him to tread lightly on the whole Somali thing too. Plenty of people want the whole refugee center moved out of Joensuu. They aren't so much afraid of Somalis though. It's more that the place will fill up with Russian mafiosi who'll do worse things than stab people."

"I've already forgotten how people around here near the border are so afraid of Russians. And are we supposed to handle Kivinen with kid gloves for some reason too?"

"Seppo Kivinen is practically a national hero, even for Järvisalo. The Great Bringer of Jobs." I wasn't used to the bitterness I was again hearing in Koivu's voice. Where had he spent last night?

"You didn't tell Kivinen we're on our way to interview Barbro, did you?"

"We don't need a husband's permission to question his wife these days, do we?" Koivu snapped. "Damn it, this isn't even food!" he said, dumping the pizza in the trash.

Just then Järvisalo put his head in the door and said he was going back to Joensuu. That man seemed to spend half of every working day in his comfortable police car. Hopefully he liked driving. Before he could leave, I told him Tuija's entire story, of which he seemed to grasp only the part about Johnny. And, as predicted, he was ready to issue an arrest warrant right then and there. My legs started to shake when he said the words. Then the trembling moved to my hands, but my voice remained steady as we discussed the inconclusive forensic findings from both killings.

After ordering Koivu to write up a report on the hospital-knifing by the end of the night, Järvisalo cleared out. I could tell from his face that the assignment rubbed Koivu the wrong way.

"I stayed at the Sokos last night. I thought that if I had to go to a hotel anyway, I might as well go to the fanciest one around. I was going to suck their minibar dry, but after seeing the prices, I didn't bother. Forty marks for a tiny bottle of whiskey. Can you believe that?"

"And what about tonight?"

"I'll stay at home. Anita has the night shift. I already started looking in *The Karelian* for apartment listings."

"It feels like that?"

"I guess I should try to talk to her first, but…in the beginning I liked how focused she was. I've never liked women who just go along with everything. But now Anita seems to want me to be like that too."

"Yes, I think you should talk to her. Maybe she's already over it and doesn't want to split up after all. But if you have problems on Saturday night, come out to the farm again. I'm going to need a dinner date." I told him about the Copper Cup Bar & Grill's stripper situation and my promise to the restaurant manager to go see if everything was legit. I wanted to bring a companion so no one would think I was on the prowl for a man.

"I'm always up for going to see a stripper," Koivu said with a grin. For that comment he got my paper cup thrown at him, which Detective Antikainen managed to dodge as he entered the room.

The Kivinens lived on a rise behind the mine in a house that had once served as the official residence of the director of the mining company. The city had been forced to take the property along with the mine area and, according to hearsay, was leasing it to Kivinen for a scant three thousand marks a month. The house stood alone surrounded by birch trees, on the crest of its own little hill. On one side was a panoramic view of the Sump and on the other stood the Old Mine. Kivinen had to stroll only a few minutes through the forest if he wanted to walk to work.

I had never been inside the house before, even though the mining company CEO's son had been in my sister Eeva's class, and had thrown a few class parties there. Based on Eeva's descriptions, the house had been a veritable castle without the towers, three stories of luxury. In that same spirit, we set out in the department's Saab instead of my Lada, since it seemed more suitable for Kivinen's driveway.

A colonnade decorated the main entrance, on the Sump side. When I rang the doorbell, I was certain a butler would answer. To my disappointment, Mrs. Kivinen herself came to the door dressed in a blue silk housecoat. I introduced Koivu, who was staring wide-eyed at the lion statues guarding the entrance hall.

"You probably came to ask about that other murder. It did happen practically under our drawing room window. I'm afraid we were asleep then though. Aren't these lions atrocious? Apparently they were an acquisition of the first director of the mining company. For some reason, Seppo wanted to save them. This house came largely furnished, you know. We still have very little here of our own."

Mrs. Kivinen was talking to us as if we were reporters rather than police officers. Maybe she expected Koivu to start snapping photographs.

"Perhaps we could sit in the library," Barbro Kivinen said, leading us from the entry into the room of my dreams. Stuffed bookcases stretched from floor to ceiling on every wall. The first two things that caught my eye as I glanced quickly around were a leather-bound set of English classics in the original language and at least a hundred volumes of Strindberg in both Finnish and Swedish. Was *The Son of a Servant* one of Kivinen's favorite reads?

Between the shelves, little tables and leather chairs were strewn. Against one wall was an oak writing desk nearly eight feet by five, and against another, a fireplace. Two large windows faced west, opening onto a hillscape of birch trees. The only thing missing was the scotch decanter.

"Would you care for coffee?"

Without waiting for an answer, Mrs. Kivinen rang a bell next to her armchair. A moment later, a woman who seemed to be an honest-to-God parlor maid—even though she wasn't wearing an apron or a white bonnet—walked into the room. Suddenly I felt as though I had been thrust into an Agatha Christie mystery. Of course if that were the case the parlor maid would have conjured up a salver of sherry and I would have had to ask for crème de cassis.

On the way over, Koivu and I had agreed that I would handle the questioning. Having recovered from the lions, he pulled his notebook out of his pocket and readied his pen. Convincing myself that this library shared the same reality as my hometown took a while. When the maid brought the coffee and cake, Koivu and I politely took what was offered, although I felt like I had coffee running out my ears.

"Did you know Jari Korhonen, the victim from the night before last?" I finally managed to ask.

Barbro Kivinen sipped her coffee black, and she did not appear to be touching the cake.

"I couldn't say I knew him personally. But I know the names and faces of all of our employees at the Old Mine. Korhonen was also one of the long-term unemployed and we were receiving an employment subsidy to keep him on." Barbro made it sound as if Jaska wouldn't have had any other opportunities to find work without this support. "I noticed him at the gala on Friday dressed entirely inappropriately and clearly intoxicated, which I admit I found slightly distressing. But fortunately he disappeared early on in the evening."

This was not putting me in a friendly mood. Apparently the same caste system dominated Barbro Kivinen's world as the one that ruled my early childhood. Why had she agreed to marry the son of a miner then? Judging from her current digs, the decision hadn't hurt her any.

"You said you didn't hear anything strange from the direction of the Sump on Wednesday night?"

"Our bedrooms are up on the top floor and the windows face the Old Mine. Would you like to come and see?"

I shook my head no.

"One can neither see nor hear anything in that direction from them. And besides, it was raining that night. An old metal roof like this is quite loud in the rain."

"You've already been interviewed about Meritta Flöjt's death, but we've received some new information since then." I decided to get straight to the point even if it might mean inviting her husband's wrath.

"Do you mean my husband's relationship with her last spring? I've been waiting for someone to dig that up."

Barbro Kivinen smiled when she saw my expression of astonishment.

"This wasn't Seppo's first extramarital dalliance by any means. I've learned there's nothing to be gained by getting upset over them. He doesn't know everything about my life either. Still, this marriage and partnership works quite well. Neither of you are married, are you?" she asked, looking from Koivu to me. "Young, single people can afford to maintain all sorts of idealistic notions."

Mrs. Kivinen poured more coffee into our cups. Not knowing what to say next, I took another piece of cake and crammed it into my mouth.

Fortunately, Barbro continued her monologue: "Of course, my husband has probably assured you that I don't know anything about the whole affair. That was very gallant of him, since it would have given me a fine motive for murder. It would look better for him if I knew about the relationship. But the affair was over in any case. Meritta Flöjt was an aesthete, and she chose Adonis over Seppo Kivinen. I don't wonder why Seppo was a little churlish for a while around May Day. Losing out to someone younger and more handsome would injure anyone's self-esteem." Barbro Kivinen's voice was as sharp as a cat's claw.

"But I suppose our same story applies to that night as to last Friday. We were sleeping blissfully, each in our own bed. And besides, I know my husband. Seppo wouldn't kill out of jealousy. He wouldn't sacrifice all of this. He's risen so far. After we moved into this house, he told me how once he and a couple of other local boys wandered onto this property and the caretaker ran them off with his German shepherds. He wouldn't endanger what he's achieved here. And the same goes for me. But now, unfortunately, I have to ask you to leave. When Seppo's secretary made this appointment she didn't know that I had a massage scheduled for two fifteen."

In her blue housecoat, Barbro Kivinen looked like a queen whose every whim must be obeyed. So we slunk away like scolded lap dogs.

"Would Mrs. Kivinen kill to keep all that?" Koivu asked as we were driving back to the police station.

"What do you mean?"

"What if Kivinen was still crazy about Flöjt and promised to leave his wife?"

"I don't know. But I can imagine just about any kind of melodrama playing out in that house. Barbro seems like a pretty cold woman. I have a hard time imagining her getting so mad she would throw someone off the Tower. And I can't see her even agreeing to talk with someone like Jaska."

"You don't like her?"

"I wouldn't go quite that far. There's always something fascinating about people who know what they want," I said, paraphrasing Barbro.

"But living with them isn't much fun." Koivu sighed.

Soon after we arrived at the station, Koivu took off to Joensuu to write his report, but promised he would come back the next day on the seven o'clock bus to accompany me to the Copper Cup and see the stripper. I tried to reach Ella, but her answering machines at work and at home said she would be away all day Friday. I left messages on both, telling her that she had been seen on the mine hill the night of Meritta's murder and instructing her to contact me immediately if she preferred talking to me instead of Detective Sergeant Järvisalo.

The little copper key was still waiting on my desk. What on earth did it open? What if Jaska had found what he was looking for at Meritta's house and then hid it somewhere? But where?

Then a new place occurred to me. The band room. I wondered if the key was still the same one used to open the other doors at the school. Calling my parents, I arranged to borrow my father's key to the school.

The band room door was as stiff as always, and I had to push on it for a while, but it opened. No one practiced here anymore except Jaska's band, since the new youth center offered much better spaces with a bathroom and windows even. Jaska and company had inherited the high school basement by accident, and presumably he and Pasi and Johnny had felt ancient compared to the crowd at the youth center. With Jaska gone, Pasi might have to find a new home for his drum kit and the keyboardist for his ties. The bass was lying on the table, along with Johnny's guitar. Only Jaska had taken his home; he had always been careful with his equipment.

I decided to start with the music shelf. Nothing out of the ordinary, just overflowing ashtrays, a dried piece of rye bread, a crushed juice carton, and piles of sheet music. Afraid of becoming too nostalgic by rummaging around in the familiar songs, I just shook the books and thicker stacks to see if anything fell out from between the pages. Then I checked in the guitar cases and drums. I dug around in the chair cushions. Nothing. The last thing was the couch. It was a fold-out model, and under the seat cushions was a storage box for bed linens. Jaska had stashed things there before.

Just as he had done recently. Under a truly disgusting blanket and pillow, I found a half-empty vodka bottle and a sack of clinking beer bottles. Jaska's emergency supply. The empty bottles hidden in the couch were sufficient to redeem for a pint at the Copper Cup. Sometimes he would bring women here, and he had probably spent the night on occasion too when he was so drunk he didn't have the nerve to go home. But there was nothing in the room or under the couch that the small copper key could have fit.

Then an idea began to take shape in my mind. Could Jaska have met his murderer here? The school building stood abandoned during the summer, so it would be a safe place to rendezvous. And a very natural place, if the person he had been meeting was Johnny.

I closed up the couch and sat down, leaning against the cigarette-smoke stained back. I had spent so much time sitting here waiting for the others, listening hopefully for steps in the hallway, wondering what if it wasn't another member of Rat Poison? What if it was Johnny? Distinguishing the different footsteps had been easy, the stamping of our drummer, Jaska's kicking and shuffling, and Johnny's quick soccer-player's steps. Even if I couldn't tell from his steps, he always flung the door open the same way.

Damn it, Johnny, where have you disappeared to?

Picking up his guitar, I started plucking something incoherent and then as if by accident fell into the first bars of "Scarborough Fair."

That's when I heard the door open and those familiar quick steps. The place had ripped me out of my police role once again, because without thinking I sprang up and screamed Johnny's name. As I burst into the stairwell, I heard the steps turn back up the stairs and the door shut with a resounding thud. In the seconds it took me to fumble it open again, Johnny had disappeared. Standing in the empty schoolyard, I called his name in vain.

I didn't bother to go after him though. He wasn't going to be able to hide much longer in a town this size now that I knew where he had been sleeping. I went back and looked at the juice carton and dried rye crust still in its packaging. The bread had been packed only the day before. If Jaska had used this as a base, then why not Johnny too? If I would have had the presence of mind to keep my mouth shut, I could have caught him. Whether I was more annoyed or relieved, I wasn't really sure.

Although I didn't think Johnny would come back, I left a note on the table telling him about the warrant for his arrest. Then I took the band room keys to the station and told the boys to check on the basement at regular intervals.

At the end of the day, I stopped by to tell my parents I couldn't return their keys quite yet. While I was there, they managed to talk me into staying for the whitefish they had smoked that morning. Somehow sitting at my parents' table felt silly—eating off the same old plates, observing how the house remained the same after I had left and changed so much.

My dad had also spoken with Uncle Pena's doctor, the one who seemed convinced that Pena's attacks were brought on by the local news—though what caused the initial stroke remained unknown.

"There was definitely something going on with Pena and Meritta," my father said contemplatively. "Over winter vacation

I spent a couple of days out at the farm felling trees in the backwoods, and once I happened to answer the phone when Meritta called. It was like Pena didn't want to talk while I was there; I remember wondering if our eternal bachelor was a little infatuated with her…"

"What did Pena say to her?" I didn't want Dad to get bogged down again on how Pena had never married because of his fear of women.

"At first I thought it must be city business. Pena asked whether she was sure that some contract said something. Then he sighed and said that she would have to do something, even though it wouldn't be pleasant. After hearing her reply, he smiled."

"And then?"

"That was all." My father spread his arms. "Then he said something about some colors. But the most interesting thing about it all was the tone of the conversation; it almost felt intimate, and I've never heard Pena use that same voice with anyone but his cats."

I knew the tone my father meant—my sisters and I called it Uncle Pena's "kitty-kitty voice." It was an utterly unmanly cooing, similar to the exaggerated way mothers talked to their babies in diaper commercials.

Pena had undoubtedly been infatuated with Meritta.

But I wondered about their talk of colors. The colors of the political parties—red, blue, and two shades of green? Or the colors of paints Meritta was using for some project? Presumably the artists' association had some sort of contract with the city. But so did Kivinen's company.

Attempting to use finesse, my parents began trying to pry out my plans for the future after Antti returned. I was the only one they had left to marry off, after all, now that Helena and

Petri had tied the knot a few weeks before Antti's dissertation defense. My aunts had asked why we couldn't combine the defense and our wedding.

"Hell's bells, now that I'm actually finishing this thing, I want to be the center of attention for at least one day," had been Antti's reply.

Hopeless knothead that I am, I let slip at the dinner table that a couple of days earlier I had been considering having a baby. They were, predictably, overjoyed. But at the point that they started counting months and explaining how I could inherit all of Helena's baby accessories if Antti and I got down to business right after he returned to Finland, I beat a hasty retreat. Any hint that they expected something of me, and I rebelled. Where did the feeling that I always had to accomplish something before I could have their approval come from? Get tens on my tests, graduate summa cum laude, go to law school instead of the police academy…and now have a baby and get engaged.

Missing out on life as a thirty-year-old just to rebel against my parents was idiotic. But did I treat Antti the same way I treated them? I would believe he loved me so long as I could show him that I could get along perfectly well without him first. I could dare to get married if he still wanted me after returning from overseas. Was that it? Was I crouched on the top of a glass mountain after all, waiting for a prince to succeed in climbing up the slippery slope? Or was I the one climbing an endless glass mountainside, the same stretch I had started on more than fifteen years ago?

Johnny is sure to like me if I score this goal. If I perform really well at our gig. If I lose five pounds. If I dye black streaks in my hair. I was like the person in "Scarborough Fair," requiring miracles of myself before I could surrender to love. Maybe it was time to grow up.

At four in the morning, while I was in the middle of an incoherent dream, the phone rang.

"Hi. It's Johnny. I…Never mind."

The call ended before I could realize it had begun.

14

I woke up to someone pounding furiously on the front door. The rain appeared to have stopped, and the sun was high in the sky. I had tossed and turned after Johnny's call, lying awake and thinking about whether the caller really was him or just a prank. The alarm clock on the dresser said 11:05. A moment later the pounding was on my bedroom door.

"First you leave threatening messages on all my phones and then you just sleep! Are you serious?" Ella yelled ferociously just outside my room. She knew where we kept the spare key behind the third step and had let herself in.

An instant later she was next to my bed with her hands on her hips, looking even bigger and more broad-shouldered than usual. Even when I managed to drag myself up out of bed, I was still six inches shorter than her.

After putting on a full pot of water for coffee, I stuck my head under the ice-cold tap for a full minute. Slowly my brain was starting to get back in gear. Tuija had seen Ella on the mine hill the night of the murder. That was what I was supposed to talk to Ella about. That and the grant for the art camp.

"I'm glad you came," I said as I poured our first cups of coffee.

"I would rather not have. How official is this discussion going to be?"

"Completely off the record."

I didn't even intend to use the tiny tape recorder I employed now and then to record conversations illegally.

"Nothing you tell me now can be used against you in court."

While Ella gathered herself, I made myself a couple of open-faced sandwiches and poured muesli on some yogurt.

"It's true what Tuija Miettinen saw. I did go back to the Old Mine on the night Meritta was murdered. But I wasn't lying when I said I didn't go back to meet Meritta or to look for my brooch that night. I was looking for Matti."

"Was Matti there?"

"I don't know. After the party we went home. I fell asleep around two and then I woke up at three to Ville talking in his sleep. That was when I noticed Matti wasn't in bed next to me. At first I thought he was just up calming Ville down. But when he didn't come back after some time, I peeked into the studio. He wasn't there either. With my mom sleeping on the couch in the living room, I knew the children would have someone with them if I left. So I decided to go looking for Matti."

Just then Mikko started scratching at the front door. As I let him out, I stopped for a moment to breathe in the scent of the spruce forest drying in the sun. The contrast between the peacefulness outside and Ella's tumultuous confession felt strangely incongruous.

"Why did you assume that Matti would be at the Old Mine?" I asked, still watching Mikko from the door as he bounded along the edge of a stand of seedling trees, harassing thrushes until he found an appropriate-smelling place to do his business.

"That brooch of mine...I probably dropped it when I went up in the Tower again looking for Meritta. That was when you were at the bottom of the Tower talking with Kaisa and Johnny. I wanted to talk to her about…"

Ella's words trailed off and she crumbled a piece of bread in her fingers. Her cheeks were glowing red. I didn't have the patience to give her the time she needed.

"About the art camp money?"

"Exactly!" Ella's voice sounded relieved. "Maria, Matti lied to you. It wasn't Meritta who used the art camp grant, it was Matti."

I had suspected as much. Now the conversation my father had overheard between Pena and Meritta was starting to make sense. Ella turned even redder, and I felt sorry for her. Matti had pulled a scurvy trick on both of them, Ella and Meritta.

"I went to ask Meritta if she could let it be. I would've been able to get the missing money from somewhere. I tried to get her to understand Matti. Last winter things were so tight. First the car broke down, and then Matti had to spend thousands on dental work. Matti was panicking that he couldn't work anymore. We just didn't have money for canvases and paints. The art camp grant money came at the end of January, and Matti thought he would have plenty of time to pay it all back before the summer. Only Matti and Meritta could see the artists' association accounts, so no one else would have ever needed to know."

"So why did Meritta get uptight about it?"

"Because they actually needed the money at the end of April to rent class space and buy plane tickets for a teacher to come from Denmark, and when Meritta went to the bank, the account had fifteen thousand less than she expected. Meritta rushed over to our house and started yelling about how she knew city politics used to work like this but that she wasn't going to be party to any more fraud. If the money didn't show up in the account immediately, she was going to contact the police."

In the previous municipal elections, Meritta had campaigned on the need to raise the level of integrity in local politics, to stop overlooking little infractions and open up every decision for public scrutiny. Irregularities in the finances of her own artists' association would have been unbearable for her in more ways than one. I thought of the millions thrown to the wind in the Saastamoinen Construction bankruptcy scam and almost laughed. That was taxpayer money too.

"So what did Meritta say to you?"

"She said that Matti must be pretty pathetic to send his wife to clean up his mess. That he would have to handle it himself."

I understood Meritta's comment perfectly, since this situation was exactly the same thing. Ella had come to tell me about Matti's blunder because he didn't have the nerve.

"Did Matti go back to the Old Mine to talk to Meritta?"

"I don't know...I haven't dared ask him."

Ella had never been the crying type; this was maybe only the second time I had ever seen tears in her eyes. The first was when one of our classmates had died in a car accident during our sophomore year. That time we had wailed together, but these tears were Ella's alone. All I did was move the roll of paper towels a little closer to her.

"So I need to talk to Matti," I said.

"He isn't home today. He's in Lieksa teaching a class. He won't be home until tomorrow morning."

"Tell him to call. I'll notify Detective Sergeant Järvisalo that I've spoken to you. And don't be so sad. If this is really just about the misappropriation of fifteen thousand marks, no one is going to be charged with anything."

But I could see in Ella's eyes that she was afraid there could be something more.

"By the way, I saw Johnny that night too, but I couldn't tell you about it until now," she said as she headed out the door.

After working for twelve days straight, not having to go into work felt unnatural. Saturday was market day in town, but I wanted to enjoy my solitude. So I fetched the papers, drank another cup of coffee, and decided to go walking in the forest. Mikko stayed to bask in the sun on the sauna steps.

Uncle Pena's farm was located in the center of a thick evergreen forest. Behind a cow pasture now overgrown with trees rose a cliff several dozen feet high. Climbing to the top, I waved to the Tower gleaming on the horizon. From such a distance it looked like a forgotten toy in a sand box. Turning, I looked toward the fragrant swamp on the other side of the rocks, where during the best summers you could find cloudberries and later in the year, cranberries. We almost never saw moose in these parts, so I was surprised to spot an unusually large gray-brown bull rubbing his antlers on a pine tree at the edge of the bog. I sat down on the rock to watch it.

At his parents' cabin in Inkoo, Antti and I had spent hours watching moose go about their business. There was always something calming about watching the controlled movements of such a large animal. Perhaps I wasn't as urban as I imagined myself to be when I moved to Helsinki. Just living in Espoo had reminded me how much I missed hiking in the woods.

Where would I be living a year from now? I was getting tired of constantly moving. And finding a job was going to be an even bigger problem. If only Antti was here with me to assure me that we could figure out how to make everything in both of our lives fit together. And to help me forget about Johnny, who the police were searching for right at that very moment. I missed Antti so much. His face, his voice, his warm skin against mine... Only the knowledge that it was four thirty in the morning in Chicago prevented me from rushing to the phone.

The moose raised its head and looked toward me. The wind must have carried my scent to it. I felt like moving closer, but I didn't want to spook it. Antti would have joked that if I met a bear in the woods, I probably would assume it was more afraid of me than I was of it.

And what if Antti and I did get married? Lately, I had seen more than enough examples of disastrous marriages. Weren't Antti and I the same as Meritta and Mårten Flöjt? Wasn't our work the most important thing to both of us? We'd at least have to think carefully about having children. We were sure to fight constantly over who had to watch them, just like the Virtanens. But Antti and I could always sense each other's need for space, and we wanted the same things. What happened to Johnny and Tuija couldn't happen to us, right? And at the very least our marriage would never turn into a business partnership like the Kivinens'.

But was I really ready for it?

On the way back to the house, I collected a bouquet of buttercups and bellflowers from the most open corner of the pasture for the living room table, putting my thoughts in order as I did so. In my mind I had created a sort of ranking of suspects, with Johnny unfortunately at the top. Matti was a strong second, and Kivinen had climbed into third.

After leaving a blank space in my list, I added Tuija's name. Just out of spite. And then, to be honest, I added Ella too. She was extremely aggressive in the way she handled her husband's business. If she had been mad enough, she could have pushed

Meritta off the Tower to protect Matti. I wasn't so sure about Jaska's murder though.

And still the list wasn't complete. I had to add Barbro Kivinen. Maybe she hadn't been as unconcerned about her husband's relationship with Meritta as she led us to believe. Somehow it was easy imagining her hitting a blackmailer like Jaska over the head with a wrench. Or would a silver-handled umbrella have been more her style?

Finally I also added Kaisa to the list, although I had previously ruled her out. She could have murdered Meritta out of jealously, but what about Jaska? Jaska could be pretty damn infuriating, and I had wanted to smack him upside the head plenty of times myself. And I could imagine the taunts he might have used about Kaisa's infatuation with Meritta. I did decide to leave Aniliina off my list entirely. She just wasn't strong enough to have pushed Meritta off the Tower, not to mention dragging Jaska's body to the Sump.

So here I was again, suspecting every person I knew of murder. Putting the flowers in a vase, I noticed the atrocious state of the living room floor and decided to do some cleaning. At least I could easily put that in order.

Later I cycled slowly into the center of town. The streets had emptied after all the stores closed, and only a tattered banner in front of city hall remained of the bustling market that had filled the square. I wasn't going to make it through the day without visiting work either. Since I was in the area, I dropped off my bike in the police station garage and stopped in to ask Timonen, who was manning the duty desk, whether there had been any sightings of Johnny. His answer was a baffled no.

When Koivu jumped off the bus from Joensuu, the first words out of his mouth were, "I need beer." We strode the few hundred yards to the Copper Cup in silence. Only once his lager and my highball were on the way did he start to speak.

"I'm going to look at an apartment tomorrow. It's already vacant."

"It's looking like that?"

"You're goddamn right it is! Guess what? Anita's already seeing someone new."

"You're kidding me," I said, even though I could tell from Koivu's eyes he was serious.

The waitress brought the drinks, and Koivu paid for both as if by accident, but I knew I'd have my chance, guessing we'd have at least three rounds over the course of the night.

"And that's not all. Guess who the dude is," Koivu said after downing a quarter of his glass of beer. "Toni 'the Commander' Raiskio. The leader of that skinhead gang."

"What? You've got to be shitting me. She seriously fell for the guy while he was lying in the hospital with a knife wound?"

"This isn't Anita's first time two-timing. When we started dating she was still seeing this guy named Sakari, and they started out exactly the same way. I knew all about it, but I thought it would be different with me." Koivu took another sip of beer. "And with a complete asshat like that!"

"Was he the one who stabbed the Somali refugee?"

"No, that was another guy, but this Raiskio freak show definitely egged him on. And Anita thinks they're in the right. I don't care what kind of a dump that apartment is tomorrow, I'm moving in! I don't want to see that head case ever again!"

Koivu had already emptied his first pint. He wasn't a heavy drinker by any means, so I was already preparing myself for the pleasure of eventually lugging his entire two hundred pounds into a taxi and onto my couch out at the farm. In other words, I needed to take it easy on the booze.

"And now I'm sitting here in this crappy bar waiting for some stripper..." Koivu suddenly started laughing uncontrollably, almost hysterically, but I didn't think the tears in his eyes were from joy.

I knew that Anita had been his first serious romance. He was twenty-six, good-looking, and had a steady job. And he was a genuinely nice guy. Plenty of women would fight for a chance to go out with him, but I guessed he probably wouldn't believe me if I told him that right now. I ordered him another pint and let him continue wallowing in his misery.

Gradually, the bar began filling with people. Miss Miranda was going to perform twice, at nine thirty and eleven o'clock. The audience was even more male-dominated than usual, and I was glad to have Koivu with me. Otherwise I would've felt like a sitting duck for every come-on artist in the place. Then I realized how horrible the situation was. If a thick-skinned woman like me didn't dare go to a strip bar without a male escort, then what about more sensitive girls? Arpikylä didn't offer that many choices for a night out.

Shortly before nine thirty, I realized that I didn't need to monitor the legality of the striptease after all, since the local police force was well represented without me. Antikainen and Hopponen were sitting at a table in the front row with glasses of beer and seemed taken aback when Koivu and I waved to them.

After his initial burst of speed downing the first two pints, Koivu had slowed down and was approaching the bottom of his third. I ordered anise Pernod and a pitcher of water. Antikainen came over to our table to sit for a while, clearly on a mission to see whether Koivu and I were getting romantic. We did our best to encourage his suspicions, with me explaining loudly that Koivu was coming to my place for the night and Koivu saying at least twice how much he had liked taking a sauna with me the time before. I was glad to see that his playfulness was returning, even though Monday was likely to be a difficult day at work. My understanding was that Antikainen had already concluded that I also had been in a relationship with Johnny.

It was easy to understand how Meritta could have earned a reputation as a wanton woman around here. That train of thought made something else flit through my mind briefly, but then I lost hold of it just as quickly when a female voice began whispering suggestively over the speakers. Antikainen suddenly disappeared back to his front-row seat. The lights dimmed. The restaurant owner, who had been watching the night's events from behind the bar, took the stage.

"Alright, boys. Now we're going to make Arpikylä history. I give you Miss Miranda!"

The husky female voice grew louder, and the restaurant lights dimmed even more. Then Miss Miranda herself stepped onstage in a pink sequined dress, boa, and tall boots. In the flesh, she looked younger and even more beautiful than in the blurry pictures on the flyer, and she was a nimble dancer. Rather early on in the show, her dress slipped off, revealing a sequined pink thong bikini. After prancing around for a while like that, Miss Miranda threw off her top, exposing regulation-size breasts. As the tempo of the music increased, she ran her feathered boa over her body lasciviously and then passed it between her legs, smiling in satisfaction, before stomping on it with her boots.

Something about the performance was so ludicrous that I almost laughed out loud. If Miranda had been a man, I definitely would have whistled and shouted to cheer him on. But this audience sat as rigid as if they were in church pews, with their eyes glossed over and their expressions focused. In the crowd I could pick out many of the town's "failures to launch" and other men alone by circumstance. Some had stayed to till the family land while the girls moved away to educate themselves. Others were stuck on the unemployment rolls or tied to their mothers' apron strings. Of course some of the prominent men of the city were also in attendance, including the vice chairman of the city council and a clutch of small-time entrepreneurs from the industrial park. One of them even had a mortified-looking wife in tow. A couple of my parents' colleagues nodded to me, shamefaced, as if caught red-handed.

Someone who had clearly seen a stripper before slipped a twenty into the girl's almost nonexistent panties, extracting a few hoots from the audience. When Miranda shoved her gyrating lap in Antikainen's face, his jaw almost hit the floor.

Finally Miss Miranda ditched her G-string too and settled down on all fours to shake her hips to the beat of the music. At this the laughter building inside me became too much, and I had to cover my mouth with my shirtsleeve to stifle a guffaw. Koivu put a finger to his lips, but I could see the laughter in his eyes too. Finally the music accelerated to its climax, and then the stage went dark. When the lights came back on, Miranda was gone.

A moment passed before the applause began, and then some in the audience started calling for Miranda to come back on, at which point the owner announced that the next performance would be at eleven o'clock.

"What did you think?" I asked Koivu.

"She's a pretty girl. A snake would have been more interesting than that feathery thing though."

"You should go suggest that," I said just before a vaguely familiar, moderately drunk man flopped down at our table.

"Hi, Maria! You remember me, don't you? Maukka Härkönen. Is this your husband?" Without waiting for a reply, he stuck out his hand to Koivu and explained, "I played soccer on the same team with Maria when we were kids."

Yes, I remembered Maukka, although the bloated man with the five-o'clock shadow in front of me didn't bear much resemblance to the skinny, pimply-faced kid who had been in my junior-high class. Maukka had been one of the least pleasant boys on the team, one of the ones who was quickest to tackle me when he couldn't get the ball any other way and then take every opportunity to feel me up. If I protested, he would proclaim that girls couldn't play soccer because they always threw temper tantrums about getting tackled.

"I hear you're a cop now and you're working Jaska Korhonen's murder case. Will you buy me a beer if I tell you what I know?"

"Tell me first," I said skeptically, since the police had already interviewed the town drunks.

"You too good for us now or something? Well, OK," Maukka continued, glancing worriedly at Koivu, "I'll tell you anyway."

When he patted my knee with his grubby hand, I felt the hair on my arms stand up.

"I don't feel much like talking to the local cops. They'd just drag me off to the slammer like they done last winter, even though all I did was take a dump in the bank's ATM. Well, I was here last Saturday and just happened to be in the john at the same time as Jaska. We were talking about his sister's murder and he said he was smarter than the pigs and knew who really did it. He said he'd outsmarted them one night by snatching something from his sister's house that proved who murdered her. He even used gloves so the pigs couldn't get his fingerprints. And guess what, Maria," he said, pushing his stinking face right up to mine, "the murderer had promised Jaska a whole pile of money if he kept his mouth shut. Tens of thousands."

Just as I had suspected. Oh, Jaska, you feckless idiot! He hadn't even taken the key to the person he was blackmailing. He must have turned greedy, maybe thinking he could use it to double his take. Or was the important thing something other than the mysterious key?

"Did Jaska tell you anything about the murderer? He didn't mention a name, did he?"

"No, he wouldn't reveal the source of the money," Maukka said bitterly. "He did say something though—that he wouldn't have thought a wussy like that could have killed his sister."

Wussy? There was a typical Jaska expression for you. It was also typical that he had underestimated his blackmailer. Maybe that meant it was a woman. Ella? Barbro Kivinen? Imagining Jaska calling Kaisa a "wussy" was difficult, but I could imagine plenty of other inappropriate words coming out of his mouth, especially if he had known about Kaisa's sexual orientation. He couldn't have meant Aniliina though.

Or maybe it was more likely he meant a man by using that particular word. Matti and Johnny definitely would have qualified as wussies in Jaska's eyes, and he had spoken with disdain about Kivinen as well. So it could've been anyone.

"So is that enough for a beer?" Maukka asked hopefully.

After I ordered him his pint, I instructed him to come in to the station Monday morning to tell his story officially. Then I hoped he would leave. Instead he remained sitting next to me with his fleshy thigh touching my leg. Being pressed between him and the wall was revolting.

"You're a lot cuter now than you were during school," he said, wrapping his arm around my neck. Angrily I pushed it off.

"Beat it, douchebag!" Koivu had jumped to his feet before I could open my mouth. Maukka glanced at him in dismay and obeyed, assuming Koivu was defending his territory.

I downed the rest of my anise liqueur. Guys just like that had defined my value as a woman when I was in school. Assuming the right to judge my looks or the way I lived my life, leaving me feeling for years as if I wasn't good enough for anyone. Scar Town indeed.

"Thanks," I said to Koivu. "He wouldn't have taken me seriously, at least not the first time."

"I thought I should intervene before you clocked him and I had to arrest you," Koivu said with a grin.

Once at the Old Student House in Helsinki, he and Antti had witnessed me sock a guy in the nose for patting my rear end at the bar.

We stayed at the Copper Cup for one more round.

Miss Miranda's second performance got the audience a little more excited, and one man even jumped on stage with her. Always at the ready, Antikainen and Hopponen pulled him off, for which Miss Miranda rewarded them with sensuous kisses. I'd have to check whether kissing violated the bar's entertainment permit, but what would my police colleagues say about that? The performance wasn't as amusing the second time, and I was bored by the time she took off her thong.

"Should we go? I have half a case of beer at home," I said once the crowd finished trying to get Miranda back onstage.

A waitress came to bus the empty glasses, and I overheard the party at the next table ask her, "Are you up next, Maija? I don't know though, your boobs might hang too low."

I would have slapped them in the face with my washcloth if I were her, but the waitress simply turned to our table without a word. I could see that she was on the verge of tears though.

Smacking a twenty-mark tip down on the table, I decided to read the disorderly conduct and entertainment license statues first thing Monday morning. Maybe there was still something I could do to ban stripping here. How would that be? I could have a reputation for being a floozy and a tight-ass all at the same time.

When we left the bar, a crescent moon was just emerging from behind the clouds directly above the Tower. Its phosphorescent glow seemed brighter than usual, making all the stories about gnomes hiding in caverns under the earth seem believable.

Koivu started talking about Anita and her skinhead again. He was having a hard time accepting that he would have to interview him again.

"There's no way I'm going to be able to be impartial. I'm probably going to unload on him the next time he says something about inferior races coming in and meddling with Finnish women."

"Do you think he'll go to jail?"

"No. He's the kind who makes other people do his dirty work. He does have a record—a couple of assaults—but that probably won't be enough. Anyway the Somalis were here waiting for their asylum applications to get processed, and that's over for sure now. So the skinheads achieved their goal."

"You aren't turning into a refugee-lover on me, are you?" I said with a grin.

"If I have to listen to that racist garbage much more, I'll definitely turn into one," Koivu said.

A taxi took us to the farm, where Mikko was waiting proudly in the yard. I had left him outside on purpose, and he had obviously done well fending for himself, since the entrails of one small animal and a half-eaten mole were waiting on the stairs. After living with Einstein for six months, I had learned not to feel sorry for cats' prey. I ate meat too, and I knew that Mikko was expecting commendation not disgust.

"I'm hungry too, by the way," I said as we walked inside. Three drinks had given me a happy buzz, and I was still wide-awake because I had slept in so late. "Let's get some bread and beer and have a little meeting. I have more information on the murders you haven't heard yet."

Koivu didn't seem as eager to try solving murder cases at midnight, but he agreed to listen to me chatter.

After I had told him everything I knew, except about Kaisa's love for Meritta, he said, "And the key? Does that have any significance anymore if Jaska already gave the evidence to the murderer?"

"I could tell you if I knew what it opened. It could be anything. And there's still the paintings. I'm sure they mean something, if we just knew how to interpret them."

Taking the key and note out of my bag, again I read the lines Jaska had scrawled:

> Hi, Maria. If you're reading this, something hap-
> pened to me. It's Meritta's. She said she didn't dare
> keep it herself so she gave it to me. It's supposed to
> be valuable. Jaska.

"It's been a week and we still don't have any idea who did this. I hope another body doesn't turn up." I sighed after staring at the note so long the letters started to melt on the page.

Maybe it was Johnny. He had a fight with his dad, so why not with Jaska too? And what was the meaning behind his call in the middle of the night?

We kept coming up with increasingly convoluted theories until Koivu looked so wasted I sent him off to bed. My own sandman seemed to have lost his way in the woods again and didn't return until three o'clock.

At ten thirty in the morning, I woke up to Koivu turning a church service up full blast on the radio. A choir with trembling voices sang: "Drawn by Thee, our souls aspiring, soar to uncreated light." I walked into the living room and turned the music down.

"Hey, don't! I like that song."

Koivu had already had time to make coffee and fetch the newspapers. The county paper had a small story saying that the investigation into the two murders in Arpikylä were continuing apace and that the police were looking for a certain person of interest for further questioning. There was no mention of Johnny's name though. According to Detective Sergeant Järvisalo, it appeared likely that the same person was responsible for both killings. I wondered how he was supposed to know that. Did they already have results back on the fiber analyses?

At noon I dropped Koivu off at the nearest bus stop and promised to come help him move that night if needed.

The rain had started up again during the night, keeping up a steady drizzle well into the day. Somehow the tiny, muffled droplets against the window sounded refreshing. I was feeling fairly upbeat, so I thought I might go for a run. While I was washing the breakfast dishes, my eyes fell once again on the key Jaska had sent me, which I had left on the table in the living room the night before. A small copper key to some old-fashioned lock. But what lock?

It was funny because a key just like that could fit the secret compartment in Uncle Pena's dresser that I had tried in vain to open. It looked just the right size, and the copper had the same patina of wear as the lock. Even though I felt stupid, I decided to try. Marching to the old dresser, I first opened the upper drawer and then the secret compartment inside.

I inserted the key into the lock.

It fit.

I turned the key carefully.

The lock opened.

Why the hell did Meritta have the key to my uncle's chest of drawers? I suddenly felt as though the air had been knocked out of my lungs. My hands didn't want to cooperate as I fumbled open the compartment and peered inside. Larger than I had expected, it could have fit a pair of shoes.

But inside the secret compartment there was only a single thick, sealed envelope without any address. Lacking the patience to steam it open, I used a bread knife. The contents of the jam-packed envelope spread over the living room table in a colorful hodgepodge: papers with small dense text that I recognized as Uncle Pena's handwriting, and then occasionally larger, breezier writing, perhaps Meritta's.

Had they had a secret relationship after all? My dad had hinted as much. But no, these weren't love letters. This was something else entirely. Most of the documents were city council and other meeting minutes. A couple of the memos were dated only two days before my uncle's stroke. What the hell? Had Uncle Pena actually been the murderer's first victim?

In addition, the envelope contained photographs of black tunnels and a map of the caverns below the Old Mine, copies of contracts related to the lease of the mine, and a report on Kivinen and his wife's holdings in other companies.

Quickly reading through the papers, I copied down the most important information in my notebook. The county's white-collar crime team could go through the originals in more detail later. Closing the box again, I hid the key at the bottom of Mikko's litter box. And then just to be sure, I poured a whole fifteen-pound bag of kitty litter over it. While I was smoothing that out, I remembered the beginning of a thought that had flitted through my mind yesterday night just before Maukka had disturbed us at our table.

That had to be it.

I needed to see Meritta's canvases at the police station one more time. And then…I didn't want to think of the difficult task before me, so I began preparing like I might for an athletic event. I pulled my hair back in a ponytail and put on my action clothes: a long-sleeved T-shirt, jeans, a loose denim jacket, and old sneakers.

Jaska had been right. The key had been important. Dangerous and important. I couldn't take any risks. Best to pick up at least one partner from the police station to go with me.

As I was opening the front door, the phone rang.

"Hi, Maria. It's Johnny."

Johnny's voice was slow and low, as if coming from somewhere far away.

"Listen, this is important. Come to the Old Mine, to the door that leads from the museum tunnel to the lower caverns. I'll be there. Don't tell anyone if you want to save me from a murder charge. I need your help, Maria!"

Just as two nights before, the line went dead before I could say anything. Staring at the handset, I reviewed everything that had flashed through my head one more time. What I saw didn't look good. Things were probably much worse than I had thought.

15

As I drove into town, I thought frantically about what I should do. Going to the Old Mine alone would be one hell of a risk. But bringing backup could ruin everything. Or so Johnny had said.

By the time I arrived at the police station, I knew what I had to do. The front door was locked, which meant that everyone on duty was out in the field. Good. No one would be around to ask me any difficult questions. Walking straight to the gun safe, I loaded my service revolver and put a box of ammunition in my pocket. The loose denim jacket I was wearing concealed my shoulder holster perfectly.

I had never been forced to use a gun before, and I hadn't even pointed one at a living person. The metal felt strangely heavy against my ribs, and the leather holster seemed insufficient insulation against its chill. I didn't want to use the revolver now either, especially since I hadn't practiced shooting in over a year.

Still, I knew I would pull the trigger if I had to.

Timonen and Järvi replied from the patrol car when I radioed. I asked them to come to the Old Mine in two hours. If they didn't see me, they should look for me in the museum tunnel. If they ran into any problems, they should get in touch with Kivinen.

Then I went to my office to look at Meritta's paintings. The flame glowing greedily in the blackness was starting to make more sense. I remembered that when Meritta claimed to have taken all of her mine canvases to her gallery, Johnny and Kaisa had been there in addition to Matti. And Kivinen may have been walking past us too on his way to give his speech.

Leaving my Lada in the station parking lot, I started walking toward the Old Mine. Johnny could wait. The rain had picked up and ran down my face like tears.

At the mine, there weren't many tourists. Perhaps they had fled the rain and were having their Sunday lunch in the restaurant. After buying a ticket from the booth, I started up the flight of steps that led up the hill. Countless tiny streams gurgled beside the slippery stairs. Like the streams, all I could do was push forward, without any way to pause and see the final destination of my journey. Just like the sand the streams carried, my own baggage seemed to scrape deep furrows in the surface of the earth. All I could do was go with the flow.

The rain rinsed the surface of the Tower, leaving it a shiny black-gray, and fog shrouded its top like a mourning veil. Almost no one was in the Museum of Mining tunnel, and only a few tourists were watching the slideshow. On the silver screen was a demonstration of how an ore wagon moved down a tunnel. From the speakers came the screeching sound of wheels.

No one noticed as I fumbled with the door to the elevator. It opened easily, and Johnny stood in the darkness beyond, although all I could see were his shining gold-flecked eyes. Suddenly I was yanked into the room. The door slammed shut behind me. And locked.

The bulb in the elevator was the only light in the small chamber. The stench of fear and old booze wafted from Johnny, but under that I detected another fragrance—a discreet, sophisticated aftershave. We weren't alone. Kivinen stood behind Johnny. In his hand shone a pistol, which he pressed against Johnny's head.

"Nice to see you, Maria," Kivinen said. "I've spent enough time listening to the town gossip to know you would come if Johnny-boy asked you to. No tricks now, or Johnny dies."

On Kivinen's head was a helmet with a headlamp, which he now switched on. In Johnny's hand hung a large flashlight. He seemed to move gruelingly slow, as if fear had left his muscles stiff. I was scared too. What the hell did Kivinen intend to do?

"Maria, would you please open the door to the elevator and lead the way? We're going on a little outing to a place not many people have been recently."

I had no choice but to obey. As the elevator began its creaking way down the shaft, I had the feeling that going back up to ground level was going to be difficult. I didn't know what Kivinen was up to, but I had finally realized which of these two men killed Jaska and Meritta.

When we arrived at the bottom, Kivinen handed me a set of keys.

"Lock the elevator. So no one can get down even if they do manage to get the door open."

If only I had known what shape Johnny was in! Had he been Kivinen's prisoner since Thursday? Based on how he was acting, I suspected he had sedatives in addition to alcohol in his system. Given that, how well could I expect him to work with me? If I could count on him reacting now as fast as he used to on the soccer field, I would throw the keys in Kivinen's eyes and shout to Johnny to hit the deck. I only needed a few seconds to get my gun out.

But I had no idea how drugged-up Johnny was, and I wanted us both to come back up alive. So I decided to continue playing Kivinen's game. Compliantly locking the elevator door, I hoped he wouldn't think to search me.

"Good girl," he said when I handed him the keys. "Did you follow Johnny's other instructions? There aren't any reinforcements up top? You don't want Johnny being charged with two murders, do you?"

I nodded obediently.

"Now Johnny's going to check to make sure you don't have a gun."

With that, Kivinen pushed Johnny against me and he began patting my back and thighs mechanically. I felt his hands stiffen when he found the holster under my arm.

Don't expose us, Johnny, keep your cool! I stopped holding my breath when his hands kept moving from my armpits to my stomach. Hopefully Kivinen wouldn't order him to open my jacket. But he believed Johnny when he said, "There's nothing here."

I had to struggle not to show my relief. Now Johnny knew that I had a weapon too. And Kivinen had shown what an amateur he was. Maybe we had a chance.

Kivinen ordered Johnny to turn on his flashlight and told me to walk first along the tunnel. I moved slowly in the light of Johnny's flashlight beam, which flickered in his trembling hands. Kivinen followed with his pistol still drawn and the flicker of his helmet headlamp forming a weaker beam a little higher up. Outside the beams of light the black silence of the tunnel sucked us deeper in.

A tomb. A grave deeper than any other, the Tower as our headstone. I saw Meritta, orange and twisted on the yellow sand,

and Jaska, a dried trail of blood running from his head into the crimson water of the pond. Down here only black, rough stone would surround Johnny and me. But I couldn't let myself think of that.

We arrived at the fork in the tunnels.

"Maria, I seem to remember you being interested in seeing where Meritta painted those damned paintings. You're about to get your wish. Walk to the right, please."

Under both tunnels crisscrossed miles of excavations, the actual shafts extending to the veins of ore. I had managed to glance at the map of the mine just long enough to know that this tunnel really did end at the cave-in area. The left-hand corridor, on the other hand, rose back toward the surface after about a mile, close to the Sump, its mouth in the basement of some building in the ore-milling area. That was another way to get back to the surface if I could take care of Kivinen. If. The anger glinting in his eyes scared me, but I forced myself to focus on the terrain and Kivinen's movements. I forced my legs to move despite their shaking.

The tunnel we were in began to decline steeply. Copper pyrite glistened in the rocks, and the floor was damper than before, with little rivulets running down the walls. The corridor was also narrower, only six feet wide. The guide rope had ended a ways back, but on the right-hand wall there were still pins to attach one.

"I expected even Meritta to have enough sense of self-preservation not to go anywhere near the subsidence zone." Kivinen's voice echoed several times off the rock walls. "But no, she just had to take the risk and see something she shouldn't have. And now both of you are going to have the honor of seeing it too."

Kivinen and Johnny were walking right next to me now. I heard them both breathing intensely and concentrated on trying to relax. The gun weighed heavily under my arm, but I was too keyed up to be able to get it out fast enough without Kivinen noticing. In the beam of Johnny's flashlight I began to see yellow sand and then a familiar-looking cavern opened out. I was looking at the picture from one of Meritta's darker canvases. We were approaching the edge of the subsidence zone.

"Stop! I don't want this thing coming down on our heads... at least not yet," Kivinen said to me, laughing. Did he know how much he was acting like a B-movie villain? All he was missing was the black cowboy hat. Or did he think he was Lee Marvin? I tried to peer into the corner where Meritta had painted the small, greedy flame, but I couldn't see anything.

"Today something very unfortunate is going to happen. Unfortunate for all of Arpikylä, but especially unfortunate for me. Sometime during the nineteen fifties, a large number of explosives was left in the subsidence zone. Now they are going to explode, unexpectedly. After all, you never know when forty-year-old dynamite might go off by itself. The most likely cause of the explosion will be Sheriff Maria Kallio's failed attempt to arrest Johnny Miettinen at the edge of the zone, suspecting him of a double homicide. Perhaps the fuse caught from a spark made by the pistol Johnny had with him. What on earth could they have been doing underground? We may never know, since they were both blown to kingdom come. The explosion will also destroy a significant part of the Old Mine buildings so continuing business will be impossible."

It sounded as if Kivinen was reading from a screenplay. But how would he fit himself into the script? Kivinen turned his head toward the corner where the flame burned in Meritta's painting.

Johnny groaned next to me when the light on Kivinen's helmet revealed a pile of explosives there.

So that was what Meritta saw. Rumors had been circulating for decades that the mining company had left behind tons of explosives in the subsidence zone that they couldn't be bothered to clear away. But according to the rumors, they were supposed to be deeper underground. Had Kivinen's father told him the precise location of the explosives and had Kivinen brought them up here?

"Will the Tower come down?" I asked, surprised to hear how firm and calm my voice sounded.

"Doubtful. It might shake a little. Of course the explosion may unfortunately also claim the lives of a few tourists. But I could never have predicted that. I've never even visited the cave-in. It was the mining company who excavated this and then left dangerous explosives down here. If anyone has to pay reparations, it will be them—"

"Maria, I didn't kill them. You have to believe me!" Johnny yelled, cutting off Kivinen.

"Of course not. Kivinen did." Something had started boiling inside me and no matter how I tried to calm myself, I couldn't stop the rage that burst out of me. "You goddamn fucking fuckhead!" I screamed, even though no amount of cursing could vent all the anger I felt. "This whole Old Mine thing was just one big fucking load of bullshit, wasn't it? Did you plan to blow the whole pile of shit sky-high from the very beginning? I've seen Pena and Meritta's notes. They suspected you were attempting bankruptcy fraud right from the get-go and that you were funneling the money through your wife's companies to offshore accounts. And, of course, the debt falls on the city's head!"

Compulsively my sweaty right hand slid toward my left side and the holster concealed there. I had never felt such a strong desire to kill. But Kivinen's pistol was still pointed at Johnny's head.

"What went wrong, Kivinen?" I continued in a more controlled tone. "Wasn't your plan cunning enough for Meritta? Or did you ask her to come with you to live in the lap of luxury after it was all over?"

"That bitch was just a spy. She was just trying to get information about me. In love with me, my ass! She had some kind of plan with that uncle of yours. Finally the whore barged in here and saw the explosives. Luckily for me she was an idealist. She wanted to save all the jobs I had created, so she didn't expose me immediately."

Click.

Finally everything fell into place. So Meritta had suspected something from the beginning. She hadn't been acting against her principles by leaving Kivinen for Johnny because she was never in love with Kivinen. Now I understood Uncle Pena and Meritta's phone conversation too. The rest of the city council might have fallen for Kivinen's con, but the two of them had been suspicious. Instead of believing in fairy tales, they started digging into the big investor's background.

"You pulled off a world-class scam, and the city fathers swallowed it hook, line, and sinker because they had been waiting for a savior like you to descend from on high. And what about my uncle? Did you cause his first stroke somehow?"

"I just stopped by to have a little chat with him the day before his stroke. Who can say what caused it?"

"But Pena knows everything! As soon as he gets better, you're done for!"

"Gets better?" Kivinen laughed again, its hollow echo joining in. "Do you really think he's going to survive after hearing about the explosion?"

The holster was getting heavy again. Johnny's drowsy eyes flashed in the dark. Kivinen obviously intended to shoot us both before he set off the explosives. He probably intended to flee up the tunnel that had forked to the left. That meant he had calculated the fuse to burn slowly enough to allow him time to escape. But did Kivinen really know how long the fuse would burn or how powerful the blast would be?

"Why did you kill Jaska?"

"That damn snooping drunk! I wish I knew when he managed to grab Meritta's purse from off her body. He was probably still slinking around after Meritta fell and he might have even seen me. He didn't even know anything, but he could have turned into a real pain in my ass. Have I satisfied your curiosity now? And Johnny must know by now why he has to die. I thought for sure he saw me on the hill the night Meritta died, but I was wrong. He's been a great scapegoat though."

"I only saw Meritta," said Johnny, his voice raspy. "I didn't see you. Just Meritta lying there twisted and dead."

I would have liked to ask Johnny why he didn't notify the police immediately and how Kivinen had taken him prisoner. But now was no time for private conversations. Again I turned to look at Kivinen, whose soiled copper-colored suit glinted under his helmet headlamp.

"Why are you doing this? Just for the money? Or do you really want to destroy our whole town?"

"It serves the shithole right!" Kivinen shouted, and gravel fell from the ceiling right in his face. "Everybody's all 'yes sir, no sir' when you have money. It was different in the sixties though.

Back then a miner wasn't even human. Did the mining company pay when my dad got lung cancer? The fuck they did! It had nothing to do with the conditions he worked in, they said. And the bastards in city hall just lined up to grovel in front of them. Being a kid here was a living hell. But what would you know about that? Your parents were teachers."

Scar Town. Maybe his desire to prove something to the city that rejected him had spurred him on, but he failed to see that in order to succeed he was ripping his scars open again and again, until they had no way to heal.

"Now it's time for some fireworks. Maria, stay there!" Forcing Johnny closer to the pile of explosives, Kivinen handed him a cigarette lighter. "That fuse on the left. Light it."

A strange elation flashed in Kivinen's eyes, and the hand holding his pistol trembled as Johnny set his flashlight on the floor and lit the fuse. When it caught, it gave off a strange, sulfuric smell.

Then I made my move.

Pulling out my gun, I shot at Kivinen's hand, hitting him in the wrist. His own gun went off, and I heard Johnny howl as Kivinen's bullet appeared to graze his left ankle.

Kivinen lay on the ground moaning. As he fell, the glass of the helmet headlamp had shattered, slicing open his face and leaving it a bloody mess. The gun in my hand itched to fire again, its barrel pointed at Kivinen's chest. His pistol had landed at my feet. Still keeping a bead on him, I crouched to pick it up. After putting the safety on, I clumsily released the clip, all in the dark. The fuse continued hissing in the corner, and I didn't know if I would be able to put it out. The flame was already too large to simply stomp out with a shoe. And I didn't even have my knife with me! Cursing, I threw Kivinen's gun far out into the black, bottomless pit of the cave-in.

"Johnny?" Picking up the flashlight, I shined it on Johnny and saw his face was a pallid green. "Come on."

"My leg…"

"Can you walk? This place is going to explode."

As I talked, I pulled Johnny upright, seeing that the gouge in his ankle was deeper than a light graze, exposing a piece of his bone. Shoving my shoulder under Johnny's right arm, we started a running hobble back up the corridor. Kivinen shouted something after us, but I didn't give a damn about him anymore. Johnny and I had to get out before the bang.

Alone I would have been able to run the half mile to the elevator in under four minutes. With Johnny limping, it took at least twice as long. He tried his best to jump on his right leg, but his breathing was becoming progressively labored. The blood from his other leg smelled warm and sickly sweet.

"Maria, I can't. It hurts so bad."

"You have to. Rest for a second."

Ripping a strip of cloth from my shirttail, I tied it around Johnny's leg as best I could and hoped that would help. Johnny moaned in pain when pieces of bone pressed against the skin, and his blood was sticky on my fingers.

When we reached the fork in the tunnel, I stopped to think for a second. I didn't know enough about old explosive compounds to know whether we should move up or head to the left, whether explosions carry more force upward or outward. Maybe it would be better to try and go up, so we continued down the tunnel leading back to the Old Mine.

Then my flashlight went out. As we stood for a moment in the infinite darkness, I heard the terrified thumping of my heart and felt the warm weight of Johnny's body next to me. We had to continue more slowly. The whole time I expected the explosion at any moment, and I kept thinking I could hear Kivinen's steps behind us.

How badly was Kivinen wounded? Had I left him to die? I wouldn't have been able to make it out in time with him and Johnny, and I wasn't sure if I could've prevented the explosives from going off if I had stayed behind to help.

Then around a bend in the tunnel the greenish light of the elevator came into view. Seeing it put new momentum into Johnny's hopping. I knew that so long as we could get up and out the door of the mine, we would probably be safe.

Setting Johnny down, I fired one round into the lock. The impact blew it to smithereens, and a hole appeared in the wall of the elevator as well. Dragging Johnny into the cage, full of hope, I pressed the Up button.

Nothing.

I pressed again, but the result was the same. Seeing the horror on Johnny's face, I knew it would require too great an effort to escape through the other tunnel. At least ten minutes had passed already, and the explosion could come at any second.

Then I remembered the ladder sunk into the wall of the elevator shaft. I could climb up it easily enough, but what about Johnny? How long would it take him to climb one hundred yards?

"Johnny, we have to try the ladder. You go first so I can push."

Johnny was as pale as quartz. I wondered when he had last eaten or at least drunk some water, and what drugs had Kivinen pumped into him.

"I can't. I'm too tired, and we won't make it in time anyway," he said in a voice that revealed no desire to fight.

But I couldn't leave him sitting there on the floor of the elevator waiting for the explosion. "Yes we will. You can get on my back." Again I was surprised to hear how calm my voice was, even though I was having a hard time getting any sound out of my throat. Leaning forward, I pulled Johnny's arms around my neck. "Don't worry. You just hold on tight."

Only the green light on the ceiling of the elevator illuminated the narrow, damp shaft. The ladder was cold and badly rusted, instantly tearing at my hands. I forced myself to climb deliberately, envisioning in my mind's eye a fuse somewhere half a mile away growing shorter by the second. Johnny hung on to my back, a 180-pound sobbing heap. The tears on his cheek mingled with my own. I was beyond afraid. One false move and we would plunge into the depths. Trying to keep myself composed, I counted the rungs. There couldn't be more than three hundred of them.

At rung 120 we encountered a narrow platform, presumably intended as a resting place. There I was able to get Johnny's weight off my back momentarily. My panting reverberated off the walls of the six-foot-wide shaft, and Johnny's voice came as a low rumble when he whispered, "I didn't tell you I saw Meritta because I thought she jumped off the Tower...because of me. Our relationship was done, even though she didn't want it to be. And then when they said it was murder—"

"Don't waste your energy talking!"

"I ran into Kivinen last night. He said he knew they were looking for me and that he would help. He probably slipped something into my beer."

I tried not to listen to Johnny as we continued our climb; the blood was pounding in my head and my legs felt heavy as copper.

"I want you to know before we die," Johnny blubbered as he wrapped his arms around me again. "I was on the rebound with Meritta. I really would have wanted to try again...with you. That was what I was going back to tell Meritta that night."

For a moment I hated the man hanging on my back. Why was he making pathetic confessions instead of fighting for his life? Apparently he also thought I was there for the taking.

I forced myself to go on and breathe calmly through my mouth so I wouldn't smell the revolting stench of blood from Johnny's leg.

At around rung 200, I was sure we would never make it to the top. The rough steel had left my hands raw and bleeding, and my muscles were pumped full of lactic acid. Then Johnny perked up and started pushing on the rungs with his healthy leg, which helped a bit. In an excited burst of adrenaline, I started rushing, and one of my feet slipped. Fortunately, Johnny reacted faster than I did, gripping one rung firmly with one hand and me with the other while I regained my equilibrium. I felt as though my heart would explode with fear before the explosion came. Even though the light in the shaft was growing dimmer, I could see we had only thirty feet left to go.

The intervals between the rungs were long, clearly not intended for someone my size. My thighs burned and I could barely lift my legs as sweat and tears stung my eyes. Johnny tried to use his one good leg, but that almost made me lose my balance again. Our cries ricocheted off the black walls of the shaft, and then a booming sound began. Somewhere below, the earth started to shake.

Somehow we managed to haul ourselves up those final yards to the elevator platform, where we lay sobbing in darkness. The rock beneath us trembled, and hysterical screams came from the other side of the thick steel door. Taking Johnny by the hand, I thought grimly that dying next to him wasn't as romantic as I once imagined it to be.

There was a sudden final bang from the tunnels, powerful even at a distance, and the gleam of the elevator light far below disappeared. From somewhere deep in the darkness came the sound of an enormous collapse. Gravel coming loose from the ceiling rained down on us, making us one with the copper-scented stone.

16

Standing atop the Tower, I gazed down over the city. Birch trees veiled the buildings with their green leaves, and the main road wound through the city empty of cars or people. The church was just as ugly as ever, and to the west the burgundy water of the Sump pond still shimmered. The evening was already growing dark, and a round yellow late-summer moon was climbing in the sky behind the Tower. Behind the nearest trees was an opening in the ground where Kivinen's explosives had ripped the previous sinkhole even wider and deeper.

One decaying house on the edge of the subsidence zone had collapsed, but no one had died or even been seriously injured. Kivinen assumed his explosives would be about three times more powerful than they were. He had said himself you never can tell about forty-year-old dynamite.

Even he had lived. Before the blast, he had regained his senses enough to flee nearly half a mile up the left-hand passageway. After the explosion, a rescue party had gone down the tunnel through the ore mill entrance and found him still breathing. His left hand was shattered and a shard of glass had left him blind in one eye. Now he was in the county jail awaiting trial.

The copper sand of the Sump glistened in the setting sun; behind it were endless forests, their gray ribbons of road winding out to the rest of the world. Great silver lakes gleamed to the northeast. Everything was the same as before—everything except the sinkhole, the middle of which was now a gray-brown festering wound after the explosion.

I had saved Johnny, but not the city. Some heroine. Old Mine Tourism Ltd had been ripe for bankruptcy since its inception. Kivinen had managed to hustle an enormous amount in business subsidies, successfully hiding most of it in Central European banks. Using front companies registered in his wife's name as subcontractors, he had managed to sink four times more money into the project than was really spent. Lawyers for the city and the Ministry of Trade and Industry were currently in the process of determining how to recover what Kivinen had swindled and invested elsewhere, but things looked bad. The case would drag on for at least several years. In the meantime, the loans Kivinen had taken out would most likely fall to the city to repay. I had heard rumors that Barbro Kivinen would be willing to continue her husband's business provided the city could ensure sufficient capital, but I was afraid that would be too much even for the most gullible wishful thinkers on the town council.

Below, on the flat top of the mine hill, a campfire flared to life. With summer over, the art camp was having its closing party. In the calm air, the smoke rose straight up, bringing the scent of burning pine to my nose. Bending down to see better, I noticed Koivu waving a wine bottle up at me.

"That's enough brooding already!"

Koivu was standing almost in the same place where Meritta had fallen. For a second I saw her orange shadow at Koivu's feet, but it disappeared quickly. I didn't believe in ghosts after all.

Slowly descending the stairs, I occasionally caressed the weathered gray walls of the Tower. It hadn't even shuddered in the explosion. The tower viewer at the top still stood solidly on its post, and even the cobwebs in the skylights remained intact. Someone sometime in the past had done good work.

Locking the door to the Tower behind me, I returned the key to Ella, who was organizing the sausage roast. The mine area had closed a couple of hours earlier, and even the restaurant was empty now. The only people who remained were a group of some thirty people from the art camp and we interlopers who had wanted to come up the hill to bid good-bye to summer.

One of the art students sat by the fire playing a bongo drum, and another pulled a harmonica out of his pocket. Johnny sat a little farther off, tuning his guitar. His left ankle was still bandaged, but he could walk with crutches. Kaisa brought him a glass of wine.

I was surprised she had made it to the party at all. The European Championships women's javelin final was only yesterday. Maybe she had wanted to get away from all the publicity after taking the gold. Sitting with my father and Koivu, watching her compete in the final, I had shouted like a lunatic after Kaisa sent her second throw flying more than seventy-three meters. I hadn't even tried to hide the tears in my eyes when the national anthem played. Koivu had confined himself to clearing his throat repeatedly.

"Aniliina says hi," Kaisa said after I congratulated her with a hug. "I stopped and saw her yesterday. She's already doing a little better."

Mårten Flöjt, Kaisa, and I had arranged for Aniliina to go to Helsinki for treatment in an eating disorders specialty clinic. She would be in the hospital until her vitals were normal again and her weight was above ninety pounds. After that, she would continue outpatient care and live with her father.

"You don't necessarily ever recover from anorexia completely," Mårten had told me over the phone. Predicting what would happen with Aniliina was difficult. At her mother's and uncle's funerals she had barely been able to stand. She had stopped putting up such a fight, letting her weak condition show. The therapist thought that was a good sign.

I brought Kaisa greetings from another hospital. Uncle Pena had told me to congratulate her on her winning throw. He could still speak only a few words at a time, but he could write quite well with his healthy hand.

The day after the explosion, I had gone with my father to tell Pena all that had happened. The familiar young doctor stood by while I attempted to formulate my sentences as gently as possible, to tell him that at least the worst hadn't come to pass, that Kivinen wasn't going to get away with fraud. The news had caused him mild arrhythmia, but afterward Pena slowly began to recover from both his heart trouble and his stroke. That he would ever be able to live at the farm alone again was doubtful, and the city council would have to look for a new chairman too. But at least Kivinen hadn't managed to kill him. I had even brought Mikko along for the hospital visit. He had meowed pitifully the whole way in the car, but was overjoyed when he saw my uncle and curled up on the hospital bed purring. We were planning a repeat visit in the next few weeks.

Koivu shoved a stick with a piece of sausage on the end into my hands. Holding the stick carefully—I'd had the bandages removed from my hands only two days earlier—I began roasting the enormous hunk of processed pork. My skin was still tender, and I was going to have a permanent scar on my palm below my left middle finger. My legs had been sore for a week after the explosion too, so I had to shelve my marathon dreams for the time being. Despite my sore hands, I had started practicing shooting again, because using a gun without being in complete control of it felt irresponsible. Even though I had hit Kivinen almost right where I intended, that was mostly a matter of luck.

Everyone at the station had spent time talking about the mine murders with a therapist, and our group sessions had brought us close enough to make me feel almost wistful at the thought of my post ending in a couple of months. Hopponen and Järvi had even invited me to join the department's baseball team.

Handing my stick to Koivu for a second, I went to get myself a bottle of wine. As I walked past Matti, he stuck out his empty glass hopefully, so I filled it up.

After the murders were solved, Matti had been singularly embarrassed. He and Ella had each suspected the other of Meritta's murder. I had done a quick but earnest investigation of Matti's grant fraud and, of course, decided not to prosecute. When I described the situation to Detective Sergeant Järvisalo, he agreed. Matti had gotten off easy, and, of course, Ella had been the one to arrange the promissory note with the bank to pay back Matti's "loan." Compared to Kivinen, Matti's scam was so pathetic that not even the city council would have bothered to do anything but laugh.

Once my sausage was nicely blackened around the ragged edges where it had burst, I squeezed half a tube of mustard on it.

"Are you sure white wine goes with that?" Koivu asked, looking in horror at my delicacy. The white stripe around his left ring finger was almost tanned now, but the wound in his heart had only begun to scab over. He was considering moving away from Joensuu, even farther north. Apparently the city reminded him too much of Anita. I secretly hoped he would decide to move back to Helsinki.

A few days earlier, I had received a strange phone call.

"Hello, this is Detective Lieutenant Jyrki Taskinen of the Espoo Police Department. As you may have heard, we have major organizational restructuring going on. As part of that, we're establishing a new unit specializing in violent crime and habitual criminality, which we're mostly staffing from inside the department. We have one problem though. We need a woman with a law degree and police training, preferably one with at least the qualifications for detective grade two. Sergeant Pertti Ström from our department and Lieutenant Kalevi Kinnunen from Helsinki recommended you. Are you interested?"

For a moment I just listened dumbfounded until I thought to ask whether I would end up being the subordinate of my old enemy Pertti Ström.

"Ström will be working in the same unit, but you would answer directly to me."

I promised to go to Espoo for a job interview the following week. The position would start in late November, so I would have time after my summer job ended to take a month off. Koivu was urging me to take the job, as were my parents. I hadn't had time to talk with Antti yet, because he hadn't been answering his phone for a few days.

The melancholy tune of the harmonica floated from the other side of the campfire, and Johnny's guitar joined in. Someone started singing the Beatles' "All My Loving." Quickly I poured more wine down my throat, thinking of Jaska, who had always said the Beatles were touchy-feely tripe. I hoped he was playing backup for John Lennon now.

Kaisa sat down next to me with a leggy blonde who she had introduced earlier: "This is Elvira, my friend. The Estonian hurdler."

She didn't need to explain any more, and I had no trouble guessing that the sparkle in her eyes was from more than just winning the gold. It looked right when Kaisa wrapped her arms around Elvira's shoulder. That was probably a greater victory than the European Championships.

Johnny switched from "All My Loving" to "Michelle." Lately I had been wondering about his sense of perspective given that he had thought Meritta committed suicide just because of him. Johnny had brushed the issue aside by claiming that he had been too messed up that night to think straight about anything. After finding Meritta's body, he had tripped going down the steps on the hill, which was where the mysterious bruises came from. We had finally had the conversation I promised to have with him after I solved Meritta's murder. But there hadn't been much to talk about. There was no way to change the past, and we didn't have any future. Still, I was happy that the only witness had been my uncle's cat when I cried the whole night afterward. But I was also sure I was never going to dream about Johnny again. At least not very often.

Taking slow sips from my bottle of wine, I looked at the city sleeping below, the city I hated as a teenager and later tried in vain to forget. I was never going to escape the fact that I was from here, born with copper in my heart.

As if to taunt me, Johnny plucked those familiar chords on his guitar again. Two could play that game though. But as I sang, instead of looking at him, I gazed down the hillside.

Are you going to Scarborough Fair?

A familiar tall, thin, dark-haired figure climbed the stairs. I wasn't entirely surprised, since the secretive glances and whispering I had observed between my parents and Koivu over the past few days made me guess some surprise was in the works.

Parsley, sage, rosemary, and thyme.

Still, my insides filled with butterflies.

I knew happy endings usually only lasted five minutes, or at best a day or two.

Remember me to one who lives there.

Then it would be time to start again, time for facing new trials. But as I stood up and ran down the stairs toward Antti, I was ready even for a short happy ending.

He once was a true love of mine.

ABOUT THE AUTHOR

Leena Lehtolainen was born in Vesanto, Finland, to parents who taught language and literature. A keen reader, she made up stories in her head before she could even write. At the age of ten, she began her first book, a young adult novel, which was published two years later.

Besides writing, Leena is fond of classical singing, her beloved cats, and—her greatest passion—figure skating. She attends many competitions as a skating journalist and writes for the Finnish figure-skating magazine *Taitoluistelu*. *Copper Heart* is the third installment in her best-selling Maria Kallio series, which debuted in English in 2012 with *My First Murder* and continued in 2013 with *Her Enemy*. Leena currently lives in Finland with her husband and two sons.

ABOUT THE TRANSLATOR

Owen F. Witesman is a professional literary translator with a master's in Finnish and Estonian area studies from Indiana University. He has translated more than thirty Finnish books into English, including novels, children's books, poetry, plays, graphic novels, and nonfiction. His recent translations include the first two novels in the Maria Kallio series, *My First Murder* and *Her Enemy* (AmazonCrossing), the satire *The Human Part* by Kari Hotakainen (MacLehose Press), the thriller *Cold Courage* by Pekka Hiltunen (Hesperus), and the 1884 classic *The Railroad* by Juhani Aho (Norvik Press). He currently resides in Springville, Utah, with his wife and three daughters, a dog, a cat, and twenty-nine fruit trees.